Praise for Ellie Alexander's Bakeshop mystery series:

"Delectable."   —*Portland Book Reviews*

"Quirky . . . intriguing . . . [with] recipes to make your stomach growl."   —*Reader to Reader*

"Delicious."   —*RT Book Reviews*

"This debut culinary mystery is a light soufflé of a book (with recipes) that makes a perfect mix for fans of Jenn McKinlay, Leslie Budewitz, or Jessica Beck."
                              —*Library Journal* on *Meet Your Baker*

"Marvelous."   —*Fresh Fiction*

"Scrumptious . . . will delight fans of cozy mysteries with culinary delights."   —*Night Owl Reviews*

"Clever plots, likable characters, and good food . . . Still hungry? Not to worry, because desserts abound in . . . this delectable series."   —*Mystery Scene* on *A Batter of Life and Death*

"[With] *Meet Your Baker*, Alexander weaves a tasty tale of deceit, family ties, delicious pastries, and murder."
                              —Edith Maxwell, author of *A Tine to Live, A Tine to Die*

"Sure to satisfy both dedicated foodies and ardent mystery lovers alike."   —Jessie Crockett, author of *Drizzled with Death*

D0016944

Bake, Borrow, and Steal

Ellie Alexander

St. Martin's Paperbacks

First published in the United States by St. Martin's Paperbacks, an imprint of St. Martin's Publishing Group.

BAKE, BORROW, AND STEAL

For information, address St. Martin's Publishing Group, 120 Broadway, New York, NY 10271.

www.stmartins.com

ISBN: 978-1-250-78944-0

Our books may be purchased in bulk for promotional, educational, or business use. Please contact your local bookseller or the Macmillan Corporate and Premium Sales Department at 1-800-221-7945, ext. 5442, or by email at MacmillanSpecialMarkets@macmillan.com.

Printed in the United States of America

St. Martin's Paperbacks edition / January 2022

10 9 8 7 6 5 4 3 2 1

This book is dedicated to Dave Erickson, a reader and baker extraordinaire, who embodied the Torte spirit of community connection, spreading joy in the form of delectable bakes throughout the Rogue Valley.

Chapter One

They say that the truth rarely stays hidden, that secrets find their way to the surface even after being buried deep for years. It was a secret that nearly three years ago had launched my life in an entirely new and unexpected direction. A small stack of letters, correspondence between Carlos, my husband, and the son I didn't know he had, had forced me to reexamine my future. Those innocuous pieces of paper and postcards had sent me packing from my life aboard the *Amour of the Seas* and caused me to spend the last few years learning how to let go and step into myself. If you had asked me then, I would have never imagined that there might be a way forward for Carlos and me. In hindsight I now realized that our time apart was a gift. A time for me to grow, to really get to know myself, and to unearth my own burdens.

Most of the credit for sparking my growth was due to my hometown of Ashland, Oregon. From the first moment

I stepped inside the front doors of Torte, our family's bakeshop, I knew that everything was going to be okay, regardless of how things turned out with Carlos. It was impossible to resist the welcoming charm of our Elizabethan village with its Tudor-style architecture, eclectic shops, world-class restaurants, and warm and inviting community nestled between the expansive Siskiyou Mountains in a remote corner of southern Oregon. Not a day passed when I didn't pause for a moment of gratitude for finding my way home. It wasn't exactly the path I had envisioned for myself, but that's the thing about life: it's often the twists and turns that lead us where we're supposed to be.

The other surprising outcome had been that Carlos had ultimately decided that Ashland was where he belonged too. Our challenges had brought us closer and made our relationship that much stronger. When he showed up with his bags in tow last spring, I figured we might have a brief few weeks of bliss before we parted ways for good—him returning to the *Amour of the Seas,* the boutique cruise ship where we first met, and me firmly planting myself in the Rogue Valley. Fate had another idea in mind. It just took me a while to realize it.

I guess I had thought that marriage was supposed to be easy. That when Carlos and I tied the knot on a blissful sun-drenched day in Marseilles, it would be smooth sailing from then on. When things got tough, I assumed the worst. It's one of my many faults—self-sabotage, spending too much time overthinking things. Being named Juliet Montague Capshaw may have set me up for unrealistic expectations in the romance department. I had always wondered if bearing the name of arguably the most romantic literary character of all time had destined me for heartbreak.

It turns out maybe not. Carlos was here in Ashland, and unless his acting skills were on par with the Equity actors who graced the Oregon Shakespeare Festival's stages, he appeared to be happy. Dare I say blissfully so?

We had fallen into an easy routine over the last few months. He moved into my childhood home on Mountain Avenue and began making it our own with artwork and pottery from our travels across the seas. Carlos had insisted on buying a high-end espresso machine for the kitchen and spent most of the summer (when he wasn't tending to the vines at Uva, our winery) building an outdoor pizza oven and constructing deer-proof garden boxes for his homegrown herbs and veggies. The summer had passed in a dreamlike blur. Between running Torte and Uva, we had also opened a small outdoor ice cream shop, Scoops, that had been a major hit. June through September brought theater-lovers to Ashland, packing the house at the Oregon Shakespeare Festival's many indoor and outdoor venues and filling the plaza with the constant chatter of vacationers lingering late into the evening over al fresco dinners.

My team at Torte had spent the busy months greeting everyone who walked through our doors with passion fruit curd cupcakes with mango buttercream, peach crisps with generous scoops of our hand-churned coconut concrete, and Bakewell tarts. Andy, our resident barista, had recently been crowned champion of the West Coast Barista Cup. His regional fame had made the bakeshop even more popular, as visitors wanted to taste his winning lattes and pose for selfies with him. He refused to admit it because he was humble and an all-around good guy, but I could tell the praise had brought him a new level of well-deserved confidence.

Managing our ever-growing staff and three unique

properties had had me yearning for fall, the season when Ashland took on a slower pace. Just last week, the festival, affectionately known to locals as OSF, had officially gone dark for the season. Tourists returned home, props and sets were packed away, and a single bulb known as the ghost light had been illuminated, sitting center stage, warding off theater demons and darkness until the new year.

The calendar had turned to November as the sun began its winter retreat, and I found myself reflecting on how lucky I was to be living my dreams. My personal and professional lives were thriving, which often made me want to stop and pinch myself. Torte was in the midst of one of the most prestigious projects we'd ever been involved with.

A fortuitous introduction from Rosa, one of our newer team members at Torte, had put me in contact with her uncle, Javier de la Garza, the director of SOMA—the Southern Oregon Museum of Art. Javier had been working for nearly three years to bring the most coveted Shakespearean exhibit to the museum—*Shakespeare's Lost Pages.*

The exhibit wasn't simply an ode to the Bard's collection of rare books and artifacts from his time. Of course it would include those, along with a miniature scale replica of the Globe, reproductions of Shakespeare's chair and neck ruff, and an interactive stage with costumes and props for visitors to get a taste of what it was like to recite lines from a sonnet. But the main draw was a newly discovered manuscript, *Double Falsehood*, which scholars had recently confirmed was a long lost play written by William Shakespeare himself. Javier had managed to secure the first showing in the United States. Typically exhibits of this magnitude traveled to bigger West Coast markets—Seattle, San Francisco, and Los Angeles. But Javier had a trick up his sleeve in the form of the Shakespeare

Festival. He had wisely leveraged the fact that OSF, one of the most prestigious repertory theaters in America, was in Ashland. There were a variety of natural tie-ins between the festival and the traveling exhibit. And there was the fact that OSF already had a broad and loyal Shakespearean fan base who were sure to make the trek to Ashland for the opening gala.

That's where Torte came in. We would be catering the opening night gala in addition to providing desserts for a variety of smaller soirées for museum donors and patrons. When Javier had approached me in July about partnering for the event, I hadn't realized that this project would become one of the largest, if not the largest, undertakings we'd done to date. Javier had grand visions. For the centerpiece of the dessert buffet, he wanted molded chocolate art pieces designed to resemble Shakespeare's desk. Not just a static desk, but a functional chocolate desk with working drawers that would open and contain hidden sweet gems inside. Technically chocolate wasn't a dessert that would have been served during Shakespeare's time, but Javier was a chocolate fan and he was giving us creative license when it came to fudging any recipes for the sake of taste.

Initially I had resisted. While my training in culinary school included a section on chocolate, I was certainly not a trained chocolatier. I suggested some names of colleagues in Portland, but Javier wanted to keep everything about the exhibit local.

"It's important that we support and include the community, Jules. This is not simply a SOMA event, this is an opportunity to highlight our friends and neighbors here in the Rogue Valley," he said over coffee during our first meeting. "Rosa is my niece. I already know how talented she is, and I've been coming to Torte for years. It has to be you."

"Yes, but chocolate sculpting is an art to itself," I explained.

"I understand. That's why I wanted to meet with you now. The gala is in mid-November, so that gives you nearly four months to prepare. I'm sure you'll be able to create something magnificent."

I wasn't as convinced, but Javier was hard to turn down, and I was intrigued by the idea of being involved in such a mysterious exhibit. Ancient Shakespearean manuscripts certainly motivated me to put my chocolate skills to the test. So did the opportunity to showcase Torte amongst the dignitaries and distinguished guests coming in from all over the country. The exclusive guest list for the gala read like an invitation to the Academy Awards. How could I say no?

In hindsight, that might have been a mistake. Not that I wasn't excited about the upcoming gala, but we had so much work left to do. Time was slipping away fast.

I had assigned Steph, one of my cake designers, the lofty task of working on the chocolate showpieces with me. She and I had been laboring over sketches for the final designs, which were much more technical than I had imagined when I agreed to take on the project. Working with chocolate at this level was a bit like constructing actual building plans. In order to hone my skills, I had dug out my old culinary school notebooks and manuals from the basement. Steph and I had watched hours of YouTube tutorials and spent a weekend in Portland with a former classmate of mine who had become a well-respected chocolatier. There were so many specifics involved with tempering chocolate in order to achieve a lush, glossy sheen, while making sure not to sacrifice flavor and constructing something solid enough that the structure wouldn't collapse or the chocolate sag and bend.

Javier had a specific vision for the gala. He had been adamant that everything in the dessert display needed to be edible, and that the entire dinner feast must adhere to Elizabethan-era standards.

We had pored over vintage recipes. Mom would collaborate with Bethany, Torte's personal cheerleader, social media star, and brownie baker extraordinaire, and Rosa, who worked as a floater in the bakeshop. They would be making opera cakes, frangipane tarts, jellies with chestnut cream, and frankincense and wild orange puddings to accompany the old English exhibit. Marty, a baker trained in San Francisco who had recently moved to Ashland to semi-retire, was going to oversee production of breads like lardy cake—a sweet bread filled with nutmeg, raisins, currants, and pieces of lard—and saffron cake—a spicy sugar bread loaded with assorted dried fruits and served with a side of clotted cream.

Not to be left out, Sterling, our sous chef in training with a poet's soul and wisdom beyond his years, and Carlos, along with a couple of the SOU students who had worked at Scoops over the summer, were tackling the main feast, which would be served in the great hall. They had been learning ancient cookery techniques through a collection of Elizabethan cookbooks Javier had lent us. The menu for the feast seemed to expand every time I talked to them, but for the moment it was going to feature a beef stew, roasted game hens, fish pies, cheese and fruit platters, and trios of thick, rich sauces. As we had promised Javier, everything would be as authentic as possible, a replica of a feast fit for a queen, with a few minor modern tweaks. We had agreed that in terms of authenticity, patrons would never know about (or would be willing to look past) our use of industrial kitchen equipment. Thank goodness. I had had nightmares about having to knead that much bread dough by hand.

I had no idea how we were going to get any other baking done in the days leading up to the gala. While tourist season had ended, we still saw a steady stream of locals and visitors in town to experience the abundance of other activities Ashland had to offer, from wine tasting to mountain biking and hiking, and a bevy of winter sports.

The motivation to make sure we stayed on track forced me to tuck away my thoughts and get myself out of bed. After a hot shower and a hot cup of coffee, I left Carlos sleeping and headed outside into the dark, star-drenched southern Oregon skies. My morning walks to Torte required a flashlight. I didn't mind. Carlos continually insisted that he would drive me to the bakeshop, but I enjoyed the quiet of a brisk walk and having the kitchen all to myself for an hour.

I breathed in the earthy scent of damp leaves as I descended the steep hillside of Mountain Avenue and made my way past the sprawling grounds of SOU. Glowing golden street lamps illuminated the pathways that cut through campus. Moonlight pooled on the red roofs of the science and humanities buildings. There was no movement in the dorms. It was much too early for college students to be awake.

I chuckled at the thought, quickened my pace, turned onto Siskiyou Boulevard, and headed straight for Torte. Even in the dark, Torte sat like a beacon with its redbrick exterior and windows that looked out onto the plaza. This morning the front windows were backlit with strings of amber twinkle lights. Leaves dangled from invisible strings as if falling from the sky. Mirror-glazed cakes in autumn maroons and burnt oranges had been arranged on tiered cake displays. I loved the bakeshop's seasonal windows, the bright teal and red awning, and the butterflies that always fluttered in my stomach whenever it was time to launch a new day of baking.

The world was full of possibilities at this hour. I unlocked the doors and went downstairs, turning on lights as I went. My first task, after warming the ovens, was to make a pot of coffee. I knew that as soon as Andy arrived he would lure me into a second or third cup with his daily special, but I couldn't start any bake without a steaming cup of coffee in hand. With the change in season, we had swapped out our daily roast to a Thanksgiving blend, a medium-dark roast with notes of sweet peaches and apples, a touch of malt and cocoa, and a spicy finish. The aromatic beans made me breathe deeply to inhale the heavenly scent as I added them to the grinder. Some coffee shops pre-grind their beans. Not at Torte. We grind our beans fresh every day—to order. Oxidation is the key. Every bean has unique compounds and complexity that give a coffee its aroma and flavor. In order to achieve the most delicious cup and bring out the subtle nuances in a roast, it's imperative to keep the beans as fresh as possible, as oxidation occurs the moment the beans are ground and can quickly alter the brew.

Are we coffee snobs? In the truest definition of snobbery, I guess I would have to say yes. But only because we want to elevate the drinking experience for all of our guests. If done correctly, coffee can offer a transportive adventure for the palate. My favorite thing was to hear a customer chatting with Andy, Torte's lead barista. He had recently dropped out of college to focus on his coffee art and roasting knowledge, but he could have taught a graduate-level course on the origins of our coffee roasts. I never got tired of eavesdropping as customers exclaimed in delight when they tasted Andy's notes of brown sugar or a hint of smoke in their cup. He shared the espresso bar with Sequoia, who tended to push Andy out of his comfort zone. Where Andy was a traditionalist, Sequoia danced to the beat of her own drum—quite literally. I would often find her swaying to the rhythm of reggae while experimenting with hemp milk for lattes. As of late, our regulars were raving about her fall Hippie Juice, a cinnamon apple cider sangria that was a happy hour hit.

While the coffee brewed and filled the kitchen with its intoxicating fragrance, I lit the wood-fired oven and reviewed our schedule for the day. Since Scoops was closed for the season and Uva had limited winter hours, I didn't have to worry about staffing for either location. However, we did have a number of custom cake orders, as well as bread deliveries and a list of pastries to stock the store's pastry case.

I poured myself a cup of the rich roast, allowing the fall fruit flavor to linger on my tongue. Coffee is an experience meant to be savored, in my humble opinion. It should be revered, sipped slowly, and allowed to linger on the palate in order for each unique flavor to come forward.

Before Steph and I attempted a mock-up of one of the chocolate pieces, I wanted to get a head start on baking, so I tied on a candy-apple-red apron with our blue fleur-de-lis logo. I knew one of the pastries I wanted to share with our customers today—apple cream cheese bars.

I started with the crust by pulsing graham crackers in a blender until they were finely ground, resembling sand. Then I mixed the crumbs with melted butter, brown sugar, and a healthy dose of cinnamon. I pressed the mixture into large baking tins and set them aside while I creamed together butter, sugar, vanilla, cream cheese, and eggs. Once the batter was smooth and silky, I added in fall spices—cinnamon, nutmeg, and a touch of cloves. I spread that evenly over the graham cracker crust and put the tins in the oven to bake. I wanted to top the bars with a fresh apple compote. A friend had dropped off the last of her apple harvest from her organic farm. I intended to use some to make batches of our signature apple butter. The rest could go in my compote.

I washed, peeled, and cored the pale red Honeycrisp apples. Then I diced them and tossed them in fresh lemon juice to keep them from browning. I sautéed the apples in a little butter before covering them with orange juice, brown sugar, and nutmeg. I would let them simmer for ten to fifteen minutes until the juices thickened and the apples were tender.

As I pulled the first trays of cheesecake bars from the oven, Andy came through the basement entrance.

"Morning, boss. It's getting cold out there." He hung a puffy ski jacket with dozens of faded lift tickets clinging to the zipper on the coatrack. "You know what that means? Snow's coming." He rubbed his hands together with enough friction to start a fire. "This is the time of year that I start praying to the snow gods every night. I have to tell you that I have a good feeling they're on my side this year."

I chuckled. "Isn't it a little early for ski season? It's only the beginning of November." While it was true that Ashland was situated at elevation at the edge of the Siskiyou Mountains, snowfall wasn't a sure thing in town, especially in November.

"Nah, it's never too early for snow." He came into the kitchen and grabbed a red Torte apron. His youthful cheeks were the same shade of red from the cold outside, and his eyes were bright. "You never know. Remember last year we had that massive Indigenous Peoples' Day storm? It dumped a ton of snow on Mount A. I'm hoping for a repeat."

"I won't complain. I love the snow too, but maybe it could hold off until after our gala event."

Andy twisted his lips into a half scowl. "Okay, I guess I can give you a week or two before I start doing my snow dance in the streets." He glanced at the bars. "What's the special today?"

"Apple cheesecake bars."

"Hmmm. I was contemplating a fall drink on my way in this morning. That gives me inspiration. I'll go get the espresso machine fired up and see what I can come up with."

"Sounds good." I took the second round of cheesecake bars from the oven. They would need to cool before I layered on the compote and my final touch—a crumb topping. For that I sliced chunks of cold butter and forked in brown sugar, oats, pecans, cinnamon, and salt. Texture is as important as flavor when it comes to pastry, and the crisp buttery crust, smooth cream cheese filling, tangy soft apples, and crunchy topping would provide a symphony of textures in every bite.

The kitchen began to fill with delicious aromas as the rest of the team arrived. My brief moment of quiet quickly transformed into a frenzy of bodies stirring vats of soup, kneading bread dough, and running up and down the stairs to stock the pastry case. Within the hour, we were gathered around the island tasting my apple cheesecake bars, which had turned out even better than I expected. To go with the bars, Andy created an amaretto clove latte that we all agreed outshone any chain coffee shop's chemical-style pumpkin latte.

As much as I enjoyed savoring my coffee in an empty kitchen for the first hour, I loved this even more. A buzzing kitchen was a happy kitchen, and even with days of hard labor and preparation ahead, there was nothing I enjoyed more than being surrounded by my creative and energetic staff. Watching them immediately spring into action without prompting reassured me that we could handle anything that came our way.

Chapter Two

A week later I found myself regretting my words. Multiple failed attempts at our chocolate centerpieces were mainly to blame. Steph and I had spent hours cutting diagrams from cardboard and measuring angles for our chocolate Elizabethan-style chair and desk. The kitchen looked more like a chaotic architectural firm. Blueprints were taped to the walls. Notebooks with sketches and math equations lined the countertops. Sticky notes with different ratios for chocolate melting points had been tacked on recipes. Chocolate debris and remnants of our many fails littered the kitchen like the leaves outside.

We had tried a variety of techniques to adhere large sections of chocolate sheets to spindly legs, including using a torch to melt it back together and testing whether the type of chocolate had any impact on the strength of the bond. White chocolate was too fragile. Melted chocolate chips had promise, but they had a tendency to get clumpy quickly. Nothing felt quite right.

I finally ended up calling my friend in Portland, who recommended we try "couverture chocolate," a specialty chocolate that contained more cocoa butter than other types, which made it much easier to work with.

"I'm glad you asked for help on this one, Jules," Steph said one afternoon a week before the gala as we fitted delicate chocolate sides to the desk drawer. Her apron was splattered with chocolate, as was our workspace. It looked like we had committed a heinous crime against a stack of chocolate bars. Chocolate dripped from the edge of the countertops and had sprayed in a random pattern, like blood splatter, on the ceiling and walls. Every night before I left the bakeshop, I spent at least an extra hour scrubbing bits of chocolate from tiny nooks and crevices in the countertops and wondering how it had found its way in. No matter how hard I tried, my fingernails always looked as if I had painted them with the glossy chocolate.

My hands had vanished under layers of the smooth, silky chocolate. "I feel like we should offer chocolate spa services," I said to Steph, noting my hands. "At this point I think we've both gone through enough chocolate to bathe in it."

Her violet-tinted eyes lit up. "That's not a bad idea. You should get Bethany on that. 'Come to Torte, where we'll dip you in a vat of chocolate while you sip a dark chocolate mocha.' That sounds about right." Steph carefully piped a thin line along the edge of the dark chocolate pieces. "This is a million times smoother. This is definitely the way to go. Your friend saved us from a slow death by chocolate."

"I agree. I should have reached out earlier. As soon as she mentioned couverture chocolate, I kicked myself for not thinking of it sooner. We experimented with it in culinary school. That was well over a decade ago, and chocolate was never my passion. I mean, as you know, I love baking with chocolate, but I never imagined myself sculpting with it." I steadied the sides. Fingers crossed, if the pieces fit together the way we had designed, this should open like a real, functioning drawer.

"Customers haven't minded our fails." Steph gave me a rare grin, which softened her features and brought out even more of the violet in her eyes. Her dark hair was streaked with matching purple highlights. As much as she tried to play the role of being nonchalant and disinterested, I had learned better. She had a kind, tender heart that she tried to protect with an armor of eye-rolling and thick black eyeliner. In the years we had been working together, she had slowly begun to peel away her steely exterior. I credited that in large part to Sterling. He and Steph had recently moved in together. They were a good balance. He tended to express his emotions through poetry and deep, meaningful conversations. Steph used design as her emotional outlet. I wondered if there was a reason that she had guarded her heart so closely, perhaps something in her past that had forced her to keep everyone at arm's length. Whatever the reason, it was her story to tell if, or when, she was ready. I wasn't going to push her, and I appreciated seeing her slowly shed little pieces of her emotional armor.

Her talent wasn't limited to cake and pastry either. Her artistic strokes were evident throughout Torte—on the chalkboard menu, the window display, and nearly every custom cake that went out the front doors in a pretty white box.

She tucked her violet hair behind her ears and bent closer to follow the line of drizzly chocolate. "That should do it."

"Okay." I held my breath as I set the next piece in place. The chocolate didn't take long to cure. After a minute, I moved my hands off and bit my bottom lip, half expecting the chocolate to collapse or shatter. Steph had been right about the customers. We had made lemonade out of lemons by putting together small bags of broken chocolate as free samples for our customers. Let's just say that we had ample chocolate to share recently.

"It looks pretty solid." Steph sounded as stunned as I felt. She wiped chocolate from her hands on a dish towel.

I knelt to check the edges. "I think it might have worked." It couldn't have been better timing. Javier and a number of his SOMA staff plus one of the board members were stopping by in an hour for one last tasting before he signed off on the menu. I wanted to be able to show him a functioning desk. The chair was going to take longer, with its filigree design and miniature details that were going to require tweezers and magnifying glasses, but if we could finish the rough construction of the desk, I could breathe a sigh of relief.

"Hey, it's still standing," Sterling teased as he passed by our workstation with a tray of ramekins hot from the oven.

"Don't go there," I warned. "And don't you dare thud your feet on the floor." I pointed to the whiteboard with staff schedules and a list of our custom cake orders for the week, where I had written the word *TIPTOE* in all caps. In addition to making a mess of the workspace in the kitchen, Steph and I had been militant about team members moving gently through the area. "Treat this space like there's always a soufflé in the oven," I had jokingly commanded a few days earlier. "We're doing delicate stuff down here, people. Delicate stuff!"

Steph shot Sterling her signature scowl.

He flipped a strand of dark wavy hair from his eye. "Touchy. Touchy. It looks great."

"Back away or you're sleeping on the floor tonight." Steph waved a finger at him. Her nails alternated with black and purple polish. Tiny black rhinestones were glued in the center of each nail. They had lost some of their dazzle after being drenched in melted chocolate.

"Man, it's like you two are stressed about an event or something." Sterling's blizzard blue eyes twinkled as he tiptoed like a ballerina toward the stove.

"He's dead." Steph reached for a flat spatula. "He comes by us again before this is put together, and he's a dead man." She held up the chocolate piping bag with her other hand.

"What are you going to do? Squirt chocolate all over him?"

"Don't test me. I might."

We focused on securing the rest of the sections, including a thin handle that needed to stick to the face of the drawer like superglue if we were going to be able to achieve the effect of opening the drawer and revealing a copy of Shakespeare's lost manuscript inside. Steph would make the parchment out of white chocolate and use an edible calligraphy pen for the text. That could come later. For now, I simply wanted to make sure we had something functional to show our client.

The new chocolate did the trick. Within a half hour, we had a four-by-two-foot chocolate desk taking up half the countertop. It was still rough around the edges, but anyone who saw it would definitely be able to recognize it as a desk, complete with an opening drawer.

"Nice work," I said to Steph, wiping chocolate from my

hands and giving her a thumbs-up. "I'm going to check in on how everything is upstairs. You need to get to class, right?"

"Don't remind me." She sighed.

"I thought you were enjoying art history?"

Steph was an art major at SOU, and we had reaped the benefits of her artistic talents at Torte. There seemed to be no medium she couldn't master, from chalk to buttercream.

"The class is fine, but it doesn't start until four, and by the time it's done, it's totally dark. It's the worst because the lecture hall doesn't have windows, so when I get to class it's light outside and then I come out and it feels like midnight. It totally throws me off. I hate daylight savings time."

"Sorry, that's a bummer."

"Tell me about it." She peeled dried chocolate from her fingers. "See you tomorrow."

I went over to the stove to check on progress with the savory tasting dishes. "How's everything here?" I asked Sterling, who was whisking a thick, bubbly white cheese sauce.

"Good. We did ramekins with the stew in the pizza oven. I've got them warming in the main oven. Marty had to do a bread delivery, but he has a loaf of each of the breads done, and Carlos went upstairs a few minutes ago to get some stuff for the presentation."

"Great. We're doing the breads, the stew, and the fish hand pies for the tasting, not the cheese boards or game hens. Is that still true?"

"Yep." He ran his fingers along the dish towel draped over his shoulder. It was a trick he had learned from Carlos. That and tying his apron halfway around his waist instead of wearing it over his shoulders.

"Our distinguished guests will be here in about twenty minutes."

"It's cool, Jules. Everything has come together. Don't stress." His eyes held a deep knowingness not often seen in someone his age. Mom called him an old soul, which fit. I knew that some of his depth had come from loss, which was one of the things that had endeared me to him from the first moment he had walked into the bakeshop.

"Do I look stressed?"

"Yeah."

I inhaled deeply, taking in the scent of hearty herb and beef stew and his cheese sauce. "You're right. The chocolate structures are pushing me out of my comfort zone, but honestly I'm feeling so much better now that we got the desk put together. I was worried we weren't going to have anything to show Javier, and it's going to take the rest of our time to add all of the embellishments to it, plus finish the chair. It's weird. We've done big events before, but this is next level. It's kind of gotten in my head. The guest list is insane. We're talking A-list Hollywood names, politicians, dignitaries. It's wild, because I had plenty of brushes with famous people on the ship, and of course here with events at OSF, but I guess it's just that this isn't exactly Torte's style, you know? We're a family bakeshop. Don't get me wrong, I'm not doubting that we can do it. It's just a lot."

"So you're stressed." Sterling gave me a playful smirk. "You know what Carlos says about being stressed in the kitchen? If he catches word of you freaking out, he'll probably ban you from the bakeshop."

I nudged him with my elbow. "Listen up, wise guy, this is my kitchen and don't you forget it."

"Trust me, Jules, no one could forget that, not even Carlos." Sterling's tone shifted. "We all hail the pastry queen."

"Now you're making me sound like a dictator."

"Ha!" Sterling laughed. "As if. I'd love to see your authoritarian side come out. What are you going to do, kill us with kindness?"

I furrowed my brow.

"No, seriously, Jules. It's under control. Bethany and Rosa have the custards and puddings in the walk-in. Andy and Sequoia have everything upstairs taken care of. They're going to close and clean while you host the tasting down here. It's fine. It's good. We've got this."

"Thanks for the pep talk." I smiled. It was what I needed to hear. I hadn't slept much lately. I would wake with dreams—or nightmares—of our chocolate masterpieces shattering in front of a swath of well-dressed museum patrons. I rarely worried about what I was baking. I might overthink scheduling and timing for an event, but I typically felt confident in our products. This level of chocolate artistry was either going to push me out of my comfort zone and expand my creative repertoire or it was going to push me over the edge.

Chapter Three

Shortly after my conversation with Sterling, I found myself seated around the coffee table next to our retro atomic fireplace in Torte's cozy basement seating area with oversized chairs, a comfy couch, and bookshelves filled with reading material and games for guests to spend a leisurely morning or afternoon lounging with a spread of our savory and sweet pastries and coffee.

I had changed into a clean apron, dusted my cheeks with blush, put on some lip gloss, and tied back all the stray hairs in my ponytail.

Javier had brought along his assistant, Zoe Joiner, a PhD student in her late twenties; Cindy Hollings, the lead volunteer docent at SOMA; and Ernest Boyd, a longtime patron of the museum who had helped fund the *Shakespeare's Lost Pages* exhibit. Carlos and Sterling brought out silver platters with lattice-topped hand pies, hearty stew, marzipans shaped to resemble brightly colored fruit, custards, and savory breads.

My nerves settled as I studied their faces with each tasting bite. I could tell from the curve of their lips and their oohs and aahs that they were impressed with our interpretation of Shakespeare on a plate.

"This is fantastic," Javier said, savoring a spoonful of custard. "I feel like every morsel is transporting me across the Atlantic to the Globe, where I'm smashed together with the other groundlings in front of the stage. Not that they ever were able to eat like this." He was in his early sixties with salt-and-pepper hair, intelligent eyes, and a kind smile. His style, like the vibe he put out, was casual. He was dressed in a pair of jeans and a black zip-up SOMA fleece.

Zoe held the stylus for her iPad and glanced around the table to her colleagues. "Anything you want me to make note of? Any changes? We need to get them down now, because we're really behind, and we don't have much time to lose." She looked like a typical PhD student with her pointed turquoise glasses frames positioned at the base of her nose. She too wore jeans and a SOMA sweatshirt.

Cindy slathered a slice of the saffron bread with honey and herb butter. "Not from me. Everything is absolutely divine. Not that anyone cares about my opinion. I'm just a volunteer, but I can tell you that I know most of our patrons by name, and I am sure that they are going to love this." She offered me a warm smile. It was hard to peg her age, but I guessed her to be close to sixty, with mousy brown hair and light brown eyes.

I smiled back with a combination of relief and pride. This tasting represented hours of collaboration and hard work. We had had our fair share of fails, so seeing our clients enjoying what we presented made the effort worth it.

There was one voice of dissent—Ernest. He appeared to be in his late sixties or early seventies with a shock of white hair that swept to one side of his head. It reminded me of a cresting wave. He was dressed in a cream suit with a burgundy tie and matching pocket square. I wouldn't have been surprised to see him dressed like that for a production at OSF, but for a cold Thursday afternoon, it was a bit much.

"I find this dry." He moved his mouth like a cow trying to digest a large clump of cud. "It's as if my bread spent an afternoon sunbathing on the beach and got burned to a crisp. This is making my mouth so parched and desperate for something to drink, I feel like I've been deserted on a remote island."

Cindy chimed in before I could answer or offer him another glass of water. It was probably a good thing that she had beat me to a response, because I might have said something I would regret. Our cake made him so parched he felt like he was on a deserted island—what?

"I believe this is bread is baked directly from a recipe popular in the late fifteen hundreds or early sixteen hundreds, right?" Cindy looked to me for confirmation. She was dressed for duty at SOMA in a pair of black slacks and a matching turtleneck with her docent name tag pinned to her chest. "This is called lardy cake, although in the area around Suffolk it's known as fourses cake. This was a special bread served for weekend tea, festivals, high days, and is meant to be dunked and dipped with a strong cup of tea. The texture—which is not the least bit dry—comes from the assortment of spices, currants, and lard. Am I correct?"

I nodded. Her knowledge was impressive. "That's right. We made some minor adjustments to the original recipe due to modern measurements and such, but this is the same bread that the Bard could have enjoyed at a post-show feast."

Ernest made a smacking sound with his lips. He reached for a water glass and swished liquid around in his mouth before responding. "I'm usually a stickler for authenticity, but I can't imagine the Bard consuming this. If you want my opinion, I think you may want to go back to the drawing board for this. I'm not sure if Javier has expressed how incredibly important the success of this gala is. SOMA's reputation depends on it. What you need to understand is that this isn't a quaint little Ashland event. Some of the most important people in the world will be attending, and we absolutely will not accept mediocrity."

I wanted to reach across the table and punch him. Instead I inhaled through my nose and forced a smile. "I'm afraid it's too late to go back to the drawing board. We can make some minor adjustments to the recipes. That's what this tasting is for, but we've already procured product and begun pre-prep." I turned to Javier. "We were under the impression you wanted each item to be as authentic as possible. Everything you're tasting is from the Shakespearean cookbooks you gave us."

Javier jumped in. "Yes, yes, you're absolutely right, Jules. We do want the menu to be as authentic as possible. Ernest, you directed that part of the event brief. If we're to be showcasing Shakespeare's tome, the food should be a reflection of that."

Ernest helped himself to a pudding. "I don't recall that being my directive."

"You wouldn't," Zoe whispered under her breath.

Javier shot her a warning look.

Zoe broke off a tiny piece of bread and nibbled it on like a bird. "Hey, Ernest, if you want to veer away from adhering to your by-the-book policy, now's as good a time as any to talk about *herstory*. It's not too late to add a section dedicated to revealing Shakespeare's true nature to the exhibit."

I was confused.

Javier rubbed his temples and blew out a long breath.

Zoe looked to me. "Ernest doesn't like to talk about this, but I'm writing my dissertation on the premise that Shakespeare was a woman. She was definitely a woman. Many, many women have been silenced throughout history, including those who wrote the canon." She shot a triumphant smile in Ernest's direction. "It makes him squirm because my theory is controversial and shatters his beloved image of the Bard."

"Absurd." Ernest bared his teeth. "There is not a single reputable scholarly argument to back up that theory."

"This isn't the time," Javier said to Zoe before changing the subject. "Jules, you mentioned that we might be able to get an early glimpse of the chocolate showpieces?"

"Sure." I motioned for them to stand. "If you want to come with me, I'll give you a sneak peek."

I found myself sucking in air again as we moved into the kitchen. If Ernest hadn't been impressed with the actual food, I dreaded what kind of feedback he was going to have about the chocolate art pieces. The rest of the team greeted our guests with a wave. They reminded me of my team on the ship, standing at the ready to do whatever was asked of them. Sterling and Carlos stood near the stove. Marty was wiping down the marble countertop, and Bethany was snapping pictures of a two-tiered forest wonderland cake adorned with red and white meringue mushrooms.

My heart pulsed in my neck as I waited for their feedback on the largest chocolate piece we had ever constructed.

"It looks like a desk," Cindy noted, checking out our confectionary carpentry skills from all angles. Her narrow nose was so close to the chocolate, I had to resist the urge to pull her away.

"The drawer opens," I said, gently tugging on the handle. The drawer slid open with ease. "We're working on designing a white chocolate replica of the first page of the lost manuscript that will fit inside here."

Javier clapped. "Bravo!"

Zoe scribbled a note on her iPad. "Just so I have this down correctly, the manuscript will be hidden inside? And will guests be able to open the drawer to reveal the text?"

"Not the entire manuscript," I replied. "That would take months. The first page will be inside and visible. One of my cake designers is a wonderful calligrapher, and she's going to copy the text word for word in edible pen."

"Got it." Zoe continued to document every second of our conversation, which I found slightly unsettling.

"I don't think it's a great idea to have the guests handle the chocolate," I continued. "It's delicate to begin with, and the more hands on the piece, the more likely something could break. One idea is that you could open the drawer at the beginning of the event and leave it open for guests to come get a closer look."

"Guests can't touch the chocolate?" Ernest scoffed. "What's the point? That's not what was discussed. What's the point if the chocolate pieces aren't functional? No, this is unacceptable. Absolutely unacceptable."

I stumbled to try to respond. Creating moveable pieces on the unsteady structures had already been a challenge; having dozens upon dozens of people handling the molded chocolate would be disastrous. Never had that been part of the conversation when Javier and I had first discussed his vision.

"Ernest, how long have you served on the board of directors for SOMA?" Cindy asked. She had moved back from the chocolate. Thank goodness. The last thing I needed was for her to accidentally knock one of the pieces off the countertop.

"I believe this is my tenth year," he said with an inflated sense of self-importance.

"In your tenure, when have we ever allowed guests to touch any artifact on display? Aside from children's interactive exhibits, of course?"

"I'm not sure I understand your point." He rolled his eyes.

Cindy wasn't deterred. "My point is that *never* do we allow patrons to handle anything that's on display. The same is true for these chocolate art pieces. More so. Imagine warm sticky hands opening and closing this intricate piece of art. It would be a melting mess in minutes. I'm surprised that you have the gall to say something so ludicrous out loud, especially when you've been lecturing anyone who will listen about the importance of maintaining the highest standards at SOMA. Why would we let the 'grubby hands of the public,' as you like to refer to some of our patrons, get their paws on something like this?" She swept her hand over the desk.

I was taken aback by her response. Not that I didn't agree with her, but it was awkward to have her lash out at him in front of everyone. I got the sense that Ernest wasn't the most loved member of the gala planning committee, given Cindy's retort and Zoe attacking him over her theory that Shakespeare was a woman.

Ernest cleared his throat and readjusted his pocket square.

Javier tried to recover the conversation. "You have outdone yourself, Jules. Really. This is quite impressive, and I know it will be the talk of the gala." He turned to Zoe. "Make sure that you include something about these chocolate sculptures in the press releases."

Zoe immediately made a note. "It will be included. Consider it already done."

We returned to the seating area. Javier walked us through the event lineup. "How much time will your team need to set up?"

"At least a couple hours. Plus, I'm going to have a crew assigned strictly to moving the chocolate showpieces. Once they are in place, they may need a little touch-up, but the big challenge is going to be getting them from here to campus in one piece." I dreaded the thought, but there was no way around it.

"Ernest and I will be entertaining some of the high-end donors who will be arriving early." He glanced briefly toward Ernest, who was finishing off the last of the marzipans. "Ah, the life of a museum director, constantly trying to raise more funds and friends. But that shouldn't impact you. If you'd like, I can arrange for Zoe to give you access to the museum the night before. That way you can have the chocolate art already in place and concentrate on setting up the dessert and buffet the night of the event. Would that be helpful?"

"That would be wonderful." I nodded. Carlos and I had decided the safest way to transport the chocolate would be in the back of our Torte delivery van with two people holding it. Fortunately we didn't have far to go. SOU was only a little over a mile from Torte, but even a short trip wasn't without risk.

Rosa appeared at the base of the stairs carrying empty trays. "Uncle Javier!" Her heart-shaped face broke out in a wide smile as she hurried over to greet her uncle. She wore her dark hair in two long braids accenting her high cheekbones and wide eyes. Rosa had been an incredible asset to the team, not only due to her warm, calming nature and skills in the kitchen, but also because she was a few years older than me. I appreciated her ability to mentor our younger staff and having someone close to my age to bounce ideas off of.

"Everyone, this is my niece Rosa." Javier introduced her after greeting her with a hug and kiss on the cheek. "She is responsible for helping to see this partnership come to fruition."

Rosa tucked the empty trays under her arm. "We are all so excited about being part of the gala. Isn't everything wonderful? We've been having fun tasting the works in progress."

"We are blown away." Javier patted his trim belly. "I don't think I'll need dinner tonight, thanks to this."

Rosa excused herself to the kitchen.

"Okay. You'll take care of coordinating with Jules?" Javier asked Zoe, getting the conversation back on track.

Zoe made more notes. "Yes. When would you like to meet? The museum closes at five, so anytime after that. Actually, the sooner the better, because I have a ton of work to do."

"Can I touch base with my staff and get back to you?"

"Sure. Let me know as soon as you can, though. I have

at least a million details to check off between now and Saturday."

"Will do. I just need to make sure I have enough hands to carry the pieces."

Javier proceeded to explain that guests would first be greeted with champagne and appetizers in the lobby, before opening the main doors to the exhibit. Dinner and dessert would be served buffet style, and the chocolate sculptures would be prominently displayed next to the original Shakespearean artifacts.

"I hope you understand what an honor it is to have a local bakeshop represented next to some of the greatest works of all time," Ernest said, narrowing his bushy white eyebrows at me.

I wondered if he and Richard Lord, my nemesis, who owned the dreaded Merry Windsor Hotel across the plaza, were long-lost cousins. They shared a similar pompous, condescending attitude.

"Oh, we are all very aware of how fortunate we are to be partnering with SOMA on this project," I replied, plastering on my most sincere grin.

Javier stood. "I think that covers everything. I can't believe the big moment is nearly here." As everyone else gathered their things, he shook my hand and whispered, "Sorry about Ernest. He likes to make sure everyone knows he's the most important person in the room."

"I know the type."

"I'll do my best to keep him out of your hair."

"I can handle it."

Javier's face lit up with a smile. "I'm sure you can."

I said goodbye to the others and gathered the empty tasting

plates. In the kitchen, Sterling was putting away the last of the clean dishes. "How did it go?"

"Good. They seemed to like everything." I didn't bother to give him a recap on Ernest. I wasn't exaggerating when I told Javier I could handle him. I did know his type. Like with Richard Lord, I figured my best approach was to let him expound on his superior taste and knowledge. It wasn't worth trying to argue with men like Ernest. Plus, I planned to steer as far away from him as I could in the days ahead and at the gala. I had enough to worry about without his condescending critiques of my pastries.

Chapter Four

The rest of the week flew by. Before I knew it, the day before the gala had arrived. I had called in reinforcements to help transport the fragile structures to SOMA. Sterling and Andy were going to be responsible for lifting the desk. Marty and Carlos would take the chair. I would drive, and Steph was tagging along to help open doors and bring our tool kit of repair supplies. After much debate and deliberation, we decided to take the sculptures through the back stairwell. It was closer, but the steps were much steeper, which made my nerves that much more jittery.

"I can't believe we're actually moving these," I said through clenched teeth as Steph propped open the basement door and a cool gust of air rushed in. The sky was tinged with purple as the late afternoon sun sunk on the horizon.

Andy and Sterling stood rigid, like the queen's guards,

with their muscles flexed and a tight grip on each side of the plywood base holding the potentially shatterable chocolate desk.

"Don't sweat it, boss. This is nothing. I could probably lift it with one hand." Andy's lopsided grin did nothing to calm my fears.

"No!" I yelled, almost expecting him to try and prove his point.

"Chill, we've got this, Jules." Sterling placed his foot on the first brick step as Andy balanced his side.

"I know. Sorry. Just be careful. Watch the hand railing," I called as Sterling and Andy lifted the plywood and continued up the stairwell.

Visions of hours of painstaking work getting smashed into a million little pieces flashed through my head as they precariously balanced the behemoth structure. Once they managed to get it upstairs and out the backdoor, which required them turning the piece sideways, the real test was going to be the van ride. I kicked myself for not calling in a favor to Thomas, my high school friend and Ashland's lead deputy, or the Professor. They could have given us a police escort to campus. It took about twenty minutes to get the desk and the chair tightly secured in the back of the van.

"Is everyone good?" I asked from the driver's seat.

"Si, we are fine," Carlos replied. He and Marty clutched the chair on another large piece of plywood.

I drove well under the twenty-five-mile-an-hour speed limit through the plaza, past the English style storefronts and restaurants, constantly checking behind me to see how the chocolate was faring. "Still good? Is anything shifting?"

Antique streetlamps lined Main Street. Instead of banners touting upcoming performances at OSF, maroon and gold banners announcing the *Shakespeare's Lost Pages* exhibit hung from each post and flapped gently in the soft afternoon breeze.

"Boss, just drive, please," Andy finally begged. "This thing is heavy, and you're making my grandma look like a NASCAR racer."

"Watch out. There's a herd of deer crossing up by the high school," Steph warned.

I slowed even more as we approached the crosswalk, where a family of deer trotted in a perfect line adhering to the flashing walk signal.

The university campus was on the next block. I made it through the intersection and kept a firm grip on the wheel. SOU's grounds rivaled those of any major university. Sprawling lawns stretched as far as the eye could see. Located on the foothills of the mixed-evergreen forest, stately buildings with Italian red tiled roofs and student dorms were mixed in with madrones, cedars, redwoods, and ponderosa pines. The university was known for being a leader in environmental responsibility and attracted students from all around the country.

Zoe had directed us to the side entrance of the museum. I pulled into the parking lot and parked in front of the large double doors. An armored van blocked the ramp to the basement level. Two security guards in blue uniforms were posted on either side of the door.

"Whoa, this is next level," Steph noted. "How much is the manuscript worth, again?"

"Millions," I replied, feeling the weight of more than just getting our structures inside in one piece. The gala *was* next level, and at this point, I could only hope that we'd done enough to prepare for it.

SOMA was designed to handle large deliveries, so hopefully getting the showpieces set up inside would be much easier than the first leg of our trip. The team worked on removing the chocolate structures out of the van while I went to find Zoe.

SOMA's architecture was its own art piece with its massive three-story windowed walls. The second and third stories formed a curved archway with crisscrossing iron slats through the glass, making it appear like a giant geodesic dome. A courtyard on the upper level offered a panoramic view of the goldenrod bluffs to the east where the tip of Grizzly Peak was dusted with snow.

A student art center, the Starving Artist, was located on the basement level with an outdoor kiln and every art supply imaginable. A sign that read ART FOR STUDENTS, BY STUDENTS—TAKE WHAT YOU NEED, BRING WHAT YOU DON'T made me smile.

Zoe was waiting for me at the door with one finger pressed to her smart watch. "You are right on time." She bent her neck slightly and peered through her bright aqua frames before making notes on her iPad. "Follow me this way, I'll take you to the exhibit room. We're running behind, so I'm going to need to make this quick."

The interior of the museum matched the exterior aesthetic with vast cream-colored exhibit halls and shiny cement floors.

I sucked in a breath when Zoe led us into the new exhibit hall. I felt like I was stepping back in time. The space had been transformed to resemble Shakespeare's London. Wooden plank paths lined the floor. A Tudor-style mural covered every inch of the walls. The room had been lit with golden electric candles and lanterns that flickered naturally, casting a warm, antique glow on faded documents locked behind glass cases and mannequins dressed with the Bard's elaborate ruff and pantaloons.

Zoe didn't give us a minute to pause. She directed workers putting the finishing touches on the exhibit out of our way and took us to a long table near the back of the room. If I had thought that Torte had been a frenzy of activity these past few days, there was no comparison with SOMA. Dozens of volunteers dressed in black scurried around the exhibit halls like skittish rabbits.

"The chair should go on this side," Zoe said to my team, showing them the table draped in a black tablecloth. An ornate candelabra sat on the center of the table. "And the desk goes on that side. We can adjust the wall-mounted and overhead lighting as needed."

I crossed my fingers as both of the structures were loaded onto the table. It wasn't until the chocolate desk and chair had been placed perfectly on either side of the candelabra that I finally breathed deeply. Our creations had survived the trip intact.

"Great work, everyone. Group hug?" I waved them closer. We formed a circle. I felt like a coach pumping up the team before the biggest game of the year. "You guys have been awesome. I know I've been a little jumpy, but we're in the homestretch—we're almost done. Head out. Get some good sleep, and we'll make the final push tomorrow."

With that, I sent everyone home except for Steph. She got to work doing minor touch-ups and adhering filagree pieces that were too delicate to transport. While she completed that, Zoe walked me through the rest of the museum.

Staff members and volunteers raced around doing a variety of last-minute tasks from dusting the ceiling to running extension cords. "How's everything coming together?" I asked as Zoe paused to inspect programs that would be handed out to each guest.

"It's a nightmare. I think I'm going to pull an all-nighter. I've been putting out fires all day while Javier is off wining and dining donors, like we have a budget for that." She ran her finger along a list of tasks on her iPad. "At this point it's going to be a miracle if we're ready."

I looked around us. Aside from the crew of staff, the exhibit appeared to be in good shape. "It looks great to me."

"You're only seeing the surface. There's so much more that goes into a show like this, and we don't have anywhere near the staff we need. We're relying heavily on volunteers, which is giving me an ulcer." She glanced at her watch. "I'm supposed to be meeting with a high-end art dealer from Seattle who has very deep pockets and has expressed an interest in partnering with us, but now I have a docent training in an hour that Cindy was supposed to be running. Apparently she's too busy with some special task that Javier assigned her. I don't believe that for one minute. What could be more important than this? And what am I supposed to say to my contact from Seattle? Just leave him hanging? This is crazy—we are way understaffed." She caught the eye of a young security guard and waved him over, then she turned to me and lifted a finger. "Hang on one sec."

I couldn't help but agree with her about staffing. I would have expected that SOMA would hire additional help for an event of this magnitude.

The security guard dragged his feet along the concrete floors as he came toward us. His shaggy hair, untucked shirt, and baggy pants didn't exactly match the aesthetic of the rest of the museum. He moved at the pace of molasses. I wondered if he was a college student on a work study program.

"Dylan, come on, hurry up!" Zoe snapped twice.

Neither her words nor her snapping inspired him to move faster.

"This guy drives me crazy," she said to me. "I swear he does this just to annoy me."

If that was true, it was clearly working.

She tapped her foot on the concrete so fast it sounded like a woodpecker trying to carve out a nest in a tree. "Dylan, move it!"

Dylan finally plodded to us. Upon closer inspection, he definitely appeared young. He was broad shouldered with dark hair that stuck out in every direction as if he had just gotten out of bed. Maybe he had. He yawned and stared at Zoe. "What's up?"

"What's up?" She pointed to a large glass case in the center of the room. "We've been over this too many times to count, Dylan. I've told you that you are not to take your eyes off of the manuscript—not for a second! That is your only job. I want you within ten feet of the display case at all times."

"You mean, like, now?" His speech mirrored his lumbering movements. I couldn't tell if he was simply a slow mover or if maybe he had smoked too much pot.

"Yes, I mean, *like*, always." She placed her glasses on the tip of her nose and stared through the lenses at him. "This is the most valuable piece of art the museum has ever housed, and we can't take any chances."

"But it's just staff." Dylan sounded confused.

"It doesn't matter. Your job is to keep one eye on the manuscript at all times."

"You mean no rounds?"

Zoe huffed. "No rounds. I've told you this already. Tim is going help out with that. I want you in here the entire time, understood?"

"So you don't want me doing my normal loop?" he repeated, wrinkling his forehead in confusion. "But that's not what you—"

"No. Stop. Don't say one more word." She cut him off. Then she looked at me and rolled her eyes. She took a second to compose herself, pulling her lips in like a fish and audibly sighing. "Dylan, let me repeat this one last time. You have one job for the weekend—do not take your eyes off that glass case, got it?"

"Yeah, sure." His nonchalant tone made it clear he couldn't care less.

"Good." Zoe made another check on her to-do list. "Okay, Jules, if you want to come with me, I'll take you to the kitchen and then we can talk through the setup for the buffet."

I gave Dylan a smile before trailing after Zoe.

"He is the worst, isn't he?" she asked, not waiting for an answer. "Javier hired him last year on a work-study program, and I've told him that Dylan is worthless. Thank goodness we're in Ashland, where nothing dangerous ever happens, because I swear Dylan couldn't catch a slug if he tried. It's not usually a very big deal, but this exhibit is worth millions. The exhibit came with its own guards who are going to be patrolling the grounds, but part of the contract was that we needed to hire someone to stand next to *Double Falsehood*. I warned Javier that we should hire additional outside security for the gala and the duration of the show, but he wouldn't listen. He said there was no extra budget for it, but I think it's a huge mistake. We should have a team of five or ten people patrolling every public space, but Javier doesn't want to hear that." Her turquoise glasses had slipped farther down her nose. She pushed them up.

"Five or ten people for one manuscript?" I repeated. That sounded drastic to me.

"The other museums that will be hosting this exhibit have entire armed security teams. We have a pothead college student who struggles to string more than three words together in a sentence. If I were running the museum, things would be very different, but I'm not, so I'm not going to stress about it. If something happens, it's not on me." She bit the side of her cheek and shrugged.

Not that I was one to judge, but she seemed to be struggling to follow her own guidance. On the way to the kitchen, we bumped into a custodian who was mopping the hallway.

"Tim! I'm so glad to see you," Zoe said, stopping long enough to introduce us. "This is Jules from Torte. She and her team are catering the gala tomorrow night, so you two might want to coordinate. We'll have our volunteer docents circulating to clear plates and glasses, but I would like extra trash and recycling set up throughout each of the halls. Guests can be so careless at events like this, especially after they've had a couple glasses of wine. I don't want to see a discarded napkin end up on the floor."

"No problem." Tim shot his finger at her. He was older. I would put him near sixty, with graying hair and rugged features that made me guess that he had spent an ample amount of time outside in the backcountry. "You want me to do a walk-through every thirty minutes, too, right?"

"That would be great." Zoe made a note on her iPad. "I've assigned Dylan to the manuscript, so another set of eyes would be good, especially checking any out-of-bounds areas.

I'll be putting up signs and roping off sections of the museum tomorrow, but you've been around long enough to know that there's always some tipsy guest who goes off in search of a bathroom only to find themselves in the artifacts section in the basement."

Tim laughed. "Oh yeah, I've shooed my fair share of drunk guests out of off-limits places over the years."

"Exactly, and I don't want to take any chances with this exhibit." Zoe looked to me. "Is there anything you or your staff need from Tim? He's been around for years and knows everything about the museum."

"Not off the top of my head. I mean obviously, trash and recycling subtly placed near the food tables would be good."

"I'll take care of that." Tim plunged his mop in a bucket of soapy water. "And I'll be around tomorrow. Holler if you need something."

"Thanks."

"Okay, good. Let's go see the kitchen." Zoe moved on. My nerves about our chocolate showpieces had calmed, but spending time with her made me wonder if stress was transferable. In some ways it was understandable. The *Shakespeare's Lost Pages* exhibit was a big deal for SOMA and the university, but teams of armed security guards patrolling our sweet little Ashland? Was Zoe high-strung? Or could there be a legitimate threat to the exhibit's safety?

I didn't have time to dwell on Zoe's emotional health. There was much to be done tomorrow, and I needed a good night's sleep. Once I finished at the museum, I went home and called it an early night, knowing that I would need all the beauty rest I could muster and an IV of caffeine to get me through the next day.

Chapter Five

Long before dawn the next day, I awoke without an alarm. Carlos rolled over and massaged my neck. "Good morning, mi querida. It is going to be a good day, si?" He nuzzled my cheek. I leaned into his caress, drinking in the scent of his crisp, woodsy aftershave.

"I'm nervous," I admitted. "It feels like the first day of school."

He ran his fingers through my hair. "Do not stress. It will be fine. It will be wonderful. You'll see."

I gave him a kiss before we got up and pulled on jeans and a sweatshirt for prep, knowing that we would have time to come home and change into our evening wear before the gala. "Julieta, how are you so happy when it is so early the moon is taking the sun's place?" Carlos asked as we finished getting ready. "No one should look so beautiful and have such color at this hour."

"You know me. I've always been a morning person. Plus, as soon as we get to Torte, there will be coffee. Lots of coffee."

He pulled me into a hug and held me in his arms for a moment. "This is why I love you." Before he released me we shared a long, passionate kiss. "Okay, we must get to the bakeshop for this promise of coffee."

Coffee fueled us and the rest of the team as we prepped every last-minute detail for the gala. The desserts would be completed at Torte. But the bulk of the dinner course—the stew, game hens, and hand pies—would be baked and assembled at the museum. SOMA's event kitchen would become a warming and finishing station for the salads and fruit and cheese trays. We simply didn't have enough room in our kitchen to get everything done. The kitchen was an organized disaster. Prep boxes, stacks of expensive nuts and cheeses, tubs brimming with fruits and dainty pastries, and piping bags had been stacked on every open inch of the countertop and island. We were left to find little sections of counter space for our daily tasks.

Thanks to our minute-by-minute schedule, the last of the prep was done by midmorning, which freed Carlos, Sterling, and Marty to begin piling the food and supplies that had overtaken the kitchen into the van and head to SOMA before lunch. I agreed that I would help see the rest of the team through the lunch rush and then meet them there later.

Lunch rush was manageable, given that we'd done so much work in advance. I went upstairs to make sure everything was running smoothly. Customers noshed on apple butter and Brie paninis and fall harvest salads in the dining room. Golden November light flooded the windows, basking the sidewalks in the plaza with warmth and illuminating the changing deciduous trees.

Andy, who was running the bar solo while Sequoia helped downstairs, was the only person unhappy about seeing the auburn glow outside on the plaza. "Man, I would have bet good money that it was going to snow. My snow gods never fail me. I don't know what's wrong. I was sure we were going to get an early snow."

"Maybe you should have made your appeal to the snow *goddesses* or put in a word directly with Mother Earth," I bantered back.

"Yeah, good thinking, boss. I'm going to do that tonight. Goddess power. I feel you on that, and the good news is that the sun is out, but it is bitter cold today. I'm not giving up on a pre-Thanksgiving whiteout." His hands worked like a dealer at Vegas, flying over the humming espresso machine with ease.

"How are you feeling about the rest of the afternoon? Are you good to close if I take off for SOMA?"

"No problem. It's been steady but not anything I can't handle. Go knock 'em dead."

"That's the plan," I said, crossing my fingers. "Hopefully our food and our presentation are going to impress the guests."

"I'm sure it will, boss. You'll probably get a ton of big events like this now. Torte's going to become the place to go for galas," Andy said, reaching for a bag of beans on the highest shelf adjacent to the espresso machine. I noticed he barely had to stretch. He was already one of the tallest members of our staff and, by the looks of it, still growing.

"Oh no, don't say that." I chuckled. As much as the revenue from the gala was nice for our bottom line, especially during one of the slower months of the year, I wasn't sure I was going to be ready to take on an event of this size again anytime soon.

"Fine, then I'll just stick to my snow dance." He moved to the beat of the overhead music and passed me a paper to-go cup across the bar. "Here, I made you a special latte. I figured you could use an extra jolt of caffeine this afternoon. It's a double latte with a touch of burnt sugar and a hint of salt."

"Sugar and salt, you're speaking my language." I took the latte. "Thank you for this."

"Hey, no worries. I like to remind you that I'm paying attention. It's like you always say—cheese and chocolate. Complete opposites, and yet they work like magic."

"So true." I raised my cup in thanks and went downstairs to do one last check on things before heading to SOMA. My trusty tool kit included fresh aprons, flat spatulas, extra piping bags of our silky buttercream, and chocolate for any final touch-ups that might be needed for the showpieces. A mix of excitement and nerves erupted in my stomach as I slung a tote bag over my shoulder and walked outside, sipping Andy's sweet and salty latte.

The plaza wasn't bustling like it would be at the peak of summer, but locals milled around, lingering over their lunch breaks on the brick benches and strolling through Lithia Park to take in nature's display of color. Brilliant red, yellow, and burnt orange leaves showered down in fall's chromatic flush. The Lithia fountains in the center of the plaza bubbled with the odor of healing sulfur. While the waters were known for their health properties, they were also an acquired taste. It was always fun to watch tourists try to force a sip down. I paused to take in the floral display in the window at A Rose by Any Other Name. Grapevines and fall foliage had been twisted into miniature wreaths adorned with acorns and sprigs of berries. At Puck's Pub an advertisement for their annual Thanksgiving buffet, complete with roasted turkey legs and garlic smashed potatoes, made my stomach growl. Two college students busked on the corner, strumming guitars in unison.

How lucky I am to live here, I thought, basking in the luminous glow around me.

A voice interrupted my moment of zen.

I stopped in midstride as the sound of a familiar booming baritone voice echoed from across the street.

"Capshaw! Where are you going?"

I looked up to see Richard Lord standing on the Merry Windsor's front porch. Richard had managed to get under my skin since I had returned home to Ashland. He owned the dilapidated hotel and had made it his mission to do everything in his power to make my life miserable. His latest escapade had been installing a summer ice cream cart to compete with Scoops. Not that we had anything to worry about. Shakescream—as Richard had named his temporary cart—served stale store-bought ice cream bars on the cheap.

The one thing I had to credit Mr. Lord with was tenacity. Regardless of less-than-stellar feedback and plenty of one- and two-star reviews online, he refused to let go of our feud, a feud that had been entirely contrived by him. I did my best to avoid him whenever possible.

"Can't talk, Richard. I'm on my way to an event." I threw him a wave, clutched my coffee cup, and speed walked in the opposite direction.

I could hear him mutter under his breath as I walked away.

I passed the blue awnings of the police station, where Thomas and the Professor stood outside chatting. Thomas was Ashland's lead deputy. He and I had been friends since high school. We had dated for a few years before I left for culinary school. When I had returned home, we had rekindled our friendship, a friendship that I had been very grateful for on many levels, but especially during the first few weeks and months of being heartbroken over leaving Carlos.

"Hey, Jules, how's it going?" Thomas asked. He wore a blue police uniform with shorts and hiking boots. Snow or no snow, Thomas wore shorts year-round.

"Good. I'm on my way to SOMA to get ready for the gala."

"Your mother and I are looking forward to the event— *Shakespeare's Lost Pages*, that does have a wonderful ring to it, doesn't it?" the Professor replied. Officially he was my stepfather, but neither of us liked that term. Since marrying Mom at a gorgeous vineyard wedding amongst the vines at Uva, he had become a second father to me. I had always appreciated his affinity for the Bard and his deep commitment to the community, and over the last few years, our personal relationship had filled a void I had felt since my dad died.

Unlike Thomas, he never dressed in a uniform. Today he wore a pair of slacks and a wool jacket. "Black tie in Ashland to celebrate unearthing a lost manuscript from the Bard, I wouldn't miss it for anything. I've been on pins and needles for days. I can't believe that we here in Ashland are going to be graced with a first glimpse of *Double Falsehood*. My head is absolutely aflutter. What an utter delight tonight is going to be."

I'd never seen him so giddy. The Professor was more versed in Shakespeare than anyone I knew, which was saying a lot, given that Ashland was Shakespeare Central. He could quote sonnets and soliloquies at will (pun intended) and rattle off random facts about Shakespeare's most obscure characters.

"It's exciting," I agreed. "Are you and Kerry coming?" I

asked Thomas, taking a couple big drinks of my latte. He had recently gotten engaged to Ashland's newest detective. Mom and I had been pressing them to set a date, but as of yet, they hadn't committed to a date, let alone a season.

"No. We're on duty tonight." He ran his fingers along the light brown stubble on his cheeks, which appeared to be getting thicker. I wondered if he was growing a beard in honor of No-Shave November.

"Someone has to keep an eye out for any scarecrow thieves," the Professor kidded. "Did you hear that a few seniors from Ashland High stole the scarecrow from Orchard Farms?"

I shook my head.

"It's part of their senior prank. They're holding the scarecrow hostage as a fundraiser for the local food pantry. I myself appreciate a clever prank and community mindset, but the owner of Orchard Farms wants us to arrest them." The Professor patted Thomas on the shoulder. "Fortunately, Thomas and Kerry have the task of finding a way to appease him." His eyes twinkled.

"Lucky you," I said to Thomas, finishing off my coffee.

"That's the life on the mean streets of Ashland, what can I say?" He tapped the police badge pinned to his chest.

"Well, on that note, I should get moving, but I'll see you and Mom later, and good luck with scarecrows, Thomas." I waved and continued up Main Street, passing the historic Ashland Springs Hotel, shops and boutiques, and the library. Fall's touch was evident on front porches with their collections of pumpkins and gourds, and in the earthy scent of the leaves crunching beneath my feet. Wild turkeys strutted in front lawns, showing off their kaleidoscope of tail feathers. Pinecones nearly the size of my palm littered the sidewalks.

Squirrels scrambled to gather fallen acorns, preparing themselves for the upcoming winter. A neighbor had told me that an early acorn drop portended a cold, harsh winter. I wondered if she was right.

The walk helped clear my head. By the time I made it to campus, I felt ready to tackle the last of the baking and setup.

I was greeted at the door by a frazzled Zoe. Her glasses hung crooked on her nose. Wispy hairs stuck out as if she had jammed her finger in a light socket. "Oh, thank goodness, you're finally here."

I glanced at my watch. It was shortly after two. "What do you mean?"

She took off her glasses and rubbed them on her sleeve. "Everyone is late. There's tons to do. Tons. I don't even know where to start. This is a disaster in the making."

"I'm not late. I'm actually early. I had planned to be here around three." I could smell the herbed game hens. "Plus, half my team is already in the kitchen."

"Fine. Whatever." Her tone was shrill and piercing. "Just focus, okay? I need to see the tables being set up soon, though, understood? We can't wait until the eleventh hour to set up the food."

"That's not entirely true," I countered. "We talked about this. You know we can't place the hot items until the guests arrive. If we set them out now, they'll be like ice when you open the doors."

"Yes, but what about the cakes and the other desserts that aren't served chilled? Can't you get those out?" She tugged at her hair. "We have to get something out. I have to be able to check something off my list."

Why was she freaking out?

"We will." I tried to make sure my tone remained calm. "That's why Javier hired us. We're professionals. We know what we're doing."

She gave her body a shake like a dog after a muddy swim. "Sorry. Sorry. You're right. I'm sorry. I shouldn't be berating you. There's just so much more to do, and I'm completely on my own. Javier is giving donors behind-the-scenes tours. Who knows what Ernest is doing. Last I saw him, he was down in the archives doing who knows what. If this gala is a bust, it's on my shoulders, and I can't take that kind of responsibility. I have a dissertation to finish. A job search to begin."

"It won't be a bust," I assured her. "Don't worry."

She forced a smile, but by the way her jaw remained clenched tight, I didn't think my words had gotten through. "I'll leave you to it. I need to go find Tim—he's been sulking in the basement, and Dylan is nowhere to be found, despite me threatening to kill him if he left his post again."

Her hysteria made me reflect on my own stress the past week. No gala was worth it, Shakespeare's lost work or not.

I left with another promise that there was no need for her to worry about the food. That was confirmed when I walked into the kitchen to find Sterling, Marty, and Carlos working seamlessly in their crisp chef whites.

"It smells amazing in here, and you guys look so professional. I feel like I'm back in the kitchens at the *Amour of the Seas*," I said, putting down my bag of supplies and tying on an apron. "What can I do?"

Carlos motioned to the door. "Keep that woman out of here. She has been in to check on us like we are toddlers at least twenty times." He sounded exasperated. "Julieta, you know that I am not easily annoyed, but this Zoe woman must be banned from the kitchen. She is stressing out the food."

"I know. I just talked to her. I'll take care of it. In fact, I'm going to start prepping the dessert table with the cakes, marzipans, and shortbreads. That should calm her down." I washed my hands and went to the walk-in to get the trays of opera cakes, frangipane tarts, and marzipans.

"Si, this is good. You keep her out of the kitchen, and everything will go smoothly."

I took the tray of marzipan fruits to the exhibit hall. I didn't disagree with Carlos about a happy kitchen, and my interaction with Zoe had confirmed that her stress level was off the charts. I would make it my mission to run interference with her for the next few hours.

As I began placing the marzipans shaped and painted like pears, apples, strawberries, oranges, and grapes on gold-edged cake stands, I heard voices nearby. Arguing voices, to be more exact. The fight appeared to be going on in the next room. I left the dessert table to go get a better look.

Ernest stood next to the glass case containing *Double Falsehood*, Shakespeare's priceless lost manuscript. A single spotlight hanging from the ceiling shone down on the case, illuminating the faded paper. The Professor's words rang in my head. It was unbelievable that we were getting to debut one of the most historical finds of the century here in Ashland. No one had seen these pages for over four hundred years. I was looking at Shakespeare's actual handwriting. It was impossible not to be awestruck.

Ernest wasn't caught up in grandeur. He waved a finger in Dylan's face. "I told you not to touch that. Not a finger."

"But Javier told me—" Dylan tried to respond.

"I don't care what Javier tells you. My money is paying for this exhibit, and what I say is the final word." Ernest smoothed the front of his tux.

"Did you talk to Zoe?"

"About what?" Ernest huffed. "I don't take orders from a glorified assistant."

Dylan backed away from him. "Okay. Whatever."

"Don't back talk me, young man. I'll have your job and your head." With that, he shook a finger in Dylan's face and stomped away.

I went back to the dessert table, wondering if I should go track down Javier. Maybe it was time for him to pull his team together and calm everyone down.

Chapter Six

Javier was nowhere to be found, so I focused on setting up the dessert display and directing Steph, Bethany, and Rosa when they arrived. We stood back to observe our work after the very last chestnut cream custard, passion fruit curd tart, and frankincense and wild orange cake had been placed on the table. The presentation looked like a scene fit for royalty, with the chocolate art pieces serving as stunning bookends for the bounty of sweets and nibbles.

One of my favorite pieces were the imprime cakes we had created to resemble the calligraphy on *Double False-hood*. To make the cakes, Steph had used our dark chocolate cake batter to pipe some of Shakespeare's most famous quotes, like "All the world's a stage" and "If music be the food of love, play on" on a sheet pan. Then we had spread our vanilla sponge batter over the top. Once the cakes had baked, we simply flipped them over to reveal the design. It's a relatively simple technique, yet it looked like we had spent hours on crafting the dainty, edible quotes.

Floral bouquets from A Rose by Any Other Name finished the whimsical feast. Botanical herbs and trees straight from the pages of Shakespeare's canon along with blood-red roses and purple pansies filled the exhibit hall. Amber tapered candles in iron candelabras cast a sparkly sheen on marzipans dusted in jewel-colored sugars. Inkwells, parchment, and quills were on display throughout the vast, long room. Framed Shakespearean quotes, pictures of the Globe and of the Bard himself hung from the walls. Swaths of velvet draped the doorways.

As I surveyed the final display, a feeling of calm washed over me. Every event needs good flow, and tonight's gala was no exception. I felt confident with how we had arranged the food stations. We had opted to display desserts and appetizers on the long tables in the hallway adjacent to the main exhibit. Volunteers would circulate through the foyer and small exhibit rooms with wine and appetizers. The main course—our stews and hand pies—would be served in the large gallery on the far side of the museum, where a troupe from OSF would be performing a variety of Shakespearean skits as dinner entertainment. *Double Falsehood* would remain locked behind closed doors until Javier signaled that it was time for the grand reveal.

"Amazing work, everyone," I said, pulling the team in for a group hug. "I couldn't have done it without you. Enjoy the rest of the night and don't come in early tomorrow. We're going to open late."

Bethany lingered, pulling over a chair to stand on in order to take a shot of the elegant display from above. "I have to capture this before I go. It's so dreamy. Those little imprime cakes are the cutest. They look like love notes. We should do more of these for the holidays. I'm seeing Christmas trees, presents, stars. Wouldn't that be cute?"

"Yeah, go for it." I gave her a grin and checked my watch. The gala doors would be opening in less than an hour. I went to find Carlos in the kitchen so we could hurry up the hill to our house for a quick costume change. When I stepped inside the humid kitchen, he was using a torch to turn the edges of his mashed potatoes on top of ramekins of hearty beef stew golden brown. "What do you think, good?" He placed the ramekin on a tray.

Instead of scooping a mound of potatoes on top of the stew, he had piped them into a cone, brûléed the edges, and tucked a sprig of fresh green parsley on the top.

"Gorgeous, and they smell so good I want to grab a fork and devour it, but we need to get cleaned up." I nodded to the clock above his workstation.

He untied the apron around his waist. "Si."

"You guys go," Sterling said. "I'll make sure everything is 'GBD, baby,' as Bethany likes to say."

"GBD?" I raised my eyebrows. "I don't know that I've heard her say that."

"Gold, brown, and delicious." He winked. "It's her new phrase. She's using that hashtag on anything and everything she can."

Carlos chuckled. He gave the crew a few last-minute instructions before removing his chef's coat and leaving with me.

We made the quick trip home and an equally speedy transition out of baking clothes and into our outfits for the event. I opted for a long navy dress, cut with a V-neck that was trimmed with tiny silver sequins. I paired it with navy heels and a cream cashmere wrap. I dusted my cheeks with blush, applied silvery eye shadow, mascara, and a pale pink lip gloss. Then I tied my hair up into a messy bun and completed the look with a silver rhinestone headband.

"Julieta, you take my breath away." Carlos waited for me at the bottom of the stairs. It had been a while since I'd seen him in a tux. He looked suave and debonair in his classic black tux that brought out his natural skin tone and dark hair. His eyes locked on mine, making my heart rate speed up.

"You don't look so bad yourself."

When I reached the bottom of the steps, he pulled me to him. "Maybe we don't need to go to the gala. I can keep you all for myself tonight."

His lips brushed across mine.

After a minute, I pulled away. "Carlos, you'll ruin my lip gloss."

He gave me a playful kiss on the cheek. "You do not need it, mi querida, you are beautiful just as you are." He reached for my hand. "I will be the envy of every man in the room tonight."

I looped my hand through his as we went out to the car. Even though SOMA was just down the street, navigating the steep incline in a dress and open-toed shoes would be challenging, and I had a feeling tonight might be a late one. Walking back up the hill at midnight when Ashland's forests critters came out didn't sound like fun.

I checked my lip gloss in the rearview mirror. It wasn't often that my baker's hours called for a ball gown. The last time I remembered seeing Carlos in a tux was on the *Amour of the Seas*. We used to host a send-off dinner on the last night of the luxury cruise. As head chef, Carlos would always make an appearance at the captain's table, where he would spend the duration of the meal being fawned over by adoring passengers. Not that I blamed them. Carlos's food was transformative. He didn't simply cook—he embodied every part of himself in each dish he served. On rare occasions I would join him for dinner, but since my shift began while most guests were finally dragging themselves to bed after a long night of merrymaking, I was usually proofing yeast for the cinnamon rolls and sweet bread they would enjoy for brunch.

A realization struck me. In the time that Carlos had been in Ashland, we had spent more time together than in all the years we'd been at sea.

Carlos steered the car with one hand and used the other to caress my fingers. "What is it, mi querida? You have a faraway look in your eye."

"I just realized how much time we've spent together lately." A lightness spread through my chest at the happy thought.

"Is that bad?"

"No, no. Not at all."

He squeezed my hand tighter. "Good, because we have much time to make up for." His eyes glinted with longing.

By the time we returned to SOMA, a line of guests stretched all the way from the museum to fill pathways surrounded by fiery red burning bush that connected the upper and lower portions of campus and led to the Hannon Library. Carlos and I passed garden art sculptures in the quad as we made our way to the long queue.

"Darling! Juliet! Carlos! Over here," a voice I knew well called from the back of the line. Lance, my dear friend and the artistic director at OSF, waved with two fingers. He wore a long gray overcoat and matching leather gloves as he stood next to his date, Arlo. They made a striking couple. Lance with his fair skin, dark hair, and catlike features. Arlo with his tall muscular shoulders, black skin, and bald head. When

Arlo had been hired as the interim managing director for the festival, Lance had immediately been smitten. So much so that he had taken to drinking beer and wearing baseball hats on the weekend. Shock of shocks, I know.

We joined them. Lance reached for my hands and gushed over my dress. "You are an utter vision, as always. What do you want from me? Must I drop to my knees and beg you to grace my stage with those cheekbones and neckline?" He kissed my cheeks before hugging Carlos.

"Ignore him," Arlo whispered in my ear.

"Trust me, that was my plan," I teased, hugging him too.

"You know, I promised that I had the perfect show for you, Juliet, and the board met this morning to finalize next season. It's happening. I'm going to make you a star." He gave me a deliberate smile that radiated smugness.

"A star?" Carlos looked confused.

"Don't ask." I shook my head. "You'll only encourage him."

Lance stabbed himself in the heart. "Ouch. That stings. And when I'm simply doing you a favor. Who wouldn't want to grace my stage?"

"Well, me for one." I pointed to my chest. "That's going to be a challenge, considering I have no interest or time to be in a production at OSF. And then there's the minor detail that I haven't acted since I was twelve years old."

"Nonsense." He flicked the thought away with his thumb and middle finger. "Arlo, back me up, please."

Arlo held his arms up in surrender. He was dressed in a black tux with a red scarf and gloves. "I'm not getting in the middle of this one. No way."

Carlos nodded. "Si, you are a wise man."

They stepped forward in line together and began talking about soccer. Arlo coached the women's softball team at SOU in his free time and was an avid soccer fan, which had bonded him immediately to my husband. Carlos had embraced life in Ashland with ease, with one exception— American football. He was disgusted that soccer took a backseat to football. "This is not football, Julieta. I don't understand. They do not even use their feet!"

Fortunately he had discovered SOU's soccer teams and quickly became a regular at matches.

"Juliet, before you dismiss the idea, let me tell you what show we're bringing to the Lizzie next year. I swear this production was made for you." He fanned his hand out in front of him. "I can picture it now. You, center stage, under a starlit sky, the audience at the Lizzie completely captivated by your rapturous beauty."

The Lizzie was Lance's term of endearment for the outdoor Elizabethan theater.

"I'm listening." Which was only true because I was excited to hear what was in the lineup for the new season, not because I had even the faintest interest in being involved in anything other than watching the show.

"Drumroll." Lance twirled his tongue. "Wait for it." He pounded his palms on his thighs. "*Waitress*!"

"Okay?" I squished my eyebrows together.

Lance let out an impatient snort. "*Waitress* as in the Sara Bareilles musical that was a smash sensation on Broadway— sold out shows for months. Nominated for four Tony Awards. *Waitress*, Juliet, *Waitress*. This is your dream role."

I shrugged. "I don't know it."

"My God, the things I must teach you. What would you do without me?" He tugged me forward as the line inched closer to the door. "It's a gem of a show, featuring a baker and waitress in an abusive relationship. It was written just for you."

I looked in front of us to Carlos. "Uh, um, last time I checked, I'm pretty sure that I'm happily married, Lance."

"Details. Details." He waved me off. "I know. Obviously not that part. But this role has everything—a waitress, a baker, and the ultimate quest of finding love. It screams Juliet Montague Capshaw. You were destined for this role. Absolutely destined."

"Lance, there are so many issues with me being involved in the production. Namely, I'm not a professional actor, and I'm running multiple restaurants in town, but the most important is that this is a musical, right?"

"Exactly. Arlo is thrilled because it will 'fill the seats,' as he and the board like to say."

"I'm definitely not your leading lady, because I can't sing."

"What?" Lance recoiled as if I had injured him with my words.

"Nope. Can't sing. Not a note. I can't carry a tune, so there's no way I could carry a musical."

"How did I not know this?" He gasped.

"It's not a secret. In fact, it's a joke in the bakeshop. Everyone begs me not to sing in the kitchen."

He scowled. "Is this some sort of ruse to get out of my show?"

I crossed my heart with my finger. "I solemnly swear I cannot sing to save my life. Ask Carlos."

Lance tapped Carlos on the shoulder, interrupting his and Arlo's conversation. "Carlos, tell me, can your beautiful wife sing? Surely she must. There's nothing that the remarkable Juliet can't do."

"Julieta?" Carlos winced. "Oh no. No." He shook his head repeatedly. "She has many talents, but singing is not one of them, is it, mi querida?"

"Told you." I punched Lance in the shoulder.

"What am I going to do now?" Lance wailed.

"Audition the cast," Arlo retorted as we made it to the entrance.

Once inside, we got pulled in multiple directions. There were touches of Shakespeare everywhere and so many familiar faces it was impossible not to get swept into conversations with old friends and fellow business owners. Javier worked the crowd, greeting everyone and thanking them for their support. I enjoyed watching trays of our crab puffs and mini cheese tarts circulating through the foyer along with flutes of bubbly champagne.

I spotted Mom and the Professor chatting with Ernest. Carlos had gone to check in on the kitchen, so I went to join them. Mom looked radiant in an ivory cocktail dress with a burnt orange wrap. The color brought out the natural honey streaks in her hair. The Professor looked distinguished in his tux, but to my surprise, he and Ernest appeared to be in a heated discussion when I approached.

"That's the problem with the anti-Stratfordian theory," the Professor said, folding his hands together. "It's shortsighted, to say the very least."

"And what? You believe some kid who came from illiterate parents, who never attended college, and didn't travel outside of Stratford penned tales of international political intrigue. Impossible! Please!" Ernest huffed. "Tell me this, Doug, how did Will Shakespeare have such a firsthand view of life in the royal court? I'll tell you. He didn't. No way. It wasn't him. It's not possible. You truly believe that a commoner, a working actor, and a provincial glover's son wrote the canon? Someone with no university degree or formal education? I'm convinced that William Shakespeare was a nom de plume for a distinguished contemporary. Someone with high standing. The actual Will Shakespeare was simply used as a front man at the time for the real writer, who didn't want to reveal their true identity."

"Blasphemy." The Professor rolled his eyes. "I'll tell you what your theory is really about—elitist snobbery."

Ernest threw his head back and laughed.

The Professor's cheeks were deep red with color. His jaw was clenched like he was doing everything he could not to explode. I'd never seen him so angry. "It's true. It's modern-day elitism. Classism. Superiority. You can't believe that a common villager like William Shakespeare didn't write the canon. It had to be a playwright from prestigious Oxford. Someone with connections. Someone with money. Am I correct?"

"Yes. Prove to me how someone without a college education wrote *Hamlet*," Ernest challenged with a nasty gleam in his eyes. He wasn't about to budge.

"Gladly." The Professor's jaw relaxed as he smiled. "I'll give you one word—*creativity*. There is no force so great in the world as the creative mind. That's been proven time and time again, and William of Stratford had one of the greatest creative minds of all time. I give you this, his very own words. 'We are such stuff as dreams are made on, and our little life is rounded with a sleep.' That's how William of Stratford penned the greatest works of all time. In his dreams. He tapped into the creative force."

I thought about ducking away as their conversation paused, but Mom caught my eye and shot me a look of thanks for rescuing her. "Oh, Juliet, you're here. Everything is wonderful, isn't it?"

"Yes, it turned out well. I can't wait for Javier to open the doors to the exhibit." I tried to keep my tone upbeat. The last thing I wanted was to get dragged into a debate about Shakespeare's true identity.

The Professor cleared his throat and composed himself. "Juliet, you look lovely tonight."

"Thanks."

Before we could continue the conversation, Javier stood in front of the large walnut doors that led to the main exhibit hall containing *Double Falsehood*. He clinked his champagne glass with the edge of his fork. "Ladies and gentlemen, welcome to SOMA. I'm Javier de la Garza, director of this incredible community resource here in the Rogue Valley, and I'm so pleased to welcome you to the US premiere of *Shakespeare's Lost Pages*. Tonight you will be among the very first people in the world to view this revolutionary discovery."

"What does he think he's doing? It's not time for the reveal yet. People haven't even eaten." Ernest threw his hands up and pushed his way through the crowd.

As Javier continued his brief introduction to how the museum had procured the exhibit and began to explain that the dinner and dessert bars had been crafted to resemble a feast from Shakespeare's time, Ernest interrupted him, yanking the microphone from his hand and pushing Javier aside.

Javier tried to recover, but I could tell from the deep creases on his brow that he wasn't happy that Ernest had barged in. "Ladies and gentlemen, let me take a moment to introduce one of our benefactors for this very special exhibit, Ernest Boyd."

Ernest proceeded to spend the next ten minutes expounding on his important role. The audience shifted uncomfortably as he dragged on and on. His welcome speech sounded more like a threatening lecture about recognizing Shakespeare as a demigod. Ernest made it abundantly clear that he was a Shakespeare "purist." He believed that there was only one pure way to perform Shakespeare's works and that the playwright who called himself, William Shakespeare the Bard of Avon was the sole creator of every piece of material on display. "While we may never know his real identity, tonight we celebrate the one, true, creator of the canon."

"Except that Shakespeare was a woman!" Zoe yelled from the other end of the room. She held a nearly empty glass of wine in one hand and rocked slightly as she spoke. I wondered if she had already been imbibing, or if the stress of the gala had finally gotten the best of her.

"What is happening?" Carlos came up next to me, his gaze moving from Zoe to Ernest. "Shakespeare is a woman? And why is he taking credit for everything?" Carlos asked, voicing what I was thinking. I was waiting for Ernest to claim that he had been responsible for the desserts and dinner buffet as well.

"You want to know the real story of Shakespeare, come find me!" Zoe hollered, her words slurring.

The crowd went quiet.

Zoe held her wineglass high. "Cheers, everyone." Then she stumbled away.

Javier seized the opportunity. Ernest's full attention was focused on Zoe sneaking out of the exhibit hall. Javier grabbed the mic from Ernest's hand and addressed the crowd. "On that note, come feast your eyes and feast your bodies on the delightful spread prepared for you by Ashland's very own Torte. Desserts and appetizers are waiting for you right here." He motioned to our display tables. "There's an authentic Elizabethan feast and entertainment waiting for you in the gallery. Please mingle, drink our delicious Rogue Valley wine, and take in the interactive exhibit halls. We have an extensive collection of art as well. Shortly we will be ready to pop open the champagne and open the doors to let you lay your eyes on Shakespeare's never-before-seen work."

He didn't wait to see Ernest's reaction. Instead he waved to the waiters standing ready with trays of wine and appetizers and encouraged the crowd to disperse.

"That was strange," Mom whispered to me as we followed the masses.

"I'm convinced Ernest and Richard Lord are related. He enjoys listening to the sound of his own voice more than anyone I know, except Richard."

She chuckled. "True, and I can tell you that Doug isn't a fan either."

The Professor and Carlos were behind us.

"Yeah, I could tell."

"Don't get him started on the theory that Shakespeare wasn't Shakespeare. It's literally the only thing that makes his blood pressure skyrocket."

"I thought his comeback was good. I'd never thought of that being an elitist perspective, but it makes sense." Living in Ashland surrounded by thespians with a vast knowledge of the Bard's works meant that I had a peripheral knowledge of the ongoing debate amongst Shakespeare scholars, like the Professor, and those in Ernest's camp, who believed someone outside of Stratford must have written the collection of plays and sonnets. But it wasn't an argument I'd had much time or interest in tracking.

"I'm going to keep the two of them apart for the rest of the evening," Mom said. "We don't have many galas in Ashland, and Doug isn't even on call tonight. He's trying to take on a smaller role and let Thomas and Kerry handle more responsibilities on his quest to retirement. Which means that I intend to enjoy myself. Drink some delicious wine. Eat those wonderful sweets we've been working so hard on, and mingle with friends."

"That sounds like a good plan. You should do just that." I kissed her on the cheek as she went to get in line for a glass of wine. I needed to check on the dessert table. As I squeezed past a couple admiring our chocolate brocade chair, I noticed Tim, the custodian, and Cindy, the docent whom I had met at Torte, standing behind the dessert table guarding the pretty dishes of custard and lardy cake as if their lives depended on it.

"Hey, what's going on?" I asked.

Cindy startled and clutched her chest. "You scared me."

"Sorry. I was just wondering if something's wrong with the dessert table?"

"Not with the *dessert,* no. The dessert is fine," Tim responded in a weird code.

Cindy's head bobbed in agreement. "The dessert is fine. We were discussing another issue. That's all."

Tim shot her a strange look.

"Not an issue." She paused, blinking rapidly as if trying to find the right words. "Uh, I guess you could say a slight mishap. That's all."

"A mishap?" I asked.

"Maybe. We're not sure." Cindy gnawed on her bottom lip.

I was confused, but before I could ask more, she stole a sideways glance at Tim and leaned toward me.

"Tim thinks that the manuscript is missing. *Double False-hood,* the one thing that everyone is here to see tonight. He thinks it's gone. As in gone. Like, vanished. Ernest is about to open the doors, and the manuscript isn't there. It's been stolen."

Chapter Seven

"Cindy, I told you not to say anything. We have to contain this." Tim scowled. He yanked us both back away from the guests who had begun filling dessert plates with chocolate pots de crème, Banbury tarts, and bite-sized honey drops.

"Wait, what's going on? You think the manuscript, as in *Double Falsehood,* was stolen?" I asked, wondering if I had heard them wrong. "The doors are locked. How could anyone have gotten in?"

Tim shrugged.

"It's missing? Like, the case is empty?" My throat went dry. An uncomfortable heat crept up my back.

"No." Tim frowned, shooting daggers at Cindy. "That's why I said we need to contain this. There's a document in there, but it doesn't look right to me. I think someone took the original and swapped it with a forgery."

"Have you told Javier?" I glanced around us. Patrons

dressed in expensive evening wear sipped wine and nibbled on cheese and fruit, completely oblivious to the fact that the highly valued and anticipated document they were here to see was potentially missing.

"That's what I was just saying," Cindy said, glaring at Tim. "Javier needs to know."

"We can't tell him now. Not with all these people here." Tim's tone was firm and unyielding.

"We can't *not* tell him," Cindy wailed. "In a few minutes he's going to open the door to the main hall. We have some of the world's leading experts on Shakespeare here tonight. Scholars. Do you know some of the names on the guest list? I do. I've memorized it. These are people who have spent lifetimes studying the Bard's works. If you think it's a forgery, they will too."

"Hold on." I tried to make sense of what they were both saying. I turned to Tim. "Why do you think it's a forgery?"

"I don't know a lot about artifacts." Tim rubbed his stubbly chin. "But I've worked here long enough to know every detail about the display cases, and the one out there is wrong."

"Wrong how?"

"It's not the same one we installed. The hinges are different. They're brass, and the others were chrome." He sounded certain.

"Are you sure?"

"Yep." Tim looked into the adjoining room. He motioned for us to follow him. I hurried behind Cindy as Tim took us to the main exhibit hall and unlocked the massive walnut doors. He motioned for us to get inside and quickly shut the door behind us again. Dylan, the security guard, stood next to the glass case with one hand on his hip. Aside from the display case, the cavernous room housed a variety of

Shakespearean art mounted to the walls. A single burgundy velvet rope wrapped around the display case in order to ensure that people didn't crowd in too close to the valuable document.

"Is Dylan armed?" I asked, wondering why Dylan's left hand was clutched to his hip.

Cindy gave me a funny look. "No, of course not. He has a Taser, but we would never hire armed guards. I mean, I think the guys outside might have Tasers too, but I'm sure they don't have guns. Why would we have guns at a museum? No, that's unnecessary."

That went against what Zoe had said earlier.

We moved closer to the display case.

"What's up?" Dylan had one elbow propped against the glass.

"Can you give us a minute?" Tim asked, reaching toward a plastic cart with a variety of cleaning supplies and tool belt on the top that was pushed up near the case. Even the bottom half of the supply cart had been decked out in black fabric to match the aesthetic of the exhibit.

"You want me to move?" Dylan scowled.

"Hang out over by the main doors for a minute." Tim directed him with a short nod toward the doors, keeping one hand on his supply cart as he moved it out of the way.

Dylan shrugged. "Okay."

"Look." Tim ducked under the velvet rope and knelt next to the case, running his finger along the shiny latches. "These are different. This isn't the same case they installed when the exhibit arrived. I'm sure of it."

"Uh, maybe you shouldn't touch it," I suggested.

He lurched backward and stared at his fingers like they were covered in blood.

"Yeah. I'm going to find Javier," Cindy insisted. "This is crazy. We have to get to the bottom of this right now. We can't let the guests in here if the manuscript is missing."

Tim stood up and grabbed her wrist to stop her. "No, it will only make things worse."

Cindy freed herself from his clutches. "Let me go. I'm telling Javier, and you can't stop me."

Tim scowled, but he backed away. "You're making a mistake. Javier has a lot riding on tonight. All of us do. No one needs to know. We can tell him after the last guests are out the door and deal with the fallout later."

Why was he so resistant to telling Javier? I understood not wanting to cause a scene at the gala, but if the manuscript was missing, informing Javier and the authorities as quickly as possible was imperative.

Cindy left to find Javier, sending Dylan back to his post.

Tim dropped the subject. "Uh, I guess I'll go get some more trash bags. I've got to take this cart to the basement before we let people in anyway. Zoe will freak out if she sees anything that's out of place." He started toward the door, pulling the cart with him. "People are already devouring the food out there."

Tim's reaction was bizarre. Why the sudden change? And trash bags were the least of my worries. If *Double Falsehood* was missing, we had to get the authorities involved immediately. How had he suddenly gone from pressing Cindy to keep quiet to pretending like everything was fine, to running off to take his supply cart to the basement?

Dylan plodded back over to his post. His eyes were glassy and dull. I wondered if he was on something.

"Did you notice anything with this case?" I asked.

"Huh?" He blinked hard, like he was having trouble understanding me.

"You've been in here alone tonight, right?"

"Yeah, so?"

I decided to be direct. Cindy was getting Javier. The Professor would be next, so there was no point in pretending like everything was normal. "The manuscript might be missing. Has anyone else been in here tonight?"

"Huh?" His mouth hung partway open.

"Look, the police are going to be involved soon. I'm asking you whether you saw anything out of the ordinary tonight. Did you leave? Have you been here the whole time?"

He wrinkled his brow tight and squinted, like he was trying to focus on my words. "Yeah, I've been here."

Progress. "Has anyone come in?"

"Yeah." He ran his fingers through his already disheveled hair. "Zoe came in to check on me. Javier was here. Ernest, Cindy, Tim. Yeah. Everyone."

That didn't exactly narrow it down.

"What about the case?" I pressed my index finger on the top of the glass. "Has anyone been near this?"

He shook his head. "No. Why?"

I gave up. "Stay here. Don't let anyone other than staff in." I left through the side door feeling less than confident that Dylan had processed my words. The side exit took me into the kitchen. As I pushed the kitchen door open, I ran directly into Javier.

"Javier, you're here, good." I could hear that my voice had a breathless quality to it.

He dabbed his forehead with a paper towel. Sweat dripped along his checks. His skin was blotched with color.

"Are you okay?"

He clutched the paper towel in one fist. "No, I've had some terrible news."

"The manuscript?"

His eyes widened, showing off the white edges. "How did you know?"

"I was just talking to Cindy and Tim." I pointed behind us with my thumb. Cindy must have made good time. She had left minutes before me.

"What?" Javier patted his damp brow again with the balled-up paper towel.

"Cindy and Tim just told me."

"How do they know?" He pressed the balled towel to the center of his head and rubbed it around in little circles.

"Sorry. I'm confused. Didn't Cindy come tell you?"

Javier shook his head. "No."

"Then how did *you* know?"

"Ernest. He wants me to clear the museum and call the police." He paused as a volunteer docent balancing two trays filed with puddings and custards passed by us. "I can't do that, Jules. We have way too much invested in tonight. Our funding has taken a hit recently, and we need tonight to go smoothly. I'm counting on some large donations coming in from the gala. If we involve the police now, it will spook investors. We need to get through the evening, and as soon as the guests are gone, I'll call the police immediately."

"The Professor's here," I noted. "Do you think we should loop him in?"

Javier hesitated. He tossed the paper towel in the garbage. "No, you're right. What am I thinking? I can't do this. I suppose it won't look good to the authorities if I keep this under wraps, will it? I can't face telling everyone. This is the worst night of my life."

I moved closer and reached for his arm. "I know. It's terrible. But the sooner you alert the police, the better the odds of finding the manuscript."

He stared at his feet. "Yes, yes. Of course you're right. Could you do it?"

"Do what?"

"Talk to Doug. I need to go have a word with Dylan—immediately. And then I have to make sure that Ernest doesn't do anything rash."

"Okay."

He took off his tux jacket, threw it over his arm, and left the kitchen. I paused for a minute to make sure that everything was running smoothly before searching for the Professor. I found him chatting with Lance at the bar. They each had a martini in hand.

"Juliet, you are without a drink. What's your poison?" Lance turned to the bar.

"I'm fine."

"Nonsense." Lance waved to the bartender. "Can I trouble you for glass of your pinot noir for the lady?"

While he was focused on ordering my drink, I leaned closer to the Professor. "Something's happened. Can I have a word with you?"

"Of course."

Lance handed me a glass of red wine. "A toast to the pastry maven—you've outdone yourself once again."

He clinked his glass to mine.

"Thanks, I have to borrow the Professor for a minute. Kitchen emergency."

Lance smiled broadly, his lids fluttering and his head tilting to the side. "A kitchen emergency. Dash away, darling. I'll keep your spot here warm."

I knew that Lance didn't buy my excuse, but I turned in a hurry.

"What's the problem?" the Professor asked after I had led him to an empty corner of the foyer.

"It's the manuscript. Javier thinks it's been stolen."

"Stolen? *Double Falsehood*?" The Professor sounded as incredulous as I felt.

"Yes, apparently the case is wrong. He and his staff think that someone took the original and swapped it for a fake—case and all."

"They've discovered this now?"

"I guess so." I filled him in on everything Tim, Cindy, and Javier had said.

The Professor was thoughtful. "I'm afraid, then, we must make haste. If there's been a theft of this magnitude, we haven't a moment to spare."

"I agree, but Javier doesn't want to make a scene. He and his staff are actually considering letting the gala go on as planned and dealing with this later."

"As the Bard says, 'Time travels in divers paces with divers persons. I'll tell you who time ambles withal, who time trots withal, who time gallops withal, and who he stands still withal.'"

The Professor had a habit of quoting Shakespeare. It was an endearing quality, but in moments like this, it left me wondering what he meant. "Do you think Javier is stalling on purpose?"

"Perhaps." He nodded. "I understand the angst of having to cause a disruption to this event, but there's no other way around it. A highly valued object is potentially missing. There's no time to delay."

He was right.

I followed him back into the foyer, where he immediately took charge. "Ladies and gentlemen, I have an unfortunate announcement. Let me introduce myself. I'm Ashland's leading detective, and I'm afraid that there's been a bit of a snag. We need to delay the unveiling of the exhibit temporarily. Please continue to enjoy yourselves and the refreshments. We'll give you an update as soon as we're able."

Everyone murmured and looked around the room, but they heeded the Professor's instructions.

I followed the Professor into the main hall.

Dylan started to leave his post. The Professor raised a finger to stop him. "No, I'll need you to stay, young man." Then he turned to me. "Juliet, if you could kindly gather Javier and the other team members, I'll place a call to Thomas and Kerry for support."

I didn't have to search far. Ernest burst inside with Javier trailing behind him. He headed straight for the Professor. "Doug, excellent," he said, invading the Professor's personal space. "Thank goodness you're taking charge. You need to arrest this young man immediately."

Chapter Eight

"Let's take a step back." The Professor's voice was calm and steady. His hands moved like he was practicing Qigong as he attempted to set a different tone. "No one is under arrest. I have yet to determine if there's even been a crime."

"There's been a crime. That manuscript is a fake! And he stole it." Ernest pointed a thick finger at Dylan. His bright red face reminded me of a tomato about to burst. "No one else could have—it had to be him! Arrest him now! Search him! He probably has it on him."

I had thought that when Ernest ran in he was going to accuse Javier of stealing the manuscript, but he thought Dylan had taken *Double Falsehood*?

"Me?" Dylan squinted, sounding equally confused. "Why would I want an old ripped book? I don't care about this thing. I'm here for the paycheck and free food, man. Go ahead and search me if you want." He held his arms out like a T.

"Because it's worth millions." Ernest sprayed spit as he spoke. "More than millions. The artifact that you either took yourself or had a part in letting slip out of this building is perhaps the most significant and priceless discovery of the century. I am personally responsible for bringing it here. I paid for it, and I want it found and returned right now! This minute!"

Javier had shut the doors behind him. "Please, let's keep it down. I can't let word get out the manuscript is missing. I don't know what we're going to say to the guests, but if everyone keeps shouting, there's no way we're going to be able to keep this quiet."

The Professor motioned both men forward. "Where's the rest of the staff?"

Javier glanced behind him. "I'm not sure. Zoe was in her office getting a donation form for a donor. I haven't seen Cindy or Tim for a while."

"I saw them," I piped up.

"Excellent." The Professor nodded. "Juliet, if you would be so kind to go round them up? I'd like to speak with the three of you next, but first I need to call my deputies for backup."

"Backup?" Javier gasped. "You're sending more police? Is that necessary? Squad cars, sirens, flashing lights—that's definitely going to put our guests on edge."

"Yes. I'm afraid it's absolutely necessary."

"We'll say that there's been a leak—a gas leak," Ernest suggested.

"Can we say that?" Javier asked the Professor, his voice filled with a faint hint of hope.

"I can't dictate what you tell the guests at this point,

although procedure for a gas leak would be to evacuate the building." The Professor had already removed his cell phone from his tux jacket.

Javier sighed with disappointment.

Dylan was still standing with his arms out as if he was anticipating being patted down.

"You can go ahead and put your arms down, son." The Professor met Javier's gaze. "I would also caution against saying anything until we have a better sense of what we're dealing with. If a multimillion-dollar manuscript has indeed been stolen, then my team and I will be interrogating everyone in attendance tonight." The Professor's eyes traveled to the glass case.

"No one at the gala could have walked off with a case and an ancient manuscript," Ernest retorted. "The heist had to have taken place before we opened the doors. For all we know, *Double Falsehood* is long gone. Why are you standing around doing nothing?"

"That could be." The Professor left it at that. He ignored Ernest's demanding tone as he placed a call. I took my cue to go find the other staff members while they examined the case and the document inside.

Rumors were already swirling in the exhibit hall. I spotted Carlos first. He was rearranging cheese and fruit platters on the buffet table. "Julieta, what's happening? People are saying that there was an accident or that we are in some kind of danger?"

"No, it's not that." I gave him a quick recap.

"Ah, I see. This is not good at all, but it is good that the Professor is here. What can I do?"

"Keep an eye out for Thomas and Kerry. They should be

here soon. Show them where to go. Javier wants to try to keep this quiet as long as possible." I stood on my toes, glancing around the crowd in search of the other team members.

"I think that is a bad idea, given the theories that are already spreading."

"Agreed," I said, before continuing on through the crowd toward the dessert table. I found Cindy and Zoe huddled together. Neither of them looked happy to see me. "They need you both in the exhibit hall," I explained.

Cindy shot Zoe a triumphant grin. "Told you."

Zoe's mouth hung open. "Is it true? Is the manuscript missing?"

I nodded. "It looks that way. I think they're confirming that now."

"How? How could this happen? Dylan! I told Javier that Dylan was a liability." Zoe's words smashed together as she spoke. She had refilled her wineglass and chugged the pale liquid as she fumed.

Why was everyone's first assumption that the stoner kid had stolen the manuscript? Yes, it was an extremely rare and valuable document, but after spending five minutes with Dylan, I ranked him as the least likely suspect on my list. It seemed like more than a stretch that Dylan would have the contacts, let alone the knowledge of how to go about stealing Shakespeare's lost work.

"I think Javier is trying to keep a lid on this for as long as he can. Maybe it would be better for you two to continue this conversation with the Professor," I suggested, suddenly aware of the fact that we were surrounded by dozens of eyes hungry for details about whatever was happening in the exhibit hall.

"Fine." Zoe stalked away.

"You haven't seen Tim, by chance?" I asked Cindy before she left.

"Uh." She opened her mouth and then closed it again before speaking. "I think he was heading for the basement. He said something about needing supplies, although I don't know why. We're in the middle of a crisis. I think garbage bags or whatever he's on the hunt for can wait."

"Right. Thanks." I left her and cut through the crowd toward the basement. I had only been down into the archives once, but the space was off-limits to guests. I ducked under the golden braided rope and made my way down the dimly lit stairs.

Once I made it to the lower level, the corridor was plunged in darkness. I felt along the wall for a light switch, without success, so instead I turned on the flashlight app on my phone and descended into the basement.

"Tim! Tim, are you down here?" I called.

There was no answer. The only sound was the echo of my footsteps on the concrete floor. The basement was a maze of storage rooms used to house artifacts that weren't currently part of any exhibits.

I tried the first three doors. They were all locked.

"Tim! Are you here?" I yelled again.

Nothing.

A prickle of fear sped along my spine, like someone had dropped an ice cube down my dress. Where was Tim? Something didn't feel right.

I tried another door and the next. Each was locked. It wasn't a surprise, given the number of guests upstairs.

I was about to give up when a faint noise stopped me.

Was it a moan?

"Hello?" I called. "Tim, is that you?"

I froze, waiting for a response.

A muffled cry sounded again.

I moved toward it.

It was coming from the last door on the left. I turned the handle, and the knob twisted with ease. A sense of dread washed over me. What if whoever had stolen the manuscript had hurt Tim?

I stepped into the room and fumbled for the lights. The room was lined with ceiling-high industrial shelving that was packed with rows and rows of neatly labeled boxes.

"Hello, is anyone here?" My voice quaked ever so slightly. Maybe this wasn't the brightest idea after all.

"Here." A weak response came from the far end of the room.

I sucked in air through my nose, squared my shoulders, and headed toward the sound. One of the industrial shelves had been knocked over. Beneath layers of boxes and the stainless steel shelves was Tim.

"Tim, are you okay?" I ran over and tried to lift the shelves off of him. They were too heavy.

He moaned again.

"What happened?"

"They fell on me." His breathing was labored.

"Hang on. I'm going to go get help." I realized after I spoke that it was hardly as if he could move.

He blinked his eyes in response.

I sprinted down the hallway and upstairs. As I crested the top of the stairs, I saw Thomas and Kerry coming in through the front doors.

"Thomas! I need your help!" I hollered, waving through the sea of people decked out in gowns and tuxes.

"Jules?" Thomas came toward me, followed by Kerry.

"Tim, the custodian, he needs help." I pointed to the stairwell.

"Slow down," Thomas cautioned. "What do you mean, help?"

"A heavy shelving unit fell on him. I can't get it off."

Carlos appeared with Lance tagging at his heels. "Julieta, what is it?"

"Tim, he's stuck under a shelving unit," I repeated.

Thomas turned to Kerry. "You want to go find the Professor? I'll help them."

She nodded. "Yep, I'm on it. Where is he?"

"In there." I pointed to the exhibit hall.

Kerry took off in that direction while I led everyone else downstairs. It took all four of us to lift the shelves off Tim. He remained frozen on the cement floor. His left arm was contorted like a mangled balloon animal. His face had lost all of its color.

Thomas knelt next to him and assessed his vitals. "Can you move?"

"My back and my arm," Tim replied, his eyes fluttering like he was trying to stay conscious.

"Okay." Thomas checked his pulse on his other wrist. He studied Tim's face. I had a feeling he was trying to decide whether Tim had sustained a concussion.

Lance, Carlos, and I stood in silence.

Thomas looked up at me. "Jules, can you call for an ambulance, please?"

Tim tried to protest by attempting to sit up. Thomas stopped him. "Stay where you are. We don't want to risk injuring you more."

"I don't need an ambulance." His breathing was shallow and labored.

"You may have a head injury. Your arm is broken for sure, and my protocol tells me that you could also have a fractured spine. Let's get the professionals here. They can take a look at you, and if they decide you don't need a ride, we'll arrange for someone else to take you. How does that sound?" He asked it as if Tim had a choice. I was impressed with how calm Thomas remained, while clearly in charge.

"Okay."

I called 911. They assured me that an ambulance was on the way. Thomas sent Carlos to find a glass of water and directed Lance to go find a first aid kit. He kept Tim calm while we waited for help to arrive. It didn't take long. As promised, before Carlos or Lance returned, a team of paramedics rushed in, carrying a backboard and medical supplies.

I tried to stay out of their way. I moved toward the other shelving units as they carefully strapped Tim to the backboard and braced his neck. My eyes drifted to the floor. Among the boxes that had fallen in the crash, there was one labeled DOUBLE FALSEHOOD—ORIGINAL: DO NOT TOUCH.

I let out a gasp and then clamped my hand over my mouth. Was that the original manuscript? And if so, did that mean that Tim had been trying to steal it? Maybe in his quest to grab the valuable document and make his getaway he had knocked the shelves over on himself.

Chapter Nine

Thomas and Carlos huddled near the door holding a now use-less first aid kit and glass of water as the EMS crew triaged Tim. Tim yelped in pain as they positioned a foam support around his head and splinted his arm. He passed out as they secured him on a backboard.

It was clear that Tim did indeed require an escort to the hospital. Once they had wheeled him out on a stretcher, I called Thomas over. "You should come take a look at this."

"What is it?"

I pointed to the box, not wanting to touch it, in case there were fingerprints. "It's labeled *Double Falsehood*. That's the name of the manuscript they think was stolen upstairs."

"Really?" Thomas crouched down to get a better look. "Hmmm. I better check in with the Professor on this before we do anything else. There could be prints on that. Can you two wait here and promise that you won't touch anything or do any snooping until I return?" He addressed me and Lance. Carlos had gone with the paramedics to assist in opening the outside doors to the building.

"Us?" Lance sang out in a high-pitched tone. "You have our word. Juliet and I take our civic responsibility with the utmost sincerity. We shall ensure that not a hair upon our heads is disturbed until you return."

Thomas rolled his eyes. "Yeah, that's a likely story." He met my eyes. "Don't touch anything, got it?"

"Got it." I gave him a solemn nod.

When he was out of earshot, Lance leaned in and rubbed his hands together. "Okay, do tell, darling. Dish."

"What do you mean?"

"Don't you play coy with me. You know exactly what I'm talking about. A stolen manuscript. A man nearly killed—practically clinging to life right in front of our eyes. We have ourselves a case. And I need details. All the details, stat!"

"Lance, you know as much as I do—" I started, but he held his index finger to my lips to stop me.

"Not another word of protest, darling. There is no time to lose. We have been handed a golden opportunity. That dashing husband of yours will be back momentarily, and this place is going to be swarming with police. Tell me everything you know—do not spare a single detail."

There was no point in arguing with Lance. "Honestly, I know as much as you do. I came down here searching for Tim and found him lying under the shelves. I couldn't lift them, so I ran upstairs to get help."

"What did he say?" Lance waved his hands, motioning for me to speak faster.

"Nothing."

"Then how did you know about the box?"

"I just happened to see it. I moved away to make room for the paramedics and noticed it on top of the pile." My eyes drifted that way. I had made a promise to Thomas that I intended to keep, but I also had to admit, I was tempted to sneak a quick peek inside. "It's a weird coincidence, isn't it?"

"Coincidence? I think not." Lance stretched one lanky leg over the debris on the floor. He moved the supply cart to the side.

"What are you doing?"

"My civic duty." He proceeded to yank a gray polka-dotted silk handkerchief from his breast pocket. He used it like a glove to open the box in question.

"Lance, what are you doing?" I whisper-yelled. "We promised Thomas we wouldn't touch anything. Like he said, the thief's prints might be on there. You're tampering with evidence."

"Technically speaking, I'm not touching anything. And I spotted a rat. Didn't you?" He tried to sell his lie by shuddering. "Nasty little vermin, these Ashland rats, aren't they? We've had an issue with them in the theater. They've chewed their way through feet of organza, silk drapes, too many costumes to count. We wouldn't want a rat to contaminate the crime scene, would we? Imagine if that were to occur on our watch. We would be personally responsible."

"You can't do that," I whispered again in warning, glancing behind me. "There's no rat, and that may be your worst attempt at a feeble excuse for snooping to date."

"Watch me." He shot me a conspiratorial look and lifted the edges of the box. Then he dropped his jaw, let out a little shriek, and let box fall again.

"What?"

"Cash!" He froze as footsteps thudded in the hallway. He leapt over the clutter of boxes and came to stand next to me. "Lots of cash."

"Huh?"

Thomas and the Professor appeared in the doorway causing Lance to go hush.

"I see that you've taken your duties seriously. Many thanks." The Professor gave us a half bow.

Thomas tugged on a pair of gloves, picked up the box, and brought it over to the Professor for closer inspection.

"Double, double, toil and trouble." The Professor quoted the Bard as Thomas removed stack after stack of tightly bound hundred-dollar bills.

Lance kicked me.

Carlos walked in at that moment. He looked to me for an explanation as Thomas piled stacks of crisp green bills on an empty shelf.

"That is a lot of money," Carlos said, his mouth hanging open.

"Indeed," the Professor agreed. "I do believe this discovery changes the nature of our investigation." He and Thomas shared a look I couldn't decipher. "If you all could kindly return upstairs, we'll need to close off access to this space and inform everyone that they're going to need to linger longer."

Thomas had already taken out his walkie-talkie and was signaling for Kerry.

Carlos reached for my hand. "Julieta, shall we?"

The Professor raised a finger. "If I might borrow Juliet for a moment."

"Of course." Carlos nodded. "I will see you upstairs." He left with Lance.

I waited while the Professor gave Thomas further instructions. He motioned to the hallway. "Walk with me for a moment."

We fell into stride together. Fluorescent lights guided our way down the long corridor. Posters of previous exhibits—Egyptian mummies and rare butterflies—lined the otherwise utilitarian space. I could hear the sound of the ambulance's siren wailing away as they rushed Tim to the hospital.

"As you know, I've always valued your insight." The Professor choose his words carefully. "Is there anything you might be able to add about Tim? Your interactions with him. Any impressions you may have had."

"How so?"

"He was the only person down here when you discovered him, correct?"

I nodded.

"You didn't notice anyone else? Those doors at the end of the hallway were locked, yes?"

"Yes." In my mind, I replayed the motions of coming downstairs. "Everything was dark. I had to use my phone as a flashlight. All the doors were locked on both sides of the hallway, and the exit doors were closed. I can't say for sure that they were locked, because I never made it that far."

"Mmmm-hmmm." The Professor paused to make a note a on Moleskine journal. I couldn't believe he carried one with him, even to a fancy soirée. "And how was Tim when you found him?"

"Pretty out of it. I couldn't lift the shelves, so I didn't stay long."

"Did he say anything?"

"No. Not really, but earlier he was resistant to the idea of telling anyone about the manuscript. In fact, the minute we said we were going to tell Javier and find you, he took off. He came up with a weird excuse about needing to bring the supply cart down here." As I relayed my interaction with Tim, I realized again how odd it was that he had rushed out in search of trash bags. "Is he going to be okay?"

"It's too soon to say for sure. They'll be running tests at the hospital. It appears that his injuries are external, but there's concern about internal bleeding and a concussion."

"Do you think he did it? Could he have been trying to steal the manuscript and hurt himself in the process?" The tips of my toes had begun to tingle in the cool basement. Perhaps I should have opted for winter tights and a different shoe, but then again I hadn't imagined myself traipsing around the musty archives this evening.

The Professor was thoughtful. "It's certainly a possibility."

"How much money do you think is in the box?"

"We will have to do a full count. Quite a lot, I would guess at first glance. But nothing on the scale of what someone might pay for *Double Falsehood,* if that's what you're wondering." He took long, slow, deliberate steps, as if trying to stretch out our conversation. The Professor was naturally tall, with classic features and an uncanny ability to read people.

"It has to be connected to the fake manuscript. Maybe it was a down payment. Have you been able to determine whether the one upstairs is fake?" I realized that I was the one asking the questions. "Sorry. I'm getting ahead of myself."

"Yet another reason to love you." He patted my forearm. The Professor and I had developed a deeper relationship over the last few years. Since I had returned to Ashland, he had endeared himself to me with his devotion to Mom. Our bond had strengthened, and he had become an integral part of my life. Lately I'd been ruminating on what an amazingly doting grandfather he would be, if Carlos and I decided to have a baby. I could picture him reading bedtime poems and singing lullabies. I could imagine him staying up late and soothing a baby to sleep, or dipping his pinky into whipping cream to offer up a little taste to his grandchild. I pushed the thought away as we neared the stairwell.

"That's quite all right, Juliet." He laid his hand against his breastbone and let out a heavy sigh. "Alas, I do believe that the original document is not what is in place upstairs. How and why it was stolen remains to be seen. It's a blow to SOMA, to Ashland, and selfishly, I'm quite distraught that it vanished before I had a chance to lay eyes on Shakespeare's long-lost work." He sighed. "I'm perplexed by the case on many levels, and to be frank, I'm a bit worried that this isn't the end of the situation."

"Really?"

He sighed. "I hope that I'm mistaken, but I fear that the worst is yet to come."

My stomach lurched at his words.

"It occurs to me that you will likely be at the museum late this evening and into the weekend for cleanup and such. If it's not too much to ask, I would appreciate it if you could keep your eyes and ears open and report anything to me that seems suspicious."

"Of course."

"I caution you to stay vigilant, though. Do not let your guard down." His eyes were serious.

"I won't." I gave him a hug and returned upstairs. I would do my best to stay alert to anything out of the ordinary, but his warning rang in my ears. *Stay vigilant.* He didn't think that I was in danger, did he?

Chapter Ten

The tone had shifted dramatically in the foyer as Detective Kerry announced that unfortunately there would be no unveiling of the lost manuscript after all, nor would anyone be cleared to leave until individual interviews could be conducted. With over one hundred and fifty attendees, that was going to take a while. The only thing I could do was make sure that guests continued to stay well fed.

Our desserts had been a hit. So much so that the buffet table looked as if it had been hit by a swarm of locusts. I cut a path through the crowd to the kitchen. Cindy was directing her team of volunteer docents to refill trays. Where was Zoe? Wasn't this her job? I was confused with the hierarchy of the museum's small staff.

"Get more food out there—stat. We are inches away from guests going into full meltdown mode. Where are my wineglasses? We need to keep the drinks flowing." Cindy narrowed her eyes on a young college student unloading wineglasses from the dishwasher. Her mild-mannered personality had gone through quite the transformation.

Her wineglasses? I appreciated her jumping in, but she was a volunteer too.

"Can I help?" I offered.

She spun around. The whites of her eyes were huge and puffy like meringues. "Oh, it's you. Sorry. I hope I'm not over-stepping. I was telling the volunteers how important it is to keep everyone as happy as possible given the terrible circum-stances. I hope you don't mind, but I'm sending my docents out with more desserts and wine. It's the least we can do."

"Not at all."

We moved to the side to make way for the volunteers to pass.

"Have you seen Javier anywhere?" Cindy asked. She wrung her hands as she spoke.

"I saw him a while ago, but not lately. Why?"

She darted her eyes from the stove to the workstation in the middle of the kitchen, then back to me. "Rumor has it, he's been arrested."

"Javier? The police have already made an arrest?" I glanced longingly at the coffeepot. I could use a hit of caf-feine to warm me up after being in the basement, and also to help me try to wrap my head around the evening's strange turn of events.

"Yes. The police think that he did it. They moved swiftly. Rumors are going around faster than the wine. I heard that they found a pair of disposable gloves, a set of wrenches, and a mangled lock like the one from the display case stashed in his office." Cindy paused and snapped her fingers at a volunteer. "More macaroons. Put out everything you can.

We have to try and keep the guests fed if nothing else. Everything is riding on tonight. Everything." Her voice was wobbly.

From what I could see, every tray had been refilled as a swath of docents in matching black slacks and turtlenecks circled in and out of the kitchen. "Wait, the police think he did what?" I asked Cindy.

She sucked in a breath. "Stole the manuscript."

I wasn't sure how to respond. Javier? I couldn't believe it.

"I hate to say it, but it makes the most sense. He had full access to the manuscript, and he's been acting odd for the last few days." She tapped her fingertips on the butcher block.

"Odd how?"

"He'll disappear for long stretches. It's been driving Zoe crazy. She found him in the basement archives this morning digging through old boxes when he was supposed to be introducing one of the guest artists. It's not like him. He's usually the model of professionalism, but yesterday I caught him and Ernest going head-to-head. I thought he was going to punch Ernest in the face."

"What?"

She bobbed her head up and down. "Now that I think about it, he started acting strange from the time the *Shakespeare's Lost Pages* exhibit arrived, and he hasn't been the same ever since."

"Do you know what he and Ernest were arguing about?"

"No. They broke apart when I walked in on them, but if I hadn't, I'm sure they would have gotten into a physical fight." She twisted a strand of her wiry hair around her index finger.

That didn't sound like Javier. My interactions with him

had been nothing but professional. I had found him to be warm and open to feedback, a true partner in planning the event. And in every interaction I'd had with him, Javier had come across as being highly intelligent. If he had broken into the old display case, why would he leave evidence in his office? It didn't make sense.

One of the volunteers had a question for Cindy. She left to answer it. I stood stunned for a moment. Could Cindy be right? Could Javier have stolen the manuscript? She mentioned that he'd been going through boxes in the basement. What if he had stashed away the money for the illegal sale and Tim had caught him in the act? Could Tim be an innocent victim and not the thief? It was a possibility. Not that I liked the thought of Javier being involved, but I couldn't dismiss it either. I made a mental note to tell the Professor about my conversation with Cindy, and I returned to the exhibit hall.

Guests were being divided into small groups for interviews with Thomas, Kerry, and the rest of the police squad that had been called in for support. This level of interrogation had to mean that they had confirmed that the manuscript had been stolen. Why else would they refuse to release the crowd?

I was at a loss for what to do next. The police were systematically conducting questioning, the dessert table had been restocked, and volunteers had followed Cindy's orders, circulating through the room with bottles of red and white wine.

The sound of a voice behind me made me nearly jump.

"Do tell, what news?" Lance strummed his thin, narrow fingers together. "What did the Professor divulge in your little tête-à-tête?"

"Not much," I said truthfully.

"Nonsense, darling. He must have said something; clearly, he wanted to speak with you. Rumors are spreading faster than even yours truly can keep up with. Hard to believe, I know. But it's true."

"I've heard, but you know as well as I do that the Professor is the last person to repeat gossip."

He gave me an annoyed sigh. "It's one of his most maddening features."

"What rumors have you heard?" I was curious if other people were repeating Cindy's theory that Javier had stolen the manuscript.

Lance reached for a marzipan in the shape of a golden pear. "Let's just say that my news feels like more than a rumor. I witnessed firsthand the police leading Javier de la Garza to the back of a waiting squad car in handcuffs, which, if you ask me, is an absolute travesty. Javier is one of my go-to sources on Shakespeare. The man is a walking encyclopedia of Shakespearean facts. He would give the Professor a run for his money. Why they've arrested him I cannot say, but surely it's a mistake." He took a bite of the sweet almond candy in his mouth and watched for my reaction.

"Are you sure?"

"Positive. It was quite subdued. I mean, perhaps they're taking him in for questioning. But why handcuffs? I would have liked for him to resist arrest or at least leave the building with a promise that his good name would soon be cleared. There was none of that. He hung his head and let them take him without so much as a single peep. Quite depressing, actually. I find it difficult to believe that such a lover of the Bard would have any hand in this."

"Me too." I gave him a brief recap of my talk with Cindy. "Do you think that the Professor found the original manuscript?"

"Perhaps." His eyes drifted to the ceiling. "This place has more hidden cameras than the Pentagon. I wouldn't be surprised if the police already have hard evidence. Otherwise this seems like overkill." He waved his hand to the crowd. I noticed that Arlo and Carlos had found a spot in the corner of the room. Their heads were bent together, staring at Arlo's phone. They must have found a soccer match to keep them distracted while we awaited our next instructions from the Professor and his team.

"What if Tim is in worse shape than we think? He didn't look so good when they took him away. I'm pretty sure he passed out. I hope he's going to be okay." My throat constricted for a moment with the thought. A theft of a priceless artifact was one thing, but a man's life could be in danger. "Maybe his assault is connected to Javier's arrest?"

"Could be," Lance concurred. "Javier doesn't strike me as the violent type, but I suppose stranger things have happened. Maybe it was an accident in the heat of the moment."

"Or he's being set up."

"That thought crossed my mind as well." Lance polished off the marzipan. "You know what this means, don't you? We are officially on the case."

"I'm not sure that the Professor would agree."

"I disagree. Consider your little chat his not-so-subtle offer of approval. He basically gave you permission to involve yourself in the case."

"Ha!" I laughed. "I can guarantee you that was not his intention."

Lance ignored my protest. "Let's focus. If we proceed with

the theory that Javier is indeed an innocent pawn in this game of theft, who could have masterminded such a heist? It had to be an art thief. Someone well versed in Shakespeare. Someone with contacts—connections. I don't buy that the scrawny college security guard could have pulled this off on his own. But there's a question of access. Javier certainly had the means to steal the manuscript, but is there anyone else who could have swiped the document without being seen?"

"I don't know. Dylan the security guard has supposedly been on around-the-clock watch, although yesterday he needed reminding to stay at his post. Tim, who got hurt, has been the lead custodian here for decades. I'm assuming he has keys to all of the exhibit halls. He would also have a reason to be in the building at night and after hours. Dylan told me earlier that everyone had been inside the exhibit hall at some point—Ernest, Cindy, Zoe."

"Excellent, excellent." Lance beamed. "See, darling? You're already in the zone."

I rolled my eyes and continued. "The problem is that doesn't rule anyone out. I mean, that is, if we take the line of thinking that Dylan was an accomplice. Any of them could have done it. The other possibility is that Dylan wasn't involved at all and whoever took it snuck in during off hours. Zoe is Javier's private assistant. She must have keys to the building, and I'm not sure about Cindy. She's a volunteer but, like Tim, has been here forever and is responsible for docent training, so it's possible that she could have keys as well."

"Well, it sounds like we have our work cut out for us, doesn't it?" He tapped his wrist. "Let's divide and conquer. I'll go talk up our security guard. He has features that could grace the stage, but hollow eyes, which just won't do. I'll

dazzle him with the idea of a role in my new production—
Waitress." His eyebrows wiggled with delight. "You didn't
think I'd forget, did you?"

"Lance." I scowled, knowing that there was no way he was
going give up trying to get me on the stage. He could argue
his case until he was blue in the face, but there was no way
it was happening.

"Fine. I'll take Dylan," he huffed. "You can try to butter up
Zoe and see what she has to say for herself. We'll regroup
soon. Ta-ta." He sashayed toward Dylan, who was blocking
the doorway to the main hall.

Lance had a way of making light of stressful situations,
but the truth was that I was worried. If someone had been
willing to steal a valuable Shakespearean artifact and injure
Tim in the process, what might they do next?

Chapter Eleven

As it turned out, tracking down Zoe was more difficult than I imagined. She was nowhere to be found in the exhibit hall. At first I assumed that she was in the middle of an interview with Thomas, Kerry, or one of the other officers, but as other guests emerged from their meetings, Zoe didn't appear. I knew that her office was located on the main floor opposite the kitchen, so I decided to go look there.

Sure enough, a yellow light emerged from beneath the door to her office. I knocked twice. "Zoe, are you in there? It's Jules."

"Yeah, come in," she replied.

She was seated at her desk. A wad of used tissues was piled in the center of her messy desk like a wobbly mountain. An empty wine bottle had been tipped over, leaving tiny droplets of wine on the desk. Her face was buried in her hands as she sobbed softly.

"Zoe, are you okay?"

She sniffled and nodded. Then she grabbed another tissue and blotted her eyes. "I'm okay. I'm so upset, but I'll be okay. I have to try to pull it together before I get back out there."

"Is there anything I can do?" I hesitated to approach the desk, but she motioned for me to sit.

"It's Javier. Did you hear? They arrested him. They found proof in his office. So stupid of him. I never thought it would come to this."

"I did hear," I said in what I hoped was a consoling tone. "What do you mean, you never thought it would come to this?"

She balled the tissue up and tossed it in the pile. "Things have been tight budgetwise. That's why this exhibit was so important to the museum's future success. I knew that Javier had been stressed and worried about keeping the doors open, but I didn't think he would do something so desperate."

"You mean steal the manuscript?"

She nodded. "I feel terrible. I should have seen the signs. I should have gotten him help. He loves this place more than anyone. Even me, which is saying a lot. That's why he agreed to partner with Ernest on this exhibit even though he felt like he was signing his freedom away. It was the only way to fund the show. We were hoping that tonight would be the start of a new trend. We were confident that our fundraising efforts would be able to stave off closures and layoffs."

"Are things that bad?"

She blew her nose in another tissue before responding. "Worse. Javier was looking at reducing the hours. Only opening on weekends and maybe one day a week. My job was on the line, which sucks because as a doctoral student I'm barely getting by as it is. Not that I blame him; it wasn't his fault. We already run a skeleton crew. There weren't many more cuts he could make. Then the opportunity for this exhibit arose, and it felt like a gift from the heavens. Javier knew we needed a benefactor, but what he didn't realize was that Ernest was going to try and micromanage every level of the show. Not only that, but he's been demanding to have a voice in what we bring in next. Things have been brewing between them for weeks now, but yesterday it blew up."

Her story matched what Cindy had told me.

"Ernest threatened to take away all of his cash, every dollar, if Javier refused to go along with his agenda for SOMA. That man is so awful. He only wants to flaunt his money. He doesn't care about art. He has no passion. He wants to gloss over history. To whitewash anything that doesn't work with his narrative. He has no desire to really explore art's complicated roots. Like with my dissertation. You saw how he blew that off. It's not some crazy out-of-left-field theory. Many, many people believe Shakespeare was a woman." She picked up the empty wine bottle, placed it in a recycling bin near her desk, and used the pile of tissues to wipe up the drops that had spilled out.

As much I was intrigued by the idea of *Romeo and Juliet* being penned by a woman, I wanted to keep her focused on Ernest. "What is his agenda?" I studied the degree certificates mounted on the wall behind her. She had done her undergraduate at the University of Washington and received her master's degree from Stanford. Impressive and expensive.

"Don't ask." She shook her head in disgust. "He wants us to have a more historic—his word, not mine—perspective when it comes to art. He demanded that we cut all of our family programming. He wants us to discontinue the new voices project that showcases the work of artists who traditionally have been left out of galleries—people of color, women, you know the drill."

Yet another reason he and Richard Lord had to be related. "I'm guessing Javier pushed back on that idea?"

"That's an understatement." Zoe sat up straighter. "He was fuming. I've never seen him that angry. I was actually scared."

"Of Javier?" That was a surprise. I leaned back against the chair. I had warmed up since being down in the basement, but the longer the night wore on, the more I could really go for a strong cup of coffee.

"Of the whole situation. Javier and Ernest have completely different visions for the museum, but Javier was in a terrible position. He was tethered to Ernest because we needed his dollars. Without funding, we can't do anything. That's why I'm so upset. I feel like I could have done more. I should have done more. It might have stopped Javier from stealing the manuscript. He didn't need to do it. We could have found another way."

"You really think he did it?"

Zoe buried her face in her hands again. "I think he was desperate. I mean, I get it. We all are. Money does that, you know? I think he probably thought he could get away with it. The forgery was good. I was even fooled by it. He probably figured if we could get through the exhibit, it would be on to the next stop on the national tour, and no one would be any wiser. Maybe that's why he hid the evidence in his office. He must not have thought there was any chance he would get caught. I'm betting he was hoping that they would assume it was stolen en route, not by the director of SOMA. He would be the one to verify that everything was intact before it was carefully packed away for travel. I hate that he felt like he had to do something so drastic to save the museum and us."

More tears flowed.

"There could be other explanations. We don't know for sure that Javier stole the manuscript." I tried to console her.

She sniffled. "Yeah, but who else could have taken it?"

I shifted to logic. "Are there other employees who had access to the building?"

Zoe brushed tears from her cheeks. "Sure. Like I said, we're a small crew, but a few of us have access. Why?"

"Let's think it through. Who else could have had an opportunity to be alone with the manuscript?"

She used her index finger to massage her temple. "Well, Tim has keys to everything. Dylan's been here late. We've been paying him overtime during the setup process."

"What about Cindy?"

"Oh, yeah—I forgot about Cindy." Zoe gasped. "She doesn't usually have keys, but I gave her a spare so that she could get in if I wasn't here. She's been doing extra training for the volunteer docents. You don't think she could have done it?"

"I have no idea who took the manuscript," I replied. "I'm trying to show you that there are plenty of other alternatives to Javier being the thief. Not to mention, this could have been a professional job. We don't know if the delivery crew or someone else involved in setting up the exhibit could have swapped the real document for a fake early on."

Zoe nodded. "I guess I didn't think of that. I hope you're right."

Her phone rang.

I excused myself while she took the call.

After I left, I realized that she hadn't included herself in the list of people who had access to the manuscript. It could have simply been an oversight, or it could be that she was intentionally trying to shift focus from herself.

I wandered toward the buffet tables, suddenly acutely aware of the fact that I hadn't eaten dinner. I filled a small plate and nibbled on the delectable assortment of savory bites that Carlos, Sterling, and Marty had prepared. I found myself caught up in conversations with friends as everyone waited for their turn with the police. Everything was delicious, but I couldn't stop eating Carlos's stew. He had braised the beef in wine with onions and garlic. Then added in an assortment of winter vegetables and herbs and simmered the pot on the stove for hours. After polishing off a ramekin and going back for seconds, I decided that I was going to adopt Bethany's GBD, because the swirls of garlic and rosemary potatoes that topped each individual serving of stew were crisp and golden on the outside, yet melted like butter in my mouth. I decided on the spot that the dish needed to become part of the winter menu.

The food helped steady my nerves and clear my head. The mood was subdued, yet oddly, a touch of palpable excitement hung in the air. Outlandish and more realistic theories circulated the room along with more of our desserts and plenty of wine. It was almost as if everyone was buzzed on the news of a museum heist.

"Things like this don't happen in Ashland," a friend of Mom's said to me as we watched Detective Kerry bring the next guest in for questioning. "I hate to admit it, but it is almost exciting."

She wasn't alone in that sentiment, but then again, neither she nor any of the other guests had seen Tim carted out on a stretcher. There was a difference between a theft and physical violence. I lost track of time as the night wore on. Eventually Thomas, Kerry, and the other officers completed their interviews. Thomas came into the main hall. He didn't need a microphone to get everyone's attention.

"Okay, everyone, I'm happy to announce that you are free to leave. We have everything we need, and we will be in touch if we have follow-up questions. Please exit the building in an orderly fashion through these doors." He pointed to the main exit, where Dylan was still posted. "I'm afraid we can't allow anyone back into any other portions of the museum tonight. The docents have collected items from the coat check and will have them outside for you."

No one from the museum spoke, which made me wonder if Javier had indeed been arrested. Otherwise wouldn't he or someone on staff have wanted to thank everyone for coming and assure the museum patrons that the exhibit would be open again as soon as they were able to sort out what had happened?

His absence made me suspect that things might be even more serious than I had thought.

Chapter Twelve

After the guests had departed, we shifted into cleanup mode. I started by helping the volunteers clear the dessert table. "Let's leave the chocolate structures for now," I suggested. "I'll come back tomorrow and figure out what to do with them."

Javier and I had discussed giving our chocolate art a semi-permanent home as part of the *Shakespeare's Lost Pages* exhibit, but I wasn't sure that would still be the case in light of the missing manuscript. We packaged leftovers while Thomas and Kerry continued interviewing the volunteers and staff.

Carlos blasted salsa music. The kitchen steamed up from running load after load of dishes in the industrial dishwasher and scrubbing pans in hot soapy water in the oversized sink. "Julieta, should we leave all of this here? Did you discuss donating the leftovers?" He ran his hand over platters resting on the stainless steel countertops.

We had a policy at Torte to deliver any extra pastries, soups, or sandwiches to the local shelter at the end of the day. I hadn't thought to ask Javier what he wanted to do with the leftover food. The guests had made good work of both the dinner and dessert tables, but there were still quite a few items left to share.

I glanced at his stack of recycled containers. "That's a good question. I think we should probably leave everything here, but once I finish putting these marzipans away, I can go ask Zoe. She might have an idea. If nothing else, we can offer doggie bags to the volunteers. They've earned at least that much tonight."

Carlos wrinkled his nose. "Doggie bag. This is a phrase I think I will never get used to. I would hope that our leftovers are worthy of more than a four-legged friend."

"American English idioms, what can I say?"

We spent the next thirty minutes organizing containers, cleaning the stove, and running additional loads of wineglasses through the dishwasher. Carlos and I were both meticulous about cleaning as we cooked and baked. It was a skill we'd been taught in culinary school and mastered during our years of working on the *Amour of the Seas*. Commercial kitchens, whether on a luxury cruise liner or in a restaurant or pastry shop, tend to be much smaller than most people realize. It's imperative to keep a clean and tidy kitchen to maximize workspace and for safety. I felt proud that my young staff had adopted my philosophy of mise en place, which loosely translated, meant "everything in its place." That required setup prior to cooking or baking, ensuring that any ingredients or spices needed for a recipe were in neat containers and ready to go. The same was true in cleaning a kitchen. We went through a formal checklist at the end of every shift, making sure that not only was the kitchen spotless but everything was back in its intended place and ready for the next day.

Once the bulk of cleanup was finished, I went to track down Zoe to ask her about the leftovers. Except, I didn't get far. My hand had just made contact with the kitchen door when a scream pierced the museum. Carlos dropped his dish towel and ran over to me.

"What was that?" His eyes grew wide as he looked around the kitchen, searching for the source of the scream.

The scream echoed again, followed by heavy thudding footsteps and shouts for help.

I opened the swinging doors carefully, just in time to see Thomas running toward the main hall.

Carlos grabbed my hand as we followed Thomas and the sound of three short high-pitched, bloodcurdling screams.

The screams were coming from the main hall.

I knew something was wrong as soon as we stepped inside. Cindy was crouched over Dylan, who was sprawled out on the floor next to the glass case.

"Help! Help!" she screamed. "He's not breathing."

Thomas dropped to his knees and checked for a pulse. Dylan's Taser sat abandoned near his feet.

Kerry and the Professor appeared moments later. Their cheeks were tinged with color, I guessed from sprinting to see what had happened.

Thomas began performing CPR. Kerry pulled out her cell and called an ambulance.

Carlos and I hung back, watching the scene unfold. I regretted gorging myself, because watching them try to revive Dylan made bile rise in the back of my throat. "Do you think he's going to be okay?" I whispered to Carlos, my voice sounding like it belonged to someone else.

"I don't know." He laced his fingers tighter through mine and kissed the top of my head. "It does not look good."

"I'm beginning to think this place is cursed." A chill raced down my arms, causing the tiny hairs to stand at attention. I wished I had my coat or something warmer. This couldn't be happening. Not again. An ambulance had already come to SOMA once tonight for Tim.

"Si, it is terrible. The stolen manuscript, the custodian severely injured, and now this." Carlos massaged my fingers as he spoke.

He didn't say what I knew we were both thinking. *Now this . . . now this . . .* I had a sinking feeling that Dylan was dead.

When the paramedics arrived a few minutes later, they confirmed it. I overheard them tell the Professor that Dylan had been tased, which had likely triggered some kind of an episode with his heart.

Everything happened in a blur. How long had this night been? It felt like only a short time ago that we had discovered that *Double Falsehood* had been stolen. Now a man was dead.

I collapsed in Carlos's arms as they wheeled Dylan's body out of the exhibit hall. "I can't believe he's dead. How? There weren't many people left. Us. The volunteers. It doesn't make sense. The police are here. Who could have done this? And how could they have gotten away? I can't believe they weren't seen."

"I know. I do not understand either." Carlos massaged my back. "It is terrible. How long has he been in here? Maybe he was killed before they let everyone leave."

I shook my head. "No. I saw him. He's been standing guard here all night. He never left his post, at least not every time I saw him. He was there when Thomas made the announcement that everyone could leave. Someone had to have killed him after that, but why?"

"I don't know." Carlos squeezed me closer.

I felt comforted by his touch, but nothing made sense. Tim's attack and Dylan's death had to be connected. How could he have ended up getting tased by his own weapon?

Thoughts assaulted my brain as we waited for instructions.

The Professor came over to us after Dylan's body had been removed. His shoulders slumped. His kind eyes were filled with despair. "Such a night," he commented, meeting my eyes.

"He's dead, isn't he?"

The Professor's cheeks sunk in as he responded. "I'm afraid so. It appears that the killer managed to obtain Dylan's Taser and use it against him. It is unsettling to say the very least."

"When could this have happened?" Carlos asked.

The Professor ran his fingers over his graying beard streaked with ginger. "We'll have to await the official report from the autopsy, but I believe it happened recently, within the last hour or so. I regret that I sent Dylan here to keep watch, instructing him not to let anyone inside without my permission."

"So Dylan was posted inside?" I asked.

The Professor shook his head. "No. At the door. This is an active crime scene with the theft, and I didn't want one of the volunteers or any staff members disturbing the area. I asked Dylan to stand guard until I returned to relieve him. In hindsight, that could have been a mistake. Perhaps I should have had one of my team take on the task." His voice broke as he spoke.

I knew that the Professor took his duty to serve the community seriously. "You can't have known that someone would try and kill him," I said, reaching out to comfort him. "Do you think that the killer was trying to force their way in? Maybe they left behind a clue. Evidence linking themselves to the theft of the manuscript. Maybe they were trying to get back in here to retrieve it."

"It's a possibility," the Professor agreed.

"What does this mean for Javier?" I asked. "If he was arrested earlier, he can't be a suspect, right?"

"To be honest, I don't know." The Professor's shoulders sagged. "The coroner will need to determine a time of death. I wish I could say with certainty that's the case, but it's much too early to make any assumptions. As my mentor used to say, 'Assumptions have no place in police work.'"

"Is there anything we can do?" Carlos offered.

"Alas, not at the moment. I do appreciate the offer, but you two are free to leave. I'll plan to be in touch tomorrow."

"Of course." I gave him a hug. "What about Mom? Should we find her? We can take her home if you're going to be here late."

"That would be wonderful. Last I saw her, she was speaking with Zoe, but come to think of it, I haven't seen her since."

Fear welled in my stomach, causing my throat to constrict. I tried to swallow, but my mouth went dry.

"You don't think she's in danger, do you?"

"No, certainly not." He placed his hand on my shoulder in a show of comfort. "I didn't mean to imply that. I meant that I neglected her with the frenzy of activity, that's all. I'm sure she's around. If you would be willing to escort her home, that would be a great relief. I have no idea how long we'll need to stay, but with Dylan's death, it could be all night."

"No problem." I gave him another hug. "Call if you need anything else."

We left the hall and went in search of Mom. The Professor didn't sound worried, but where was she? Nearly everyone had come running when Cindy began screaming. But not Mom. I couldn't imagine why anyone would want to hurt her, but after the strange turn of events tonight, I wasn't about to take any chances.

Chapter Thirteen

Fortunately my fears were unfounded. Mom and Arlo were in the kitchen restocking the containers of leftovers. Arlo had removed his jacket and rolled up the sleeves on his crisp white shirt. Mom's silky orange wrap was draped over one of the barstools. She had tied on a black apron in its place.

"Whew, you're here," I said, allowing my shoulders to relax. "We were worried about you."

"Worried about us. Why?" She sounded surprised.

Arlo set a hand pie in a plastic tub. "Did we miss something?

"Didn't you hear the screaming?"

Mom shook her head and looked to Arlo, who shrugged. "No, was someone screaming?"

Her hearing had been waning the last few years due to genetics and long-term exposure to whirling mixers and blenders. "Yes, I'm surprised you didn't hear it. How long have you been in here?" I wondered if it was going to be time to stage an intervention and force her to go visit an audiologist. Up until now, she'd been resistant to the idea of hearing aids.

"Only a minute or two. Zoe needed help carting some things downstairs, so Arlo and I offered our services. Why?" She stared from me to Carlos and then back to Arlo again, whose dark eyes mirrored her confusion.

I felt relieved that her hearing wasn't so bad that she had missed Cindy's piercing screams. "There's been a murder."

Mom dropped a container on the counter. "What?"

Arlo's jaw hung open. "Who? The custodian who was hurt earlier?"

I shook my head. "No. The security guard." We told them about Dylan.

Lance swept in just as I had finished relaying what had happened. His tie was askew. Empathy filled his eyes as he blinked back what looked to be genuine tears. "I can tell by your faces that you've heard." He gave his head a shake. "A heist sounded like a game of a cat and mouse—or since I'm in the kitchen, should I say a game of cat and *mousse*—that I can get behind, but this. This is terrible." He didn't even laugh at his attempt to lighten the mood with a joke. Instead he strode toward Arlo and reached for his hand.

"It is very sad." Carlos sighed. "Any loss of life. So unnecessary. And for what?"

A solemnness fell over all of us. We stood together in silence for a moment.

Mom spoke first. "I think we're all feeling the same thing. Let's take a minute for Dylan and his family." Her chin quivered as she spoke.

I closed my eyes, feeling grateful for Carlos's solid grasp, and held Dylan and his family in my heart. Whether he was involved in the heist or not, he didn't deserve to die.

Lance cleared his throat. "I'm hearing Henry Wadsworth Longfellow's words in my head, 'There is no grief like the grief which does not speak.'"

"Well said," Arlo noted.

Carlos nodded.

"Yes, thank you for that, Lance." Mom pressed her hand to her chest. "I should go check in with Doug," she said, shaking her head and pulling her wrap tightly over her shoulders. "He must be upset. What a terrible night. He's been looking forward to this for weeks, and now an innocent young man has died."

"You guys don't need to stick around," I said to Lance and Arlo. "We can finish up here."

"I think it might be time for us to make our exit." Arlo gazed at Lance with tender concern, which warmed my heart. I could tell that he had picked up on Lance's sadness too. I gave them each a long hug before they left. "We'll talk tomorrow, okay?" I promised Lance, who blew me a kiss and nodded without saying another word.

As much as Lance teased about our sleuthing and tried to insert himself into whatever the current topic of gossip was, he had deep sense of caring that he didn't always let many people see. I was glad that he'd found Arlo. They balanced each other beautifully, like the sweet and salty latte Andy had made for me earlier.

Carlos finished making sure everything was in its place. "We will get the rest done tomorrow, si? It is late, and you look tired."

"Yeah. I'll figure it out with Zoe tomorrow." I had forgotten to tell him about my conversation with her. It didn't matter. Given that a man had just been killed, there was no need to waste energy worrying about leftovers.

We took Mom home first. She and the Professor had purchased a house on the banks of Emigrant Lake just on the outskirts of town. They had wisely decided that they wanted a place that was new to each of them to start their lives together. "Good night, you two. Try to get some sleep," she said, blowing us each a kiss when Carlos pulled in front of the house. "I've learned over the years that there's nothing that compares with a deep, restorative sleep. Tomorrow is a new day." With that, she got out of the car and went inside.

By the time we made it back to our house, exhaustion had set in. I peeled off my dress, pulled on my favorite winter pajamas lined with cozy fleece material, and climbed into bed. The minute my head hit the pillow, I was asleep. However, I woke about an hour later with visions of Dylan's body and a shadowy figure dressed all in black chasing me down the museum's empty basement corridor. My sleep was fitful. I woke nearly every hour with one nightmare after another. Sometime around four, I gave up and went downstairs to make a pot of French press.

While water boiled on the stove, I ran through the events of last night in sequential order. How had the gala gone so wrong? First there was the announcement that the manuscript had been stolen, then Tim had been injured, and last was Dylan's murder. What was the connection?

The kettle let out a soft whistle. I poured boiling water over coffee grounds and let them steep, my thoughts returning to the crime. Could it be that the manuscript was still at the museum? What if the thief had tried to sneak it out, but something or someone had foiled their plans? That made the most sense in terms of Tim. He must have discovered the thief and they retaliated. Maybe they thought they had killed him. I wondered if the Professor had police protection for Tim at the hospital.

That still didn't explain Dylan's death. Unless he too had figured out who the culprit was, or maybe witnessed the thief trying to make another getaway.

You're not going to figure it out in this very moment, Jules, I told myself as I poured the nutty dark roast into a coffee mug that I had warmed in the microwave and added a splash of cream. I savored my coffee for a while, trying to push away the nagging questions vying for space in my head, before heading upstairs to get dressed for the day. Carlos was snoozing as usual, so after I changed into jeans, thick socks, and a warm pullover sweatshirt, I decided to bundle up in my parka and ski hat to walk to Torte. There was no need to wake him. It was Sunday, which meant that we opened a bit later. Aside from a few early risers, the bakeshop wouldn't see a steady stream of coffee lovers until ten or eleven, when the brunch crowd began to trickle in.

The bitter November air outside took my breath away as pinkish light glowed on the ridgeline. I stuffed my gloves into my coat pockets and half jogged down the hill, past piles of crisp brown leaves, wild bunches of rosemary, and rhododendrons with the last of their magenta blooms clinging in a final show of color.

There was no sign of police activity on campus as the clock tower chimed, welcoming the morning. Hopefully the Professor, Thomas, and Kerry had been able to get some sleep last night. I wondered if they had made any progress on the investigation after we left.

Andy might get his wish, I thought as I turned onto Siskiyou Boulevard. A hard frost had turned grassy lawns white.

Clouds blocked the sinking moon. I passed stately houses where pumpkins and gourds rested near front doors and along porches. A few Halloween decorations remained in windows as a reminder of the changing season. One house farther down near the library had already put up a Christmas tree, its jewel-toned lights and star shimmering a festive hello as I passed by.

My fingertips were numb by the time I made it the bakeshop. Instead of starting my day by brewing another pot of coffee, I fired up the pizza oven, grateful for the heat it generated. When we had decided to expand into the basement space a couple years ago, we uncovered a completely unexpected surprise—an actual working wood-fired oven built into the exterior wall. We had ended up designing the kitchen around the fireplace, using it as our focal point. Not only did it provide natural heat, but the scent of applewood, the crackling of logs, and the earthy flavors that it infused into everything we baked in it had made me wonder how we had ever managed without it.

With a cheery fire burning, I turned on the main ovens and surveyed what we had in stock in the pantry for today's brunch specials. I decided on a pumpkin roll and sweet potato and chili hash.

I started with the pumpkin roll by creaming together butter and sugar, adding in vanilla and rum extracts along with eggs and a trio of warming spices—cloves, cinnamon, and nutmeg. Then I mixed in puréed pumpkin and blended the batter until it was a lovely pale orange color. I sifted in flour, baking soda, salt, and grated in a touch of fresh ginger. I lined baking sheets with parchment paper and spread the batter evenly. Once the cakes were in the oven, I began making a creamy filling. I whipped room temperature cream cheese with mascarpone cheese, rum, sugar, a splash of orange juice and zest, and more warming spices.

The cakes didn't take long to bake. I allowed them to cool and turned my attention to the hash. For that I peeled and chopped sweet potatoes, red onions, and garlic. I warmed olive oil in a nonstick skillet and sautéed the veggies until the onions had caramelized. Next I added smoked paprika, chili powder, salt, white pepper, and roasted chilies. I stirred the mixture together and allowed it to sweat for a few minutes. Then I cracked eggs over the top of the hash and left them to cook.

While the eggs were cooking, I returned my attention to my pumpkin rolls. I spread the luscious, creamy filling liberally over the top. To add some texture I sprinkled them with toasted pecans and mini chocolate chips. Then I rolled the cakes into logs, dusted them with spiced powdered sugar, and cut them into two-inch slices. We would finish them with a dollop of fresh whipped cream.

By the time the team began to arrive, the kitchen smelled divine. Andy and Marty came in together.

"You're slaying me with whatever you're baking," Andy said, his cheeks red from the cold. "It smells like Thanksgiving and Christmas mashed together in here."

Marty agreed. "I'm with the young man. The aroma is a sensory treat. I'm smelling heat and sweet."

I grinned. "Good nose. That's from my pumpkin roll and sweet potato and chili hash. You guys should give them a try and tell me what you think."

They didn't need any extra encouragement before diving in.

"This is awesome, boss," Andy said through a mouthful of pumpkin roll. "It gives me an idea for today's coffee special. I'll go ahead and eat the entire loaf and then get started, is that cool?"

I chuckled.

Marty held a piece of the cake on the tip of his fork. "This sponge is so light and airy yet packed with flavor. It's quite impressive, and actually, I'm with the kid on this one, too."

Andy scowled. "Remember, we're not calling me that anymore? I serve wine at our Sunday Suppers, so don't mess with me, man."

"Many apologies." Marty caught my eye and winked. Andy was only twenty-one, and as the youngest permanent member of staff, we liked to tease him about his age.

"This time of year my wife used to love for me to bake her a chocolate babka. What do you think of that for our bread of the day?" Marty asked. "It should go nicely with this chili hash." He had finished his serving of the spicy potato and egg dish.

"Count me in." I had learned how to make the Eastern European sweet bread in culinary school. The yeast-leavened bread required patience and a double rise, but the final result was layers of chocolate and toasted hazelnuts twisted into a brioche loaf and topped with a crumbly chocolate streusel.

Sterling and Steph were the next to arrive. Steph grunted a hello before immediately grabbing cake orders from the bulletin board and stuffing AirPods in her ears.

"How was the gala?" Sterling asked as he tied on an apron.

"Well, it was interesting." I filled him and Marty in. I noticed that Steph paused her music to listen in, but kept her headphones glued to her ears.

Andy came downstairs with a tray of coffees. "Okay,

everybody, I want your honest opinion on this. I'm calling it an autumn latte. It's a traditional latte with the same spices Jules used in her pumpkin loaf, along with a splash of maple syrup, fresh grated orange zest, and a zing of orange juice."

The coffee was like drinking the best of fall in a cup. The sweetness of the syrup balanced beautifully with the notes of citrus and spice. By grating fresh orange zest on the top of the foam, Andy had ensured that not only was the coffee a delight to the taste buds, but every sip offered a sublime ambrosial aroma. It was a treat to the senses.

"Andy, I don't know how you do it, but you manage to make every drink you create better than the last." Marty raised his coffee mug in a toast.

"We should bottle this," I said, taking another sip.

As always, Andy's humility came through with his sheepish grin. "Thanks, everyone. So it's a go for the Sunday special?"

"Yes," we all replied in unison.

Andy went back upstairs to finish prep work. Sterling and I talked through a lunch special. "What do you think about a butternut squash soup, since we're going all in on fall? We have plenty of squash, and I saw a bunch of fresh sage in the walk-in. That with some heavy cream, chicken stock, and caramelized onions should make a nice base for a soup."

"That sounds great."

"We can pair it with a turkey panini with apple butter, fontina cheese, and spinach." He made a note on the whiteboard.

"Okay, now I'm really hungry." I placed my hand on my stomach.

"I was also thinking of pumpkin and apple crepes for another sweet special," Sterling continued.

"That works for me." I loved the fact that my team was invested in the creative process.

Once we had our plan for the day, he shifted the conversation back to Dylan's murder. "Does the Professor have any leads?"

I shook my head. "I don't know for sure. Rumors were running rampant last night, but I have no idea what was real and what was speculation. I'm hoping to see him or Thomas or Kerry at some point today. We still need to pick up our supplies from the museum, and I need to confirm whether or not they want to keep the chocolate showpieces. If they don't, we can put them on display in the front windows for a while. It would be a shame to waste all of the hours we put into them on one night, especially a night that was cut so tragically short."

Sterling began dicing onions and garlic for the base of his soup. "Do you think the manuscript was really taken yesterday? That seems so brazen, doesn't it? I would think an art thief would be more discreet."

"That thought crossed my mind too," I replied, peeling a large butternut squash. "None of it makes sense. The timing, and why Tim and Dylan? Unless it's all connected."

"Why kill the security guard? I talked to him a couple times while we were setting up. We made sure to give the staff samples and offer up dinner while we were prepping, and he kind of seemed like a pothead to me." Sterling poured olive oil into a stock pan.

"Right? Yeah, that was my impression too. Unless he was a great actor, he didn't come across like a criminal mastermind, that's for sure." I discarded the peels in one of the composting tins on the counter. "It's so senseless. A young life cut short. I agree with you. I can't imagine any possible way he could have taken the manuscript himself, but I guess there's the possibility that he was involved. Maybe he was someone else's pawn, and they killed him to make sure he stayed silent."

"That could be." Sterling tossed the onions and garlic into the hot pan, which immediately sent an intense fragrance wafting through the kitchen.

"The whole thing was a disaster."

"Yeah. What a bummer to have the event shut down," Sterling commented.

"I know. I feel so bad for Javier. He had put as much effort into securing the exhibit as we put into the food."

As if on cue, Rosa came in through the back door. Typically she was calm and steady. Her naturally grounded aura made her a favorite amongst our customers and the staff. This morning she was the opposite. She slammed the door behind her and raced into the kitchen without taking off her coat. Her eyes were bloodshot and puffy.

"Jules, you've heard, right?"

"Heard what?"

"Javier. My uncle. He's been arrested on three charges— theft of Shakespeare's manuscript, attempted murder, and murder." She blinked rapidly, as if trying to process what she was saying.

Chapter Fourteen

So the rumors were true. Javier had been arrested. I couldn't believe it. Despite Zoe's claim that he was desperate to save the museum, I refused to believe that Javier could have done something as drastic as steal a priceless artifact, not to mention hurt anyone. It was so out of character.

Tears fell from Rosa's eyes. Her nose dripped. "Please, you have to help us. You know Javier. He couldn't have done it. Any of it."

I motioned toward the cozy seating area adjacent to the kitchen. "Let's go sit down."

She wiped her nose on the back of her coat and followed me.

"Do you want a coffee, something warm to drink?" I asked as I turned on the gas fireplace next to the couch. Flames lapped toward the chimney, sending out a radiant heat that did little to warm the chill running down my forearms.

Rosa wrung her hands together. She twisted a topaz ring on

her left hand and shook her head. "No. No. I can't drink anything. I'm sick to my stomach over this. Javier is a scholar. He reveres Shakespeare. You know how long he worked to bring the lost manuscript here—years. He never would have stolen it. Never. And it isn't possible that he could have killed anyone. Not Javier. Not my uncle. You know him, Jules. You have to help. What can we do?" Her voice cracked.

I scooted closer and placed my hand on her arm. "I know. Javier is such a kind soul. I can't imagine him hurting anyone. Are you sure they arrested him on every charge, even Dylan's murder?" I found it more plausible that Javier could have been involved in the manuscript's disappearance. Not that I wanted to believe that either, but between that and murder, the latter was much harder to stomach.

"Positive." She nodded again and again, like she was trying to force herself to believe it was true.

I thought back to my conversation with the Professor last night. Did that mean that the coroner had confirmed that Dylan had been killed before Javier was arrested?

"He called me from jail," Rosa continued, her voice breaking." They haven't set his bond yet, but he told me not even to try. He sounded so strange. Like he's already given up. He said the price for his bail was going to be way too high because they think he tried to kill a custodian and a security guard. The police are acting like they don't know my uncle. But they do. He is the kindest man on the planet. He would never hurt anyone. Never."

"Did he say anything about the theft or murder when you talked to him?" I caught Bethany's eye as she passed us carrying a tray of pumpkin roll slices, almond butter shortbread tarts, and blackberry and apple crisps upstairs. She mouthed, "Is there anything I can do?"

I shook my head.

Rosa didn't notice. She stared at the fire, her voice sounding wispy like it hurt to speak. "Yes. He said he's been set up. He thinks someone did this to him on purpose. He thinks someone has been planning this. Planning to steal the manuscript and put all of the blame on my uncle. Why? Who would do such a thing?"

"Does he have any idea who could have set him up?"

She gave me a pained stare. "No. Well, at least he didn't say if he does. That's why I need your help. You're close to the Professor. The Professor knows Javier. They've been friends for many years. I can't imagine how he could have arrested Javier. Will you please talk to him on my uncle's behalf? There must be another explanation."

"Of course." I patted her arm. "I can assure you that you're right. The Professor must have a reason. I know that they're friends and they share a connection around Shakespeare. Maybe he's trying to protect Javier."

"But why would he arrest him?" Her ring was perched at the tip of her finger. She spun it round and round at a dizzying pace.

"I'm not sure." I thought for a moment. "Do you know anything about the museum's finances? The most logical explanation would be that whoever took the manuscript did so for money. I want to believe that hurting Tim and killing Dylan was an accident. An act of desperation."

"Maybe. I don't know about motive." She sighed. "As to SOMA's finances, I don't know that either. Not really. Javier mentioned that donations had been down, but we never talk much about his work, other than how excited he was to bring the exhibit to Ashland. That's one of the reasons I know that he never would have taken the manuscript. He's been like a kid the night before Christmas. He loves Shakespeare. He always has. My first memories are of him reading passages to us at family holidays. He would dress up as Shakespeare for Halloween. He's volunteered at the festival for years and sees the same show dozens of times. He has been a scholar of Shakespeare's work his entire life. He would never chance taking the manuscript. He talked at length about how worried he was about the handling of the document and transferring it between the delivery crates and the case. It's so old that the pages are fragile and delicate." The confusion in her voice turned to anger. "He and the Professor used to be in a Shakespeare club together. They used to put on performances, quote sonnets, things like that. How could he arrest an old friend?"

"Are you talking about the Midnight Club?" My dad had been a member too. For many years the group met at the Black Swan Theatre after hours to dissect the Bard's work and create offbeat new plays. The Professor's office was filled with old photos of him and my dad in pantaloons goofing around on the stage.

"Yes, that's the name of it. Why would the Professor turn on his friend?"

"I'm sure he has a good reason."

"Will you talk to him, please?" Rosa practically begged. "I don't know what else to do. I'm sick with worry."

"I promise, I will."

Rosa clasped her hands together. "Thank you."

"Do you want to take the day off? It should be fairly slow since we're in the off season. Maybe you should go home. I know how stressful this must be."

"No. I want to work. It will be worse if I sit at home and worry," Rosa insisted.

"Okay, but if you change your mind, just go."

She forced a smile, shoved her ring down to the base of her finger, and went to put her things away. I had told her the truth, that I believed the Professor must have had a valid reason for arresting Javier, but I agreed that it seemed impossible that he could be a thief, let alone a killer.

There wasn't much I could do at this early hour, so I busied myself with baking. By the time we were ready to open the doors to our first guests at seven, the pastry case had been packed with slices of my pumpkin roll, apple spice cupcakes topped with Swiss meringue buttercream, bacon, pesto, and egg breakfast sandwiches on handmade cheddar biscuits, and an assortment of breads and pastries. Our chalkboard reflected our daily specials, including apple and pumpkin crepes, sweet potato chili hash, and Andy's orange and maple latte. Typically we rotated Shakespearean quotes on the menu, but today's from P. D. James read "It was one of those perfect English autumnal days which occur more frequently in memory than in life."

I loved hanging out behind the espresso bar and watching customers' delight as they ogled the pastry case and tried to decide between ordering a classic Americano or Andy's special. Or taking a peek at the work done by our youngest budding artists, which was shared on the bottom half of our chalkboard menu. We kept that space sacred for kids to create pictures, play tic-tac-toe, or just doodle. In order to make sure that we kept every customer happy, regardless of age, we also had a basket with toys, puzzles, and books to keep kids engaged while drinking hot chocolates and vanilla steamers.

It never got old to hear customers rave about our baked goods. I enjoyed every grain of salt and sore muscle that went

into kneading our sourdough bread, and the reward of seeing people's faces light up when they sunk their teeth into a
salted chocolate caramel tart was worth more than whatever
ended up in our till at the end of the day.

As expected, the morning began slowly with regulars
stopping in to bring home boxes of cake doughnuts and
cherry turnovers. A handful of customers lingered over pots
of French press in the window booths, but it wasn't until
closer to ten that things really began to pick up. I was bringing a fresh tray of panna cottas and sweet potato chili hash
upstairs when I spotted Lance waiting by the pastry case.
"Darling, there you are. I've been waiting for hours." He was
dressed in his version of casual attire, a pair of slacks and a
cashmere sweater with a matching buffalo plaid scarf and
black leather gloves.

"Considering I went downstairs to grab this about two
minutes ago, I would say that hours is an exaggeration."

He scoffed. "Can we go talk somewhere more *private*?"

"Let me put this down." I took the heavy tray behind the
counter, where Rosa was ringing up orders. "Are you okay if
I go chat with Lance for a minute?"

"Is it about Javier?" She sounded hopeful, her eyes land-
ing on Lance.

I wondered how she knew. Were Lance and I that obvious?

"Maybe." I nodded.

"Oh good."

Two older gentlemen who spent every Sunday morning
playing chess were packing up their board. "You want to
go grab that table?" I said to Lance. "I'll be there in a second."

Andy and Sequoia appeared to have everything running
smoothly at the far end of the counter. "Are you good?" I

asked, watching Sequoia pour a foam maple leaf on top of a chai latte.

"You bet, boss. Slinging drinks. My favorite way to spend a Sunday, except for shredding it on Mount A's slopes. I just told Sequoia that tonight's the night. I'm calling it now. Chance of snow? One hundred percent."

I hadn't seen a recent forecast. "Is that true?"

Sequoia shook her head. "Only if you're Andy."

Andy pretended to stab himself in the heart. "Hey, that hurts. I'll have you know that I've predicted snowfall better than the weather guys. Every—single—season. You want to put a friendly wager on it?" He held out his hand.

"Like what?" Sequoia's almond-shaped brown eyes flecked with gold caught the light as she gave him a friendly, yet challenging stare.

"Like the winner gets to decide the specials board for an entire week."

I laughed. When I had first hired Sequoia, she and Andy had butted heads. They had very unique styles when it came to artisan coffee. Styles that complemented each other. Andy was more of a traditionalist, preferring to use whole milk and strong shots of espresso as the building blocks for his creamy drinks, whereas Sequoia dealt in alternative products—hemp and almond milk, chai, and matcha. It had taken them a little while to figure out that their personal slants on coffee were actually a benefit, not a detriment.

"Deal."

They shook hands.

"You are our witness, boss." Andy pointed to me.

"Don't put me in the middle of this." I pulled two ceramic Torte mugs from the shelf and poured our breakfast blend for Lance and me.

"Just wait and see. It's going to be a winter wonderland out there by three o'clock." Andy shot his fingers like a gun at the clock. "I'm calling it now."

"Now you're pinpointing a time. That's brave," Sequoia said with a tilt of her head, causing her dreadlocks to swing across her neck.

"I call it confidence," Andy shot back.

I let them continue to banter and balanced the coffee mugs on my way to meet Lance. I handed one to Lance and set mine on the table to scoot into the booth.

"Nectar of the gods, many thanks." Lance removed his gloves with the precision of a surgeon, then raised his coffee cup to his lips. "Listen, I don't have much time. I'm swamped with meetings today. We have a full docket of planning for the new season, but I must know, what else have you learned? What did I miss last night?"

"Nothing."

"Nothing, ha!"

"Really. Carlos and I took Mom home. The Professor and his team must have stayed pretty late."

"Juliet Montague Capshaw, stop holding out on me." His playful attitude had returned.

"What do you mean?"

"What do *I* mean? What do *you* mean?"

"Lance, if you have meetings to get to, we can't do this all morning."

"Agreed. That's why I want you to divulge everything you've learned. That's what partners in crime do, after all." He loosened his plaid scarf.

"Honestly, I don't know anything. Javier was arrested. Rosa is distraught, rightfully so. I promised her I would talk to the Professor later. That's about the extent of what I know."

He twiddled his fingers together. "Well, then it sounds like I'm the one who has news for you."

In classic Lance fashion, he paused for dramatics.

"I've learned that our custodian Tim is up, awake, and coherent." His eyes burned with an elated knowingness.

"Really, okay? I mean, that's good news, but why are you looking at me like that?" I wasn't sure what I was missing.

"It is, isn't it? But wait, there's more." A mischievous twinkle appeared in his eyes. "Evidently he's awake and *talking*."

Chapter Fifteen

"He's talking?" I repeated.

"Yes." Lance flashed his signature impish smile, which I knew could only mean one thing. He was up to no good. "He's talking, so he must know who the killer is."

"How do you know this?"

He peered over the top of the mug. "Please. I have my sources."

"At the hospital?" I cradled my coffee in my hands.

"Everywhere. Everywhere." He took a long, slow deliberate sip of his drink. "So, shall we?"

"Shall we what?"

"Pay our dear friend Tim a visit?"

"We can't do that," I protested. "Plus you just said you have a full day of meetings."

"Exactly. No time like the present." Lance set his coffee

mug on the table and picked up a glove. "I think our dearest friend Tim would appreciate a pick-me-up visit from his friends and a box of Torte's pastries to perk up his spirits. Call it community kindness."

"Lance, you're too much."

"You think I jest? I assure you I'm serious. Deadly serious." His voice filled with emotion. "Truth be told, after last night, I will admit that I'm shaken. I had just had a chat with Dylan before he was brutally killed. He wasn't going to win any awards for being the smartest person in the room, nor could he have remembered a single line or stage direction had I cast him as an extra, despite his alternatively handsome jawline, but my God, to have been murdered moments later." Lance shuddered. "I may have been the last person to see him alive, Juliet. I intend to do anything and everything I can to help bring his killer to justice."

"I get it." It was true. I understood Lance's need to right such a terrible wrong.

"Excellent." He pulled his glove over his long, lanky fingers like a debutante dressing for a ball. "Go box up some delightful treats. Put them on my credit card. Grab your coat and meet me here in five."

When I didn't move, he shooed me away. "Make haste. I'm due at a dreaded budget meeting at eleven sharp, so chop-chop."

Lance had an uncanny ability to talk me into pulling the craziest stunts, and yet I couldn't argue that I did want to talk to Tim. If he really was awake and coherent, maybe he could tell us who had pulled the shelving unit down on him. He might be the key to clearing Javier and closing in on Dylan's killer.

I asked Rosa to package an assortment of sweet and savory treats. While I waited for her to fill one of our pastry boxes with blueberry crumble muffins and pecan zucchini bread, I had a moment of hesitation. Was this a bad idea?

Yes. Undoubtedly.

Lance was notorious for pushing boundaries and walking a thin line between semi-innocent meddling and obstructing justice.

When Rosa handed me the box, her face was decades lighter than it had been earlier. "Thank you for helping, Jules. It means so much to me." Her hands trembled as she spoke. "It means more than I can ever tell you. I know Javier has been wrongly accused, and he needs all the help he can get." Her voice was breathless and her cheeks bright with color.

How could I refuse? I grabbed the box and hurried downstairs to get my coat before I changed my mind again. What would Carlos say if he was here? I had a feeling he wouldn't be thrilled with Lance and me trying to interrogate a potential witness. Good thing he was still asleep. I reached for my coat and returned upstairs to find that Lance had paid for the pastries and ordered a to-go cup of coffee for Tim as well.

He brushed his hand toward the door. "Shall we?"

"Why do I have a feeling I'm going to regret this?"

"Regret spending time with moi? Never. Shudder the thought." Lance looped his arm through mine and opened the door.

Ominous gray clouds, tinged with purple, greeted us outside. The temperature felt like it had dropped since my walk earlier this morning. Andy might win his snow bet after all.

"Bundle up," Lance commanded as we turned onto Main and headed north to the hospital.

"Do you think they'll even let us in to see Tim?" I asked.

"Absolutely. Simply follow my lead." He motioned toward Main Street. "After you."

Following his lead had had disastrous results in the past. I considered turning around and heading back to the bake-shop, but I couldn't resist—I wanted to know if Tim really did have an idea who had tried to hurt him, and wanted to get a sense of whether he had been involved in the heist. Since he'd been at the hospital when Dylan was tased, we naturally had to rule him out as a killer, but there was the possibility that he had been working with someone. Maybe he'd left the dirty work to his accomplice.

"What if Thomas or Kerry are on guard in front of his room?"

"Juliet, trust me. I have a plan."

I wasn't sure I believed him, but it didn't take long to walk less than a half mile to the hospital. Lance sauntered straight to the reception desk. "Good morning. My friend and I are here to pay a visit to Tim."

"Tim who?" A grouchy woman in her late forties glared up at him.

"Uh, Tim the custodian from SOMA. He was brought in last evening. Terrible accident. Terrible." Lance's dancer-like posture shifted. He sagged his shoulders to mirror his words.

The receptionist wasn't buying it. "I need a last name."

Lance glanced at me and raised his eyebrow.

I shrugged and shook my head. I didn't know Tim's last name.

"Obviously, I haven't had my morning java." He held up the coffee cup. "I'm having a brain freeze. I'm sure it's due to the icy weather outside, and I'm sure you must know who

I am." He paused. "Lance. Lance Rousseau, artistic director at the Oregon Shakespeare Festival. Couldn't you make a little exception?"

The reception wasn't impressed. "Nope. I need a last name. Hospital policy." She used her pencil to point at a sign on the wall behind her.

Lance frowned. Never one to shy away from a challenge, he wasn't easily deterred. He leaned closer and lifted the lid of the pastry box with the utmost care, as if he was about to reveal a precious gem inside. Then he offered her the box of pastries. "I don't suppose there's any chance you could be buttered up to point us in the direction of Tim's room with this delectable box of pastries, handcrafted with love by Ashland's pastry muse." He motioned toward me with his thumb.

I felt my cheeks burn.

The receptionist scowled. "No last name, no entry."

Lance sighed. "In that case, give us just a moment." He motioned for me to join him at a small lounge area. "That always works. My name, Torte pastries—but not even so much as a flinch. She can't be swayed. I'm at a loss. What now?" His voice was laced with irritation.

"What do you mean? I thought you had a plan."

"I did have a plan. Dropping my title and offering up a box of coveted Torte pastries always works. She's a tough nut to crack." He paused for a minute. "Can't you make a call? Someone at the museum must know Tim's last name."

"Lance, first of all, who am I going to call? I highly doubt that anyone on staff is even allowed in the building at this point. Not to mention that the receptionist is totally onto us. There's no chance she's going to let us in to see him, last name or not."

"Oh ye of little faith." Lance scanned the foyer, as if

searching for another way into the patient corridor. "How do you feel about playing the role of medical assistant?"

"No way. That is not happening."

Lance's outlandish schemes had gotten me into awkward situations in the past. I wasn't about to try and sneak around the hospital with him.

Fortunately Thomas and Kerry appeared at that moment. They had come from the patient corridor. Thomas stopped in midstride when he saw us. He was dressed in his blue uniform, shorts and all, only with one difference. Today he had a pair of tight black running pants under his shorts. Kerry was better prepared for any impending snow in her thick black leggings, wool-lined boots, and oversized black and gray poncho sweater. Her long, velvety rust-colored hair was tied in a loose ponytail.

"Do I even want to ask what you two are doing here?" Thomas raised both eyebrows as he approached us. "What are the odds that this is a pure coincidence?"

"Slim to none," Kerry murmured under her breath.

"Why, doing our civic duty of course," Lance shot back. I had to credit him for being able to craft a witty response in a matter of seconds. "Juliet and I were absolutely distraught after witnessing our dearest friend Tim's accident last night." He placed his hand over his heart and closed his eyes momentarily. "We figured the least we could do was pay him a visit and offer some of Torte's delicious and healing pastries."

"Healing pastries?" Kerry tried to contain a smirk. "That's rich."

"That's really rich, even for you, Lance." Thomas fought back a smile. "Come on, why don't you two step outside with us."

We followed his instruction, returning outside to the inclement weather. Not more than five minutes could have passed, but it felt like the temperature had plummeted even more. I shivered as we huddled beneath the overhang. A mixture of frozen rain dripped from the sky, splotching on the cement like exploding water balloons.

"Okay, you two, we know what you're up to, so enough with the act." Thomas directed his attention to Lance. "You want an update about Tim, right?"

Lance shifted his tone, sounding innocent and naïve. "If it isn't too much trouble, an update on his condition would certainly put our anxiety over our dear friend at ease, wouldn't it, Juliet?"

I didn't bother to answer.

Thomas rolled his eyes. "You'll be happy to hear that your *dear* friend is awake and responsive."

Lance let out an exaggerated sigh of relief. "Oh, most excellent news."

Kerry gave him a stern warning, her green eyes narrowing at him in that dreaded mom look of warning. I half expected her to tell him that if he wasn't careful, she was going to send him to time-out.

"I don't suppose he was able to relay what happened last night, was he?" Lance was unfazed by their disapproval.

Thomas and Kerry shared a look. Kerry gave Thomas a half shrug. I guessed it to be a sign that she was fine with him divulging what they had learned, because Thomas nodded. "He is alert and was able to tell us what he remembers from last night, though it's not much. It turns out that he sustained a blow to the head when he fell, and the doctors believe that his short-term memory was impacted. In fact, they said he's lucky that he didn't suffer a traumatic brain injury. Additionally, he's pretty beat up. Two fractures in his arm and cracked ribs. They've got him on some heavy pain meds." He paused. "This stays between us, agreed?"

Lance and I both nodded. I rubbed my hands together as fast as I could to try and create enough friction to keep warm.

"Tim doesn't remember much. That could be from the concussion or it could be from the medication they have him on, or maybe a combination of both. The one thing he does recall is that Javier asked him to go check out the basement because apparently a guest reported seeing someone headed downstairs, past the off-limits signage."

I wasn't sure whether that was good news for Javier. That could mean that he was nowhere near the basement archives, or it could mean that he had intentionally sent Tim downstairs in order to try and silence him. That also didn't match what I had witnessed. Tim took off to the archives of his own accord to return the cart and get trash bags. Could he be lying, or was his memory fuzzy?

"The bad news is that's the extent of Tim's memory right now," Thomas continued. "He doesn't remember anything that happened after that. Not even you finding him, Jules. He only remembers waking up in the hospital bed this morning. The doctors don't know how long it will take him to recover his short-term memory, or if he even will. So we're not much farther along in the investigation than we were yesterday. We were hoping that Tim might be able to identify who tried to kill him, but it doesn't look like that's happening anytime soon."

"What does that mean for Javier?" I finally spoke up.

"It means he remains in custody for the time being," Kerry replied with a scowl. "I can't expand in great detail, but we found evidence that clearly indicates his involvement. The Professor feels terrible about it, but we have to follow procedure until we can prove or disprove his role in this one way or another."

She confirmed the rumor Cindy had told me last night—the police had firm evidence linking Javier to the theft. This wasn't going to be news that Rosa would want to hear. And, it made me more resolved to want to find out who had stolen the manuscript and killed Dylan, to help clear her uncle's name.

Chapter Sixteen

Thomas and Kerry walked with us to the plaza. I was happy to be moving again as the cold permeated my outer layers and settled in my bones. My nose dripped. It had gone numb, and my cheeks felt the sting of the frigid wind. Clouds heavy with moisture shrouded the mountains, making it feel like midnight.

Lance hammered Thomas for more information while I asked Kerry about wedding plans. "I haven't heard any news about the wedding. Have you guys made any progress?"

She kept her pace quick. I wasn't sure if it was because she didn't want to talk about it or because the icy particles of freezing rain were slowly morphing into fat snowflakes. Peaked rooftops along the plaza were dusted with white. Andy had been right. The icy precipitation was dropping the temp. Fast. White flakes the size of fluffy cotton balls began to stick to the grass and bushes. "Not really. I'm still in favor of keeping things simple and going to the courthouse, but having some sort of celebration is important to Thomas." She hesitated for a moment. "I don't want to deny him that."

That was thoughtful of her. "I'm sure there's a way to compromise. What about something small?"

"Yeah, that's what I'm thinking." She rubbed her shoulders. "It's freezing out here."

"I know." I blew warm air into my hands, not that it did much good. "Look, I don't want to overstep or get involved if you don't want it, but I'll say it again—we would love to host the wedding at Torte or at the winery. But absolutely no pressure if that's not what you want. This is your wedding."

"I know, I appreciate it, but I'm leaning toward outside somewhere. Spring is my favorite season." She intentionally huffed, letting out a puff of air like smoke. "I prefer not to see my breath like this when I'm outside."

I laughed. "Yeah, an outdoor winter wedding might be a bit chilly, but spring is perfect. What about Lithia Park? You could do it in the Japanese Gardens or at the bandshell. Something really simple. Like a picnic wedding. We could do picnic style food for you. Bite-sized sandwiches, fruit salads, miniature cakes. Elegant, but easy. Everyone could bring their own blankets. You wouldn't even need flowers, although I'm sure Thomas's mom won't let you get away without some flowers."

Kerry laughed. "Janet has been so helpful, and yes, you're right, she will want to do the flowers, but it's not like I would resist that. Thomas is her only son, after all." We made it to the base of the plaza. A wintery calm fell over town as dainty particles drifted in the air and gathered on the sidewalk.

We stopped at the corner. Torte sat like a beacon glowing

in the storm. The snowfall cast a magical glow over everything.

"I kind of love the idea of a picnic wedding." Kerry ran her finger on the railing above Ashland Creek, where snow was already freezing, creating an icy sheen around the metal guardrail. "That could be good. Casual is my speed. The thought of having to do a processional in a long white dress in front of hundreds of people makes me nauseous. It's not my scene. The same goes for a big, fancy reception. Having to go table to table to make small talk with people gives me a minor panic attack. You know me, I'm an introvert. But a picnic, yeah. That could be good," she repeated, as if warming to the thought.

"I don't blame you. That's why Carlos and I got married while at port in the South of France. It was just us, which was romantic, so don't feel like you have to do something small either. If you want it to be Thomas and you, that's totally fine. You don't have to try and please the community. We'll support you in whatever you want."

She smiled. "Yeah, but like I said, it's different for Thomas. Isn't marriage supposed to be about learning how to compromise? Finding that balance. I don't want to start off our married life with one of us feeling cheated. Ashland is special to Thomas, you know, since he grew up here. He wants to include his friends, his family, the community, which I totally get. It's different for me, though. I don't have the same kind of connection here, but I want him to be happy, too." She trailed off, gazing down the street toward the park. "No, a picnic sounds cool. I love Lithia, and it will be beautiful in the spring. Maybe we could hire a band to play music. I wouldn't need a long dress or anything. I could wear a cute summer dress. Yeah, I like it. I'll talk to

Thomas, but I bet he will be into the idea too." Her green eyes were bright. "Thanks."

"Of course. It seems like you, and I'm serious about doing the food."

"I'll keep you posted." Before she and Thomas crossed Main Street to the police station, I gave them the box of pastries. I knew they would be appreciated and devoured. Lance and I headed the opposite direction to Torte. He left me at the door. "Well, that was a bust."

"At least we didn't end up getting arrested for posing as doctors and trespassing in off-limits areas of the hospital."

He gave his head a half shake. "Please, like that would ever happen. I would have simply explained that we were doing research for a role. It works like a charm every time."

"Do you want to come in for another coffee?"

"I wish, but duty calls. I'm needed for artistic meetings. You'd think they could survive without my direction, but apparently not. What's worse is that Arlo scheduled a budget meeting for today. He's forcing me to review numbers and do math on a Sunday—the nerve." He threw his hands to both sides.

I knew that budgeting wasn't Lance's forte. His ambitious vision for OSF's future came with a hefty price tag in the form of cutting-edge staging, hiring top-notch talent, and producing groundbreaking shows that challenged current cultural norms. The theater community revered him for it. The finance department—not so much.

"Let's plan to meet up later," Lance continued. "Lord knows I'm going to need a martini. Say Puck's for a happy hour? Four o'clock? Bring that Spaniard of yours, and I'll see if Arlo will tag along. In the meantime, I'll do what digging

I can between squinting over Excel spreadsheets, and you keep those pretty pastry ears wide open."

"I'll do my best."

"I never doubted it." Lance blew me a kiss and sauntered across the plaza. A thin layer of white snow coated the street and sidewalks. Bethany was going to love this, I thought as I went to close the front door. I was sure she was already dreaming up snowy photo shoots.

At that moment, Richard Lord's bulky frame blocked me from pulling the door shut.

"Juliet Capshaw, what do you think you're doing, sneaking about town?" His voice rumbled like a jet plane as he yanked the door handle. His red, white, and blue tartan golf pants and matching argyle sweater made my eyes dizzy.

"I'm at my own bakeshop. How is that sneaking about?"

He tossed his head to the side. "I just saw Lance prancing across the street. Everyone knows that you two pretend you're part of Ashland's team in blue."

His words made me recoil slightly. Not that I cared about Richard Lord's opinion of me, but I wasn't exactly thrilled with the idea of everyone in town gossiping about Lance's and my involvement in the investigation. "Did you need something, Richard?"

He peered inside. "Looks like business is slow for you, huh?"

I turned to see a small line at the counter and a handful of tables occupied, which was on par for a Sunday morning. I ignored the comment.

"Sounds like word is getting out." His eyes narrowed in a mixture of pompous delight.

"What are you talking about?" I tried to create more friction with my hands as I shifted from side to side. I didn't have time to play Richard's bizarre games, and it was freezing.

"Rumor has it that the almighty Juliet has bitten off more than she can chew. I have it firsthand from a variety of my esteemed friends that last night's gala was subpar. Subpar. Bland, cold food. Mediocre desserts. Childish chocolate displays. There's talk that Torte was involved in the heist. I'd hate to see a fellow business owner suffer the consequences of being associated with such a scandal." He gave me a sneering wink.

What? I wanted to punch him in his bloated belly. What was he talking about? Everyone at the gala had seemed to enjoy the food and desserts. People had gushed about the chocolate structures. There was only one person I could think of who would have had less than kind things to say about Torte—Ernest.

"Listen here, young lady: I know that you like to think of yourself as the queen of Ashland with all of your new business ventures, but you're not the only entrepreneur around. Some of us have ideas for Ashland and the plaza, too. Big ideas. Ideas that might take money out of Torte's fat pockets."

I had no idea what he was talking about.

"Consider yourself warned, Capshaw. Big things are coming." With that, he shot his finger at me, turned, and with lumbering footsteps like Bigfoot, headed toward the Merry Windsor.

I wasn't about to let Richard Lord or Ernest get inside my head or get the better of me. He could think whatever he wanted, but I didn't have to listen. I hurried inside, grateful for the burst of heat and delicious smells as I opened the door.

Andy caught my eye immediately. "Hey, boss, what's happening out there? It's looking like snow to me, like real *S-N-O-W*. Snow." He danced around the espresso machine.

I brushed little flakes from my coat and walked over to the espresso bar. "Andy, I have to give you credit. You called it. Not only is it coming down, but it's starting to stick."

"Sequoia, are you listening? You're not having any problems hearing over the hum of the grinder or anything, are you?" Andy teased, pressing his fingers on the grinder and pulsing beans. "I'm telling you both that by three o'clock, we're going to start seeing people cross-country skiing in the plaza. I can't even imagine how much fresh powder is falling up on Mount A."

"Honestly, I'm not sad about losing this bet. The snow is pretty, and I'm sure you're going to come up with a snowy drink that we'll all love." Sequoia was a gracious loser.

"You think I'm going to play nice?" Andy let out an evil cackle. "Never! I'm going to make you the sugary, sweetest drink you've ever tasted. I'm thinking marshmallow fluff, cotton candy, bubble gum, Jolly Ranchers, some sprinkles thrown in for fun, and a mound of whipped cream taller than my fist to top it off."

"Help me," Sequoia pleaded, looping her hands together in a prayer pose. "So much sugar."

Sequoia preferred natural sweetness for her coffee specials—stevia, coconut milk, honey, and agave.

I knew Andy was messing with her. I also knew there was no chance he would serve something so cloying sweet on our menu. But, I wouldn't have put it past him to make his candy crush drink just to force her to taste it.

"Remember, Jules is neutral. She can't save you from this. We had a bet." Andy filled a tamper with the fresh ground beans. "What's the saying? All's fair in love and war? How about all's fair in snow and coffee?"

Sequoia wrinkled her brow. "I don't think that works."

"No, it doesn't." Andy laughed. "But I don't care because it's turning into a whiteout. Pure powder, baby."

I left them to their argument and went downstairs to find that both Mom and Carlos had arrived during my absence.

"Julieta, you left me sleeping," Carlos complained. "You should have woken me."

"It was early." I tried to wink, forcing my face to contort in a weird way. I don't know why I bothered to try. I've never been able to pull off a subtle wink. "I couldn't sleep, so I decided to bake."

"Trying to keep this one of out of the kitchen is like trying to herd cats," Mom said, swatting me with a dish towel. A vat of our sugar cookie dough sat on the counter, where she had liberally floured a section to roll out the dough. She pushed the sleeves of her camel turtleneck up to her elbows.

"The pastry was calling me. I couldn't resist. I think it was a combination of knowing that we're done with the gala and trying to piece together what happened last night." I changed the topic. "On that note, how late was the Professor out?"

I went to the sink to wash my hands with our rosemary lavender soap.

"Late." Mom reached below the counter to get the large wicker box filled with cookie cutters. "I think he finally came to bed around four. Probably about the same time you were starting your day."

"Did he learn anything new?"

Mom tucked her hair behind her ears, then began laying out an assortment of snowflake cookie cutters. "Not of any substance. They're waiting on an official cause of death for

Dylan. Talk about a tragedy. I had no idea a Taser could be deadly. Doug said it's not common, but definitely possible. I know that he sent Thomas and Kerry to the hospital to interview Tim this morning. They're hoping he'll be able to tell them who assaulted him, or get a sense of whether he could be involved."

"That's off the table." I told her about my conversation with Kerry and Thomas.

"Doug said he would call when he's ready for us to go pick up our supplies at the museum," Mom noted. She placed a large ball of dough on the floured surface and began rolling it out. "I'm sure he can tell you more. That is, if he knows more then."

Rosa came into the kitchen with an empty tray. Her eyes were swollen and bloodshot. I wondered if she'd been crying again. "You're back already. That was fast. Did you learn anything?"

"I'm afraid not." I told her that Tim was responsive, which was good news, but that he didn't remember anything that happened after going downstairs.

"At least it's not another death to pin on my uncle," she said, not sounding relieved as she stacked egg and sausage bagel sandwiches and slices of veggie quiche on the tray.

Carlos came over to her holding an oversized ceramic coffee mug. "I made this for you, Rosa. I thought it might help." His voice morphed into easy lyrical Spanish. "Café de olla."

Rosa pressed her finger to her chin. "Thank you. That's very kind of you." She took the mug and held it like a fragile egg.

"What is a café de olla?" Mom asked.

"It's a Mexican coffee with orange rind, star anise, cloves, piloncillo, and cinnamon," Carlos replied. "I can make you one, Helen. It's a wonderful winter warmer for the heart and the soul."

"That does sound wonderful." Mom nodded twice. "Yes, please."

"Anyone else?" Carlos offered.

Sterling raised his hand. "I'll take one, but first I have to ask, what's piloncillo?"

Rosa cradled her mug with both hands as she took a long drink, closing her eyes to savor the flavor. "It's Mexican cane sugar," she said to Sterling. "We also call it brown sugar. I think it has a flavor almost like molasses, but there's no molasses in it."

"Si," Carlos agreed, as he passed around coffees for the rest of us. "I would guess that caramel richness comes because the sugar is not refined or processed."

One sip of the black coffee transported me to the ship, when Carlos had made it for me for the first time. "This is even better than I remember," I said, inhaling the romantic, almost smoky spice.

"Yes, this is just how my abuela makes it." Rosa gave Carlos a grateful smile.

I considered relaying Kerry's input that the Professor hadn't wanted to arrest Javier, but I didn't want to give her false hope. She finished her coffee and returned upstairs with a fresh tray. Carlos and Sterling called me over for a brainstorming session.

"What do you think about an impromptu Sunday Supper?" Sterling asked.

"You mean, like, tonight?" Typically we planned our Sunday family-style dinners at least a week or more in advance.

"Yeah. I know. It's spontaneous." Sterling looked toward

upstairs. "But it's a snow day. Your mom is making sugar cookie snowflake cutouts. Marty's got some amazing bread going. We don't get snow this early in November very often. What if we put together a snow-inspired dinner? Nothing fancy. Soup, bread, salad. I have a feeling people are going to be out and about enjoying the snow tonight. Bethany said she could post it on social. Almost like a pop-up."

I wasn't convinced. "I mean, I love the idea, but are you sure you want to do another event after last night? Aren't you wiped out?" I addressed everyone, expecting some resistance to the idea of putting on another event, whether a small Sunday Supper or not. Even with Carlos's strong Mexican coffee, I still couldn't shake the haze that lingered over me.

"This is why it might be good, Julieta." Carlos spoke up. I had a feeling he had intentionally kept quiet to give Sterling the floor. He had taken our young sous chef under his wing. Sterling was a natural in the kitchen and had a sophisticated palate, something no amount of training or culinary school could teach. For as long as I'd known Carlos, he had made it a priority to bring young chefs up in the culinary world. There was never a time on the ship that he wasn't sharing his knife skills or tips for layering seasonings into a dish with the younger team members in his kitchen.

Having him at Torte had been a huge boost for our culinary staff. Not just Sterling, but he and Steph and Bethany had collaborated on a line of unique cupcake flavors like dark chocolate with Chinese five spice and plum custard, Italian cream, and Biscoff cookie with cookie butter filling. With Marty, Carlos talked bread for hours on end. They taught one another new techniques for proofing dough and firing thin herb-crusted focaccia in the pizza oven. Rosa wasn't left out either. She and Carlos had bonded over their shared heritage and different touches on dishes, given Rosa's Mexican influence versus Carlos's Spanish roots. I loved listening to them mock debate the best version of tortillas. Rosa insisted that traditional corn flour was the only way to make a tortilla, whereas Carlos argued the case for his mother's recipe for egg-based tortillas.

Everyone in the kitchen was a winner in their debates, since we got to taste their signature styles on the plate. That was the thing I enjoyed most about my career path. Food allows everyone a place at the table. Sharing a meal can break down barriers like nothing else. Carlos and I had often discussed that if only we could bring world leaders together for an evening centered around food, perhaps that was the path to peace. And never had that been more evident at Torte. Regardless of Richard's attempts to get under my skin, I knew that we had created a place where everyone who gathered was welcomed with a heaping plate of deliciousness and love.

"It might be nice to open our doors on a snowy night for the community to gather," Carlos continued. "As Sterling said, something simple like soup and bread to warm everyone's spirits. I think maybe people will want some comfort after the news of the theft and murder, si? Isn't this what you have said about Ashland and what I am learning? That we must come together to heal, and there's no better way to make healing happen than by breaking bread."

"Sure." I nodded. "I'm game if you guys are. What do we need to do?"

"We need a menu." Sterling rolled up his sleeves. In addition to the hummingbird tattoo etched on his forearm, he had recently gotten a yin and yang tattoo on his wrist. I didn't ask, but I suspected his new artwork might have something to do with him and Steph moving in together. "What about a soup trio? We have the butternut squash. Then we talked about one of Carlos's childhood favorites, fabada Asturiana, a white bean and pork Spanish-style stew. We could round out our triple soup offerings with a classic chicken and dumpling. That's what my mom used to make for me on snow days."

"Soup and snow are always a match," I agreed.

"I'll bake a few extra loaves of bread that we can serve hot from the oven." Marty joined the conversation. "I've got a honey bread rising as we speak, and it can take its sweet time to rise away. As my guy Paul Hollywood says, 'You've got to get it right to get the growth in the loaf.'"

"I'll do a winter salad," Carlos offered. "Greens, toasted walnuts, cranberries, and herbed goat cheese tossed with a cranberry vinaigrette."

"That just leaves dessert," I replied. "I'll put my head together with Bethany and Steph and then task Bethany with getting the word out. Depending on what SOMA wants to do with the leftovers, we can probably share some of those too."

Bethany came back shortly from deliveries. She brushed snow from her curly hair. As was typical, she wore a bright red hoodie in Torte's colors with the words YOU BUTTER BELIEVE IT across the chest. "It's amazing out there. Andy's freaking out upstairs, because he totally called it. I think there are at least two inches, and it's still coming down." Her cheeks flushed. I was sure in part because she came in from the cold, but it could also have had something to do with mentioning Andy's name. She'd had a crush on him for a while, and as of yet, I still wasn't sure whether or not he reciprocated her feelings. I'd seen subtle signs that made me think so, like offering to teach her how to ski, but if he was interested, he was moving like molasses when it came to actually asking her out. Mom and I had both told her she should make the first move, but she claimed that wasn't her style.

I asked her and Steph their thoughts on a quick and easy dessert for our soup, salad, and bread Sunday Supper.

"You know what I'll say," Bethany teased with a grin. "Brownies, of course!"

Bethany had gotten her start selling and delivering brownies out of her home kitchen. We had met at Ashland's annual chocolate fest and immediately hit it off. She was at a stage where her delivery business had outgrown her space, and we needed extra help. So part of our partnership was offering her Unbeatable Brownies (which had a cultlike following) at Torte.

Steph nodded. "It's a good idea. They're fast, easy, and everyone loves a good brownie."

"How about a chocolate with blood orange, and a chocolate orange ganache glaze?" Bethany suggested. "I'm talking, like, thick and luscious ganache that's the consistency of mayonnaise. I'll use orange blossom water, fresh orange juice, and grated orange to really pull out the flavor of the dark chocolate. Finish it with a touch of flaky sea salt. Oh my gosh, I'm drooling at the thought." She pretended to wipe drool from her chin.

"Yeah, and I can do a cranberry blondie with cream cheese frosting," Steph added. "We can pipe them with snowflakes. Do them in the same style that Mrs. Capshaw is doing with the sugar cookies."

"Oh my God! Yes, that's adorable," Bethany gushed. She clapped twice, peering over Mom's shoulder to get a closer look at the snowflake cookies.

Steph stuck out her tongue. "Adorable, come on, Bethany. How dare you call my ideas adorable?" The tiniest tug of a smile spread across her lips before she returned to scooping buttercream into a piping bag.

"I'll post this on social media right now," Bethany said to me. "I bet we sell out within the hour."

I wasn't sure about that, but I was glad that Sterling had suggested the idea. He was right. After the terrible turn of events last night, it would be good to gather around Torte's welcoming table and watch the snow fall outside.

Chapter Seventeen

Sunday Supper preparations were in full swing as the snow continued to come down in an endless swirl of white. Bethany had called it. Reservations poured in within minutes of her posting the soup, salad, and bread menu on our social media. The first snow had everyone eager to get outside and hungry for comforting eats. I had a feeling that last night's terrible turn of events had something to do with it too. Our tight-knit community had weathered stronger storms in the past, and we would get through this together.

Shortly after noon, the Professor called to let us know we could access SOMA's kitchen and begin the cleanup process. We had made a good dent last night, but there was plenty to do, and I still hadn't heard from Zoe about what she had decided about the chocolate sculptures. "I'm going to head up to the museum to get our things," I announced to the kitchen.

Carlos was in the middle of chopping garlic and onions for his Spanish-inspired stew. "I will drive you."

"You? You will drive me? In the snow?" I tilted my head and pursed my lips.

"What? You think I cannot drive in snow?" He held up his chopping knife.

"Let's see . . . you grew up in the sunny Mediterranean and spent—what, fifteen years?—at sea. I am positive you can't drive in the snow."

"We should teach him, boss." Andy had come downstairs carrying a tray filled with tasters of his winning coffee creation. "I'll take you up to Mount A. That will be a crash course in winter weather driving for sure."

"Except I think the goal is to avoid the crash part," I joked.

"Fair point. Fair point. But seriously, Carlos, if you want some snow driving practice or you want to learn how to snowboard, I'm your guy. My grandma teases that I was born with a pair of ski boots strapped to my feet." He offered Carlos one of the drinks. "Speaking of coffee, I warned you guys. I won the snow dance, and now Sequoia has to spend the rest of the day talking up my newest special."

"Dare I ask what it is?" I winced, pretending to brace myself on the counter for impact.

"You bet!" Andy's grin spread across his freckled cheeks. "I'm naming it after my grandma's favorite Dean Martin song—'It's a Marshmallow World.' She's already been playing Christmas music, and I know this sickeningly sweet concoction is going to make Sequoia's teeth ache. It's a blend of our house-made milk chocolate and white chocolate sauces with a touch of marshmallow fluff and a hand-pulled marshmallow on the top. Not only does Sequoia have to make these beauties this afternoon, but I'm going to put

'It's a Marshmallow World' on constant rotation for her listening pleasure."

He chuckled as he passed around drinks.

Bethany held her cup up. "Oooh, I should take this outside and get some pictures with the snow as a backdrop." She met Andy's eyes, sucking in her cheeks. "It's really good, and I don't think it's too sweet. Couldn't we offer this as a hot chocolate too?"

Andy clapped her on the shoulder. "You read my mind. Thanks for always having my back, Bethany. You're the coolest."

Blotches of red dotted her cheeks at his compliment. She cleared her throat and hurried to take another sip of her coffee.

I tasted his winning drink. To my surprise and relief, the coffee wasn't actually cloyingly sweet. He had deftly balanced the milk and white chocolate ratio and our square-cut marshmallows dusted with fine powdered sugar finished the drink off with a hint of whimsy. Who doesn't love a marshmallow on a snow day?

"This reminds me of the hot chocolate you used to make, Mom."

She was up to her elbows in sugar cookie dough. "I haven't had a chance to taste it yet, but I'm sure it's great." She smiled at Andy.

"Si. It is nice. I prefer my coffee black, but I can see that this will be a favorite with the kids and latte drinkers." Carlos diced veggies with flourish. "Andy, I would like for you to teach me to ski. It's something I have always wanted to try. I have been waterskiing many times. It cannot be that different, can it?"

"Not at all. Only slightly colder maybe." Andy had passed

out all of his tasters and had begun gathering supplies to re-stock the espresso bar. "Let's do it. We'll get you up on the mountain and shredding." His arms were loaded with a va-riety of milks—almond, coconut, and hemp. "Do you want a hand at the museum? Sequoia and Rosa should be able to deal with the lunch crowd, no problem. Things are steady because everyone wants to come in to warm up and then get back outside into the snow."

"That would be great." I went to get my coat while he took the milk upstairs.

Mom stopped me on my way out. She pressed a six-inch snowflake cookie cutter into a large rectangle of dough. "Check in with Doug, would you? I'm a bit worried about him. It's never fun to make an arrest, but certainly much worse when you have to arrest a friend."

"I will." I gave her a knowing look before heading upstairs, where Sequoia had a line of Andy's Marshmallow World coffees waiting at the bar.

"This is seriously painful," she said to me through clenched teeth as she plunked a chunky marshmallow on top of each drink. Her eyes told a different story. "Just wait for our next bet. I'm going to make you serve pure hemp lattes for a week," she threatened Andy.

He waved toward his body with both hands. "Bring it."

"Let's go and put poor Sequoia out of her misery." I dragged Andy to the door.

As we stepped outside, I couldn't believe how the snowfall had transformed the plaza. It looked as if every storefront had been frosted with our fluffy white buttercream. Snow came nearly to the curb and weighed down the sturdy branches of evergreen trees.

"Man, it must be up to four or five inches now," Andy exclaimed. "I can't even imagine what it must look like up on the mountain."

"I'll tell you what. After you help me gather our stuff from the museum, why don't you head home and get your ski gear?"

"Really? Are you sure? You don't need help with the Sunday Supper?"

"No. We're fine. Plus, when do you get to snowboard in November?"

Andy threw his hands up. "Like, never. I mean, like, actually never. Mount A won't open until we get steadier snow, but one of my friends works ski patrol, and he texted me to say they're grooming some trails and testing the lifts today and I could come up and help."

"See? It was meant to be."

"Cool." Andy got into the passenger seat. "I'm going to pack up that kitchen and load this van faster than you've ever seen."

I chuckled as I steered through the snow. Growing up in the Rogue Valley at an elevation of two thousand feet meant that, like Andy, I had learned how to drive in inclement weather from the moment I obtained my license. Even before. Dad had taken me up to the parking lot at Mount A and out to Hyatt Lake to teach me how to avoid a skid or spinning out on the snow.

It was a running joke amongst locals that we could always tell who was a recent transplant from California because, come November, the slew of Priuses once seen zipping around town under sunny skies were immediately traded in for Subarus with snow tires and all-wheel drive.

Traffic moved slower than normal along Siskiyou Boulevard, but I didn't mind. The atmosphere was like a party. Striped stocking caps and snow boots filled the sidewalks. Kids had found any corner possible to begin constructing snow people and tossing snowballs at each other. Shops and restaurants advertised impromptu snow day specials. The bike lane had been commandeered by snowshoes and sleds.

"See? I'm not the only one." Andy flashed a thumbs-up at a group of teens sledding down the hill next to the library. "Snow days are awesome."

"I totally agree."

However, when we arrived at campus, the lightness of the mood evaporated. There were a number of police cars parked in front of SOMA. Caution tape barricaded the entrance, and officers patrolled the building.

"It looks like they're still investigating, huh?" Andy commented.

"Yeah, or maybe there's been a new development." I hadn't expected to see such a large number of officers on-site either, but then again, I'd never been responsible for tracking down a rare artifacts thief and killer. I pulled into a space in the back and got out of the car.

The Professor greeted us at the door. He was wearing jeans, snow boots, and his tweed jacket. A pencil was tucked behind one ear, and he held his Moleskine journal in his left hand. "Ah, Juliet, most excellent. I'm glad you were able to arrive without any trouble. We're trying to finish up quickly as it sounds like the storm may be getting worse as the evening rolls on. Forecasters at the Medford weather station have updated their estimates. We may see up to a foot of snow before this over."

"Yes!" Andy pumped his fist.

"That wasn't the reaction I was expecting." The Professor's eyes twinkled.

"Sorry. I'm sure it's a pain for you guys, but I can't wait to get up to the mountain."

"Do be careful. The roads going up to Mount A could be dicey."

"No worries." Andy shot him a thumbs-up. "Like I told Mrs. C earlier, I'm a safe snow driver."

"It is a serene sight, isn't it?" The Professor shifted his gaze toward upper campus. "I'm reminded of these words: 'I wonder if the snow loves the trees and fields, that it kisses them so gently? And then it covers them up snug, you know, with a white quilt; and perhaps it says, "Go to sleep, darlings, till the summer comes again."'"

"That's lovely," I said. "Is it Shakespeare?"

"No, that's from none other than Lewis Carroll, who penned, among other things, *Alice's Adventures in Wonderland*."

I wondered how the Professor retained so many quotes in his head. Watching his tender expression reciting such pleasing and calming words brought an unexpected ache to my chest. I flashed to the future—a vision of him sitting in a comfy chair facing Emigrant Lake, reading *Alice's Adventures in Wonderland* to his grandchild.

"What do you want me to start with, boss? Put me to work." Andy's question shook me back into the present.

"Uh, why don't you start with the supplies. They're all in plastic tubs and labeled. If you can bring those out here and load them up, that would be great."

Andy gave us a salute and headed for the kitchen. "I'm on it!"

I appreciated his enthusiasm, even if it was because he was

eager to get up to the mountain. I turned to the Professor. "Is Zoe here, by chance?"

"Not as of yet, but I'm assured that she's on her way. Assuming that she can make it through the snow." He walked in stride with me as we entered the building. More caution tape had been strung up between the exhibits. Yellow evidence markers served as a reminder that a gruesome crime had occurred here. Police officers took pictures, documenting the scene and bagging more evidence.

The reminder that Dylan had died here last night made me queasy. I sucked in a breath and tried to concentrate on the task in front of me. "Okay. I need her direction in terms of the rest of the leftovers and our chocolate showpieces."

"I'll be sure to alert you as soon as she arrives." He gave me a solemn nod, letting his eyes linger on mine for a moment. "Are you feeling well, Juliet?"

"Yeah, I'm okay." I pointed around us. "It's just this. It's so sad that someone had to die, and he was so young." I thought of Andy, Steph, Bethany, Sterling. Dylan was about the same age as my young staff. He had had his entire life ahead of him. A life cut short for what? An old play. It was so senseless. "How's the investigation coming along? Any new developments?"

He frowned. "Not as many as I had hoped. I presume that you've heard about Tim?"

I nodded.

"Indeed, it's a shame. Not only for our case, but for him. The doctors sounded cautiously optimistic that with time, he may regain his short-term memory, but alas, time isn't on our side."

"Do you think it's connected? The theft, Tim's attack, and Dylan's death?"

"At first glance it appears that way, but one must never operate under assumptions."

"You don't really think Javier could have done it, do you?"

He vacillated. "What I think and where the evidence leads are variant trajectories at the moment. As you know, Javier and I have been friends and fellow admirers of the Bard for many years. I wish I could say with complete authority that there's no chance of his involvement, but for now the evidence says otherwise, and I am bound by duty to follow the evidence, even if it doesn't lead me where I personally want it to."

"Doesn't it seem unlikely that someone with such a high regard for Shakespeare and art in general would do anything to jeopardize a piece as valuable as the manuscript?"

"Without a doubt, but in this line of work, we deal in facts, not supposition." He stopped in midstride, opened his notebook, and flipped through the pages until he found the page he was looking for. "On that note, you reported discovering Tim in the basement archives at approximately seven forty-five. Is that correct?"

"I'm pretty sure. It could have been a few minutes later. I had looked at my watch shortly before I went downstairs because I'd wanted to make sure we had plenty of pastries to keep stocking the dessert table before the big unveiling."

"And Tim was semi coherent when you found him?"

"Barely. He was mumbling but not really saying much."

The Professor checked his notebook again, flipping toward the back. "One of the nurses at the hospital who was assigned to care for him last night mentioned that he kept repeating what she thought sounded like 'not the show.' Does that sound at all like what you heard him mumbling?"

I shook my head. "No. No, I don't think so. Honestly, I'm not sure. It's possible, but I can't say with any confidence I heard that. I wasn't with him long. I went to get help right away because he was in such bad shape and I couldn't lift the shelving unit off of him on my own."

He closed his notebook and returned it to his breast pocket. "I understand, and I appreciate you not trying to force your memories to match my narrative."

"Do you think it means anything? The show—could he be referring the exhibit? Maybe that means he saw who took the manuscript."

"It's certainly a possibility, as is that the nurse is well intended in attempting to decipher what she heard, yet wrong."

"I don't envy you. How are you holding up?"

A sadness invaded his eye. He tried to shake it off, literally, rolling his shoulders and forcing a smile. "Juliet, I'll tell you the truth, this one feels personal to me. It's an assault on Shakespeare and on a friend. A federal team will be arriving to take the lead in the investigation. I've called in help on this one, and I'm not sure what my role will be moving forward, so to say the very least, I'm highly motivated to learn as much as I can before the case changes hands."

"Is that normal?" I felt terrible for him. He was in an impossible situation. He had to stay neutral in the investigation, but I knew it must be wearing on him to have arrested a friend.

"With a theft of a priceless artifact, yes. This is beyond the scope of what my team can handle."

That made sense. "Is there anything else I can do?" We had made it to the kitchen.

He took the pencil from his ear and tapped the tip of it to his palm. "I appreciate it. No, just continue to stay aware, listen, and do get in touch right away if you hear anything—even the most minute detail."

"I will." I left him with a hug and went to help Andy with the rest of our supplies. Not surprisingly, he had made quick work of the boxes and tubs we had left in the kitchen.

"What's next, boss?" He rubbed his hands together and then snapped his fingers. "Put my muscles to work."

"I don't know if I have another task for your muscles yet. The problem is Zoe. I don't know if we should take the extra food back to Torte. She never clarified what she wants to do with the chocolate showpieces. The Professor said she's supposed to be here soon." I didn't want to force Andy to wait with me. "I'll tell you what. Why don't you take the van back to Torte and unload everything you've gotten so far. That way you can take off for the mountain. It might be a little while before Zoe shows up."

"No, I can wait, boss, otherwise, how will you get back?" Andy looked concerned.

"Don't sweat it. If Zoe wants to keep everything, I'll walk back. I love the snow too. And if not, I'll call the bakeshop and have Sterling and Marty come back for me with the van. We're not going to move the chocolate pieces in the snow anyway. It's too slippery."

He looked unsure.

"Really, it's fine. Go!"

"Okay, if you're sure." He hesitated.

"Andy, this is a direct order—go snowboard!" I pushed him out the door. "But, like the Professor said, be safe and drive slow."

"I will." He grinned and took off, hollering, "You're the best, boss," as he left.

I did want him to be able to experience the fresh snow, but selfishly I knew that waiting for Zoe was the perfect excuse to do a little snooping on my own.

Chapter Eighteen

I left the kitchen and went down the hallway to Zoe's office. The door was unlocked, so I went inside. Catalogues and reference books were stacked nearly as high as her desk. As someone professionally trained to have everything in its place in the kitchen, I wanted to offer up my organizational services to tame Zoe's cluttered office. A bookshelf was equally crammed with books and dictionaries devoted to Shakespeare. I noticed a number of titles that dove deep into the theory that Shakespeare had actually been a woman. A poster to left of her degrees depicted just that: Shakespeare with long hair and a woman's curvy frame. It read THE FOLIO OF THE FIRST FEMINIST.

An oversized calendar took up half the space on her desk. A variety of notes, reminders, and meeting times covered every square inch of the calendar in brightly colored Sharpie. On top of that, sticky notes had been placed on different days, with lengthy lists of additional tasks. Piles and piles of un-opened bills with PAST DUE stamped in red had been bundled with a rubber band.

How did she get anything accomplished?

If Lance were here, I knew he wouldn't waste the opportunity to rifle through Zoe's desk drawers, but that wasn't my style. Instead I made mental notes about the events listed on her calendar on the days leading up to the theft and murder. It appeared that Zoe had had a private meeting with a donor from Seattle and Dylan the day before he was killed. She and Ernest had gone to breakfast the morning of the gala. There was one word next to the meeting time circled in hot pink—Javier.

They went to breakfast to talk about Javier? I wondered what that conversation had been about, as well as why she had met with Dylan the night before. It could be nothing. After all she was Javier's assistant and seemed to be involved in every aspect of organizing the gala. But was there a chance these meetings could have been something more?

What if she and Ernest were in it together? They could have set Javier up. Maybe that was why she met with Dylan. Had she asked him to abandon his post in order to gain access to the missing manuscript? That would explain his role. What if her attitude toward him had been a farce? Maybe that was what she had wanted us to think. She could have pretended to be irritated with his slacker style, when in reality that was exactly what she needed. What if she and Ernest had plotted to hire Dylan in order to steal the lost manuscript themselves? It made sense. Dylan took his orders directly from her. She could have told him to leave and seized the opportunity to strike when the museum was empty. Or maybe Dylan was their third?

Was I grasping at wild theories?

Maybe.

I walked around to the other side of the desk and took a seat in the chair. It was good timing, because Zoe came in at that moment.

"Oh, hi, I wasn't expecting to see anyone." She sounded flustered and shoved a tote bag behind her desk before sitting down. Her glasses were fogged over. She took them off and rubbed them on her fleece sweatshirt. "Have you been waiting long? Did I forget that we were meeting? My brain is fried after last night, and it took me nearly a half hour to scrape the snow off my windshield and get it defrosted. Where did the snow come from? I know I've been consumed with the gala, but I didn't hear anything about getting a winter storm this early."

"Me neither. However, my barista, who happens to be an avid snowboarder, predicted it this morning. And, no you didn't miss a meeting. I'm here getting our supplies."

"Oh, good. A foot of snow is the last thing we need at the moment. Have you heard that there's a team of federal investigators coming? How could Javier put us in such a horrible position?" She placed her glasses on the top of her head, using them like a headband to pull her hair back from her face.

"We don't know for sure that Javier is responsible."

Zoe gnawed on her bottom lip. "Yes, we do. He's been arrested. They wouldn't have taken him away in handcuffs last night if he didn't do it. I hate to say it, but it adds up. I'm still in shock about it, and now I'm wondering if we're going to have shutter the museum's doors for good. I'm probably out of a job, which is what's funding my student loans. This entire situation is a disaster. I'm not going to be able to finish my dissertation or pay my rent."

"I agree. It's terrible, but don't give up on Javier yet. I know the police are exploring every angle, and hopefully Tim will be able to shed some light on what happened."

"Tim?" She sat taller.

"Did you hear that he's awake?"

"He's awake?" she repeated. "Tim's awake?"

I gave her the brief rundown of what I knew, hoping it might spur her to keep talking.

"Good. That's good news, such a relief." She moved a stack of paperwork to the side of her desk and knocked over a container of pens, which spilled onto the floor. She didn't bother to pick them up.

I couldn't tell from her tone whether she actually believed her own statement.

"What did you know about Dylan?" I asked, changing the subject. "Do you think he had any enemies? Could there be another reason he was killed?"

She flared her nostrils. "You mean other than the fact that he was a sloth? Sorry. I know it's not nice to speak ill of the dead, but he drove me crazy. A snail could have run circles around him. And it wasn't just that he was slow either. Let's just say that he wasn't the sharpest tool in the shed. I tried to fire him, but Javier wouldn't hear of it. Now I wonder if that was because he knew that he could use Dylan as his pawn in this ugly game. It makes sense. What other reason would he have had to keep Dylan on payroll?"

I had to admit that she had a point.

"I didn't tell Javier this, but I had a meeting with Dylan the night before the gala. I told him in no uncertain terms that he was walking on the narrowest tightrope. I was so fed up with him just roaming around the museum like he owned the place. He had one job—to keep his dazed and confused eyes on the manuscript. I warned him that if he screwed up, I was going to force Javier to fire him."

"How did he respond?"

"Same as always." Her glasses slipped down. She took them off her head and placed them on the tip of her nose. "He shrugged it off and shuffled out of my office like nothing had happened. I'm telling you, he was worthless. Why did Javier keep him around? That's the question to ask yourself—that, and why is Javier the one behind bars right now?"

I decided to press on. "What about Ernest?"

"What about him?"

"I had heard that he and Javier weren't getting along."

"Who did you hear that from?" Her tone was sharp.

"I don't remember," I lied, not wanting to reveal that Cindy had been my source.

"Ernest and Javier have different visions for SOMA's future. That's all. You know that. You witnessed it yourself. Ernest is a traditionalist. Javier knew that and agreed to partner with him anyway. I warned him it was a mistake. He shouldn't have been surprised when Ernest tried to push his own agenda—after all, he is the single largest donor the museum's ever had."

"Really?"

"By far." She nodded. "His money came with strings attached, and Javier knew that from the start. I warned him after our first meeting with Ernest, and I've warned him at least a dozen times since. I know Ernest's type, but Javier wouldn't listen. He was so caught up in the excitement of bringing Shakespeare's lost manuscript here that he had blinders on. Money like that isn't carte blanche. He should have realized it. And he should have listened to me."

"Do you think Ernest could be involved with the theft?"

"Ernest?" She scowled. "Doubtful. He's much more cerebral than Dylan, but he isn't exactly nimble. How could he have done it? Plus, he's a purist. That's one of the ongoing battles he and Javier had. It's not like he needed the money.

He doled out his donations to us like bread crumbs. We've been getting by on nothing while he flaunts his wealth and has me organize thousand-dollar dinners for him and his buddies." Her eyes drifted to the bundle of past-due bills on her desk.

I wondered just how bad SOMA's financial situation was. "You mean he's a purist about the kind of exhibits the museum is hosting?"

"That and more. The Shakespeare exhibit was the start, but Ernest wanted to have a direct role in what we brought in next. Like I already told you, he's not a fan of any modern art or supportive of our family programming. He made that clear from the start, but again Javier blew it off. He was so singularly focused on securing the exhibit that he wasn't thinking. If he had been more rational, he would have realized that he was making a deal with the devil."

A deal with the devil? That was dramatic to say the least. "You think that Ernest is the devil?"

She seemed to notice the pens on the floor and reached down to pick up a few of them. "It's a figure of speech, but in my opinion—yes. He was going to destroy everything we've worked to establish here at SOMA. My entire dissertation is on community engagement when it comes to art under the lens that Shakespeare was woman. It's a fascinating discussion point and is going to engage an entire generation of young girls in a way that they've never experienced art history before. That's one thing that Javier and I share in common. Not Ernest. He intends to slash all of our programming to families, students, and members of the community for whom art has been out of reach. Last night was a tiny preview of his style. He wants art to be accessible only to the most affluent members of our community. He wants it to be stuffed and dated, like a gross taxidermy animal. He doesn't understand art that's messy or that forces us to think outside of our sphere." She swiveled in her desk chair and pointed to her poster of Shakespeare as a woman. "Like that. There's mounting evidence that Shakespeare was a woman. Ernest wouldn't hear of it. He refused to even consider the idea, despite the fact that some of the world's most renowned scholars have posed the question. The clues are there in the pages of the canon. They're not even subtle. Female power, strong female friendships, a push for equality, and more. I'm writing my dissertation on the subject, and my opening line is from Emilia in Othello. 'Let husbands know / Their wives have sense like them.'" She removed her glasses and tossed them on her desk. "Shakespeare's work is rife with heroines, but I challenge you to find many heroes. No, it's obvious if you open your eyes and start to pay attention. Shakespeare was a woman. The only question I haven't found the answer to yet is whether she was one woman or many."

Her impassioned speech mirrored Lance's philosophy about the theater.

"Don't get me wrong, I'm as excited as anyone to have the Shakespeare exhibit here, but we need art to be encompassing and inclusive. We have to raise multiple theories, even if it puts into question our own beliefs. That's the role of a museum in the community. And it wasn't just that with Ernest. Javier had to fight to get the children's section included. The costumes, stage, and drawing area all would have been scrapped if Ernest had gotten his way, and with his endowment directing our future, I'm afraid we're doomed to become a dusty relic."

She wasn't mincing words, I had to give her that. And I was intrigued by the idea that Shakespeare could be a woman. It made sense, and it fit the times.

"No one would have published a woman writer in the fifteen hundreds. What a brilliant plan to write under a pen name and conceal her true identity. Many women writers would follow her lead. The Brontë sisters, Louisa May Alcott, Mary Ann Evans (better known as George Eliot) all wrote under male pseudonyms." Zoe inhaled deeply through her nose and squared her shoulders. "I'm sorry. I shouldn't be ranting. Was there something you needed?"

I wanted to ask her more about her dissertation, but I had work to finish before our Sunday Supper, especially if I was going to meet Lance for a quick happy hour drink. "I was wondering about the leftover food. Would you like to keep it, or should we take it to the bakeshop and donate anything we can't use to the winter shelter and the police? I'll give them whatever they can take and then we can share whatever is left with our customers too."

"Sure. That would be good. We're not going to be able to reopen anytime soon, so it will just go to waste here."

"What about the chocolate structures?"

She sighed. "I don't know. Can you give me a day or two on those?"

"You bet. Moving them in the snow probably isn't a good idea anyway."

"True." She glanced at her calendar.

"I'll go gather the extras," I said standing.

Zoe nodded. "Thanks. I'll let you know on the chocolate once I have some sense of whether or not we'll be able to open the exhibit halls again."

I left her with a smile. I wasn't sure that our conversation had given me any new insight into Javier, but her perspective on Ernest and Dylan added another piece to the puzzle.

Chapter Nineteen

On my way to the kitchen, I ran smack into Ernest. *Speak of the devil,* I thought to myself. He let out a grunt and recoiled as if I had mowed him over. Since I was half his body weight, it would have taken a lot more than a bump to cause him to lose his balance, but he made a wild gesture with his hands and caught himself on the wall.

"Watch where you're going. You nearly knocked me over." He coughed and sputtered, then staggered upright. The more time I spent with him, the more I wondered if he and Richard Lord were related. He made himself large, pushing out his chest and straining his thick neck toward the ceiling.

"Sorry." I genuinely hadn't intended to run into him, but his reaction was ridiculous.

He puffed out his chest even more. "Well, be careful. Everyone is on edge after last night."

"I know. It's so sad about Dylan."

"Dylan?" Ernest scowled. He yanked a folded white handkerchief from his ill-fitting black winter jacket and dabbed his forehead.

"The college student who was killed last night," I reminded him.

"Oh, yes. That." He didn't sound broken up about Dylan's death. "I was referring to the most important piece of Shakespeare's canon that's gone missing."

Not that I didn't agree that it was terrible that the manuscript had been stolen, but in my mind, there was no comparison between that and Dylan's brutal murder.

Ernest looked to the kitchen. He rubbed his rotund belly. "I don't suppose I could bother you for a snack. Not that I was blown away by what you served last night, but it's been a trying day what with multiple conversations with the authorities and my contacts in the art world."

"Sure, suit yourself." I opened the door, opting to put on my most professional face. His snide comment about our food made me even more sure that he and Richard Lord must be friends. But it was his words "contacts in the art world" that really gave me pause. We had established that the thief/killer had to have been connected. Ernest readily admitting that he had those connections made me wonder yet again about his involvement.

He followed me through the swinging doors. "After all, I paid for this. I should be able to eat what I want."

I wasn't going to argue with him on that. Instead I went to the fridge and removed the containers we had packed last night. Without asking what he wanted, I began assembling a plate with a bit of everything. "How did it work with the exhibit?" I asked, hoping that my tone sounded casual.

"What do you mean?" Ernest found a box of marzipans and popped two miniature bananas in his mouth at once.

"As the lead patron for the exhibit, how involved were you?"

He scoffed. "I was involved in every aspect, of course. I financed the *Shakespeare's Lost Pages* exhibit. Without me, the exhibit would have gone to Seattle or San Francisco for the premiere. Javier needed my expertise and oversight not only to secure the exhibit but to make sure the guest list was on par with the kind of patrons we want as future partners and to be the face of SOMA as we launched a new campaign to raise funds for the museum's next evolution."

"Do you think there's any chance he could have done it?" I busied myself prepping the food in hopes that he would open up.

"Done what?" he asked through a mouthful of marzipan. For someone who wasn't impressed with our food, he sure had a way of scarfing it down.

"Steal *Double Falsehood*?"

He shrugged. "Javier doesn't seem like the type. He needed cash for the museum, but that's why he has me. No, I don't buy it. His only motivation for stealing the manuscript would be financial, and he didn't have to worry about that any longer. I made sure of that."

I handed him the plate. "Why?"

"We signed a deal. I have a very robust vision for SOMA's future, and I made that clear to Javier, and I made him an offer he couldn't refuse. I agreed to fund the next three years of exhibits with a few minor stipulations."

"Like what?" I checked to make sure the last load of dishes we had run last night was clean and then began unloading the dishwasher.

"Standard boilerplate. Javier knows art," he said through a mouthful of food. "I won't deny that. His education is top notch. That's one of the many reasons I agreed to continue my patronage. However, he needs someone with a clearer vision of SOMA's future. Someone who can ensure that we attract the right kind of artists in residence, the right kind of exhibits, and the right kind of clientele. As well as someone who can set realistic fundraising goals."

"And that's you?"

He tucked into a hand pie. Flaky pieces fell onto his shirt as he devoured it in a few bites. "Part of the role of serving as a benefactor is understanding where there are holes in an organization."

Since he was being so forthcoming, I decided to ask him outright about their argument. "I heard that you and Javier had been fighting about funding and programming."

He took a minute to chew and swallow before answering. "Who did you hear that from? That sounds like hearsay to me. Javier and I disagreed on what was going to be shown next at SOMA, but that comes with the territory. It's business. It's expected, and ultimately he understands that finding a compromise was worth keeping the museum's doors open and staff employed."

Ernest didn't strike me as the compromising type.

"And Javier agreed?"

He nodded because his mouth was too stuffed to speak. I waited for him to finish. "That's why I won't believe he's involved with the theft. What's his motivation? The man might be misguided in his need to make art accessible to all, but he was a Shakespeare devotee. I don't see it. That's what I told the police. My contacts in the art world agree. You have

to understand that I have a high standing in the art community, and I will not allow this situation to taint that."

That was the second mention he'd made of his contacts
in the art world. It made me wonder something aloud. "How
would someone go about selling the manuscript? You can't
exactly waltz into an antique bookshop and offer it up for
sale, right?"

He choked on a crumb. His face turned as red as our rasp-
berry macarons. He clutched his neck and forced the piece
out. It took him a minute to regain control of his breath
before he spoke. "Certainly not. That would take superior
knowledge of the art underground. You'd have to lay low
with it for a while. A long while. A piece as valuable as this
is going to be on everyone's radar. Whoever took it would
need to know how to use a decoy. How to make contacts
with shady dealers. This isn't your average street theft. Whoever stole *Double Falsehood* absolutely knew what they
were doing."

Did that make Javier more likely? Perhaps that was why
the Professor had arrested him.

Ernest had finished his plate and handed it to me for more.
"I suspect it was an outside job. I believe Dylan must have
been involved. Not that he was intelligent enough to mastermind the heist, but I would bet that someone paid him off,
used him to gain access to the manuscript, and then killed
him when they completed the job."

I loaded second helpings onto his plate. Could that someone be him? He wasn't shy about touting how connected he
was in the art community. But what would his motive be?
He certainly didn't need the money.

"Thanks." He didn't waste any time devouring the cup of

stew I had heated up. "This event has highlighted the need to clean house. Depending on what happens with Javier, I might need to do that myself. There are a few other people I have my eye on who may possibly be accomplices."

Again I was taken aback by his candor.

"Like who?"

"Cindy, for one."

"The volunteer docent?"

He nodded. "There have been rumors going around for a while now, long before this exhibit arrived, that she's been stealing from SOMA. And you know what they say: desperate times call for desperate measures."

"Stealing what?" My thoughts flashed to finding Tim in the basement. Could he have caught Cindy in the act? Was the box of cash Cindy's?

"The docents are volunteer positions, but apparently Cindy has taken it upon herself to dip into the donation funds. There's a plastic lockbox at the front of the exhibit hall where guests can drop in cash donations. She was caught pocketing the cash. Javier let her off with a warning after she gave him a sob story about one of the guests telling her they put their money in as a special tip for her services. I told Javier to ban her on the spot. Lock her out. Take away her keys. Her museum privileges. He wouldn't hear of it. He believed that she'd made an honest mistake. Please. There is very clear language in the volunteer docent contract that spells out the fact that monetary or other gifts for service are not allowed. Everyone connected to this establishment seems to be money hungry. And that is a big problem for an art museum."

I couldn't argue with that. Ernest stuffed his face with the second serving of leftovers and asked for boxes to bring home with him. I complied by packaging up more dinner and dessert items.

"Watch your back around here," he cautioned as he lumbered toward the door. "You never know who might be lurking."

His words made me shudder. Not because I was concerned about strangers hiding in the hallways but because I had to wonder if our conversation had been his way of trying to lead me off his trail. Sure, a motive was the only thing in question, but he had had the means and the opportunity to steal the manuscript. Plus, unless he was lying, he had more connections in the art community than anyone else at SOMA. If I were him, I would have employed the same tactic. Shift suspicion to Dylan and Cindy. He was either a crafty liar or he was telling the truth.

Either way, I knew what I needed to do next—find Cindy.

Chapter Twenty

As it turned out, I didn't have to search far nor wide for Cindy. She showed up shortly after I had called Torte and asked the team to bring the van to finish loading our supplies and the food we would share with the community. Cindy burst into the kitchen wearing an ankle-length puffy parka, snow boots, and a stocking cap with a fuzzy pink pom-pom on the top. Her hair, which stuck out from the hat, was damp with snow and plastered to her cheeks.

"Oh my goodness. I didn't realize anyone was in here. I wouldn't have barged in." She shot her eyes in all directions as if she was expecting someone to jump out from behind the fridge. She stuffed her hands in her coat pockets and looked around. "Are you here alone? You're the only one here?"

"Yep. I'm gathering the last of the leftovers. My ride should be here soon. We'll be dropping off a large donation at the winter shelter and the police station, and then offering up delicious free bites at the bakeshop for the next couple days. Zoe said to share with any staff or volunteers. Would you like me to package up a dinner and dessert box for you?"

"That would be wonderful. For me? Wow, sure. Thank you." She tugged off her stocking cap and stuffed it in her coat pocket. "That never happens. That's so nice of you to offer."

"No problem."

Cindy kept her hands buried in her coat pockets as she came closer. "Was Ernest in here? Did I miss him?"

"Yes. He left a few minutes ago."

She let out a large sigh. "That's a relief. I don't think I could have handled seeing him today."

"Really?" I kept my focus on boxing up food for her. "Why is that?"

"You've met him, right? He's the worst on regular occasions, but now that Javier has been arrested, he thinks he's in charge. He's been ordering us around since last night." She plopped down on a bar stool. "No, that's not true. He always orders us around. I've had to try and keep the other volunteers pacified. They were threatening to walk out and not help at the gala because we're all so tired of him dictating orders to us. We don't need to suffer his abuse. We do this for the love of art. I don't know how he gets off ordering us around, anyway. He's not in charge. Javier is."

"Ordering you around?" I repeated, trying not to sound too incredulous. It shouldn't have shocked me, given my interactions with Ernest, but why would he treat volunteers with so little respect?

"Can you believe it? Yeah. It's been horrific. He's not in charge of anything. He's a donor. I understand that he made a large donation to SOMA, which is generous, but I don't understand why Javier gave him so much power to begin with.

It's gone to his head, and now I fear that there's no turning back. He's going to stage a hostile takeover while Javier is locked up."

A hostile takeover. That was quite an accusation. And why? Why would Ernest want control of SOMA?

Cindy continued on. "I'm sure I sound crazy, but you have to understand that Ernest has been out to get me from the moment we met. Not just me, everyone. He wants to run this place and ruin it at the same time. The rest of the board won't hear of it, but he's been trying to discredit Javier and cast doubt on his ability to manage SOMA. He hasn't even been discreet about it. He's been doing it in plain sight. He wants to privatize the museum and make this place his own little shrine to his vision of Shakespeare."

That did sound slightly crazy. "Out to get you?" I found myself repeating everything she was saying.

"Yes. He hates the docents. He thinks volunteers cheapen the place. He claims that I was stealing donations. That's ludicrous! Did you know that I've been volunteering here longer than he's been in Ashland?"

I shook my head.

"I've been a volunteer here for over two decades. He thinks he owns this place because he has money. That's not true. This is a public art space. It's meant for everyone to enjoy, not just his rich friends." She sucked in a breath and kept talking. "I know why he's coming after me—because I threaten him. I know more about the museum and our patrons than he does. He doesn't want volunteers involved in the museum. He wants to hire professional docents and raise admission prices so that they're out of reach to the general public. Ernest wants art to be exclusive. He doesn't believe that art by definition is a shared experience. If he were to get his way, this museum would turn into a private club, only allowing in the most exclusive members of the community."

I wanted to get back to the donations. "Why did he accuse you of stealing?"

"Ugh, I can't believe I'm having to defend myself against this. I've been a loyal volunteer for nearly two decades. I mean, do you have any idea how many hours of my time I've given to this organization?" She didn't wait for me to answer. "It must be hundreds if not thousands, and then there's my own money that I've poured into the museum—coffee, lunches, this outfit." She pointed to her black turtleneck and slacks. "As volunteers, we're required to purchase our own attire. SOMA doesn't even give that much, and I've never asked because I'm here for the art. I care about the mission. Ernest can't say that."

I didn't doubt her claims, and yet she hadn't answered my question. "Why is Ernest accusing you of taking money?" I pressed.

She pursed her lips and gave her head a half shake. "It's not a big thing. I happened to be short on cash, and Zoe wasn't around to approve of taking money out of petty cash, so I took some of the money from the daily donations to pay for stamps and envelopes. She's been running around like a chicken with her head cut off lately. We needed them for a mailing campaign. It wasn't a big deal, but Ernest saw me taking the cash and threw a fit. I told him that maybe instead of berating volunteers he should put his money where his mouth was. If he's so loaded, why didn't he make sure that we have the funds we need for the museum's daily functioning?"

"There's not enough cash to buy stamps?" I asked. If that was the case, then SOMA was in much more dire straights than I had thought.

"No, that's my point." She sounded irritated, like she was addressing a child who wasn't comprehending what she was saying. "I simply borrowed the cash from the donations because Zoe wasn't around and Javier was nowhere to be found. They asked me to manage the mailing for the gala, and I couldn't very well send out invitations without envelopes and stamps. I kept a meticulous list of everything I spent money on—receipts and all—and a ledger to the penny of what I'd *borrowed* from the donations. Zoe could reconcile the two. That was her job, not mine."

Cindy's excuse sounded believable, but I couldn't dismiss her physical reaction. She had become more and more agitated as she tried to explain her side of the story. While we had been talking, she had shed her coat and gotten up from her bar stool, where she paced back and forth in front of the counter.

She seethed with anger as she paced around the kitchen. "Ernest has some nerve trying to throw me under the bus. Why would he do that? I've dedicated my life to the museum. I didn't have to volunteer my time. I could have walked away at any point, but I didn't because I care. I care about SOMA. I care about art. I care about what this place means to the community. Can Ernest say the same thing? No. No way." She blew out a long breath. "I have a theory as to why he's trying to put all of his attention on me."

"What's that?"

"I think he did it." She stopped pacing and folded her arms across her chest. "I think he stole the manuscript. I think everything that went down last night was because of him—setting up Javier, killing Dylan, all of it."

"But why?" I heard myself asking before I had fully formulated a question. "The police seem to think that whoever stole the manuscript did so because of its value. Why would

Ernest need to steal it? Isn't he one of the wealthiest people in the Rogue Valley?"

"Yeah. He didn't do it for money. He did for the prize." She curled her lip in disgust. "I understand why the police think that the thief was after money. It makes logical sense, but they're wrong. They're very wrong. This didn't have anything to do with money. It's about greed. Ernest is crazed when it comes to Shakespeare. He masterminded this entire exhibit for one reason and one reason alone. To steal the manuscript. He has everything he needs. Did you know that his net worth is near one hundred million dollars?"

I felt my jaw go loose. "No. To be honest, I had no idea anyone in Ashland had that kind of money." It was true that the Rogue Valley had seen an influx of wealthy retirees over the last few years, but that level of wealth was a different story.

"Yeah. He made his money in the auto empire. He doles out tiny checks to the museum when he could easily fund all of our programming for the next fifty years without making a dent in his income." She shook her head in disgust. "But that's not why he took the manuscript. I mean come on, think about it. Even the world's best art thief would have serious difficulties trying to sell the piece. That's why I'm sure this wasn't about money. It's ego. It's the need to possess something so valuable. Something that no one else in the world can have. That's why I know that Ernest did it. He stole the manuscript for his private collection. And, trust me, he's been plotting this for years. This was no crime of opportunity. Ernest had a singular mission—to make Shakespeare's lost play his."

Her words made the hairs on my arms stand at attention. Could she be right? Could Ernest not only be an art thief, but also a killer?

Chapter Twenty-One

Cindy caught my eye, forced her lips tighter, and gave me a half nod. "It makes sense, doesn't it? It had to be Ernest. He wants the coveted prize of owning Shakespeare's lost play. He wants to be able to conceal *Double Falsehood* in some secret safe in his mansion up in the hills so that when his rich friends come visit, he can flaunt his prize. Money doesn't matter to him. He'll never try to sell it. That's why he is trying to shift the focus and start rumors about me stealing a couple hundred bucks from petty cash. That's why he's been after Javier. I'm telling you it's a setup. He doesn't want anyone taking a close look at him."

I took a minute to let her words sink in. Could she have a point? "Did you share this theory with the Professor?"

"Of course. I told him all of this and more last night. I knew the minute the manuscript went missing what happened. Ernest has been sneaking around the museum for weeks under the guise of doing 'important' work for the gala. Yeah, right. I saw through that excuse from day one. Do you know that I caught him sneaking around in the archives right before the manuscript went missing?" She didn't wait for a reaction. "Well, he was. He was down in the archives right before the gala. Why? He had no reason to be down there. He gave me some lame excuse about keeping his finger on the pulse of everything that was happening at the museum."

I didn't have to press her for more. She kept talking. "He was sneaking around down there in the dark. When I confronted him, he claimed that he had been giving a potential donor a personal tour, but that was a lie. He was there alone. I know why. I know what he was doing. He was stashing the manuscript down there and planning to come back and get it later." She picked up the package of food. "Thanks for this. I need to go find Zoe."

"You bet." I smiled. After she left, I tried to make sense of her theory. On one hand, it made sense. The difficulty of selling the priceless document couldn't be overlooked. That thought lent credibility to Ernest being responsible. But I also couldn't discount the money I had seen when I had found Tim, not to mention his injuries and Dylan's murder. I had been operating under the assumption that all three were connected, but maybe it was time to open my mind to the possibility they might not be. There was also one detail that kept spinning in my head: in revealing that she had seen Ernest in the basement archives, Cindy had also outed herself. Why had she been down there? As much as I wanted to believe her, I couldn't rule out her involvement either.

Carlos and Sterling showed up shortly after my conversation with Cindy. We made quick work of packing up the rest of the food. The snow was nearly five inches deep when

I left with them. "You didn't let this guy drive, did you?" I asked Sterling.

Sterling scowled. "I don't have a death wish."

Carlos pretended to be upset. "How can you tease like this? Just because I have not spent time in the snow does not mean that I cannot drive in it. Give me the keys." He held out his hand.

Sterling quickly clutched the keys and kept them out of Carlos's grasp. "Sorry, man. I can't help you. Boss's orders." He winked at me.

"Let's swing a delivery by the shelter and then I'll take a few boxes over to the police station when we get back to Torte." I got into the back of the van next to the aromatic stacks of food boxes. The car was toasty warm, and the windows fogged up from our body heat.

"The snow it is so beautiful," Carlos noted as Sterling drove. "Everything is white. It's as if Mother Nature opened giant bags of flour and shook them over Ashland."

I grinned. "How's our spontaneous Sunday Supper coming together?"

"Good. Easy. It is nothing with this team. Everything is done." Carlos clapped Sterling on the shoulder. He beamed with pride. I knew that helping mold his young protégé was yet another reason Carlos had fallen under Ashland's charm.

Sterling waved him off. "Nah, it's just because we opted for soup and bread. It's hardly like we're offering guests a three-star Michelin dinner."

"No. No. Never say this," Carlos interrupted, his voice turning serious. "I would always tell my young sous chefs not to be so focused on the idea of fine dining. Yes, fine dining has its place, and I too enjoy eating a special meal every now and then, but food is about service with love. This is what we must embrace if we want to truly become chefs. I do not care if you serve me a basic omelet, a bowl of soup, or a seven-course dinner, it is the love and energy we infuse in our food that counts."

Sterling caught my eye in the rearview mirror. We both laughed.

"What?" Carlos spun his head around. "You agree, Julieta, si?"

"Yes." I grinned. "I just think that we've heard this speech before."

"Exactly. And we must tell it again and again because we cannot forget. A beautiful bowl of stew can become a transformative experience. It is touch, it is the awakening of all of our senses. This has nothing to do with how much a meal might cost or if the presentation is on a stark white platter. Food is connection. It's family. It's coming together around the table. If we lose sight of that, well, then I must turn in my apron."

I loved his passion.

"It's true, but that would never happen at Torte," Sterling assured him. "Helen and Jules have taught us well."

"Si, si. I know this. I did not mean to imply differently." Carlos sounded apologetic. "It is that I get so frustrated by chefs having to try and prove themselves with food that does not feed the soul. I am not worried that Torte would take this path, but I do not want you to ever believe that a humble bowl of soup cannot be a masterpiece."

We arrived at the shelter. I dropped off the food and then had Sterling let me out in front of the police station on the plaza. "I'll give the team some sustenance for the investigation," I said to them. "A group of federal agents is arriving, so I have a feeling any food will be welcome. Oh, and, Carlos, when I get back, Lance and Arlo want to grab a quick drink at Puck's. Does that work for you?"

"A drink would be good, si."

I was hoping that I might be able to get an update from Thomas or Detective Kerry before meeting Lance and Arlo. The police station's blue awning had vanished beneath the snow. Tiny icicles clung to the edges. When I went inside the station, it was packed with men and women wearing navy blue coats with the word "FBI" in bold print. Apparently the team had already arrived.

The Ashland police station was more like a glorified welcome center. There was a small reception area, desks for Kerry and Thomas, the Professor's office, and a holding cell. More than four people was a crowd, and there had to be nearly a dozen law enforcement officials crammed inside. Not only that, but it didn't look like police stations I'd seen on TV or in the movies. The walls were painted a soft pale blue and paid homage to Ashland with playbills and posters from previous shows at OSF as well as framed photos of some of southern Oregon's most spectacular outdoor regions like Crater Lake, Mount Ashland, and the Rogue River.

I considered leaving, but I caught Kerry waving from the back of the room. "Jules, what do you need?" she called.

"I come offering sustenance." I held up the boxes.

Kerry squeezed through the throng of people. "Please tell me there is chocolate in one of these." She ogled at the containers as she came closer. "Or I'd take doughnuts as a close second."

"Would I come without chocolate?"

She smiled and motioned to the door, reaching for her coat

and wrapping it around her shoulders. "You want to step outside for second?"

I handed her the boxes as we went out into the snow.

"It's so pretty," she commented. "Growing up in Southern California, I always dreamed of snow and a white Christmas, but instead we would grill a turkey outside and go to the beach."

I was shocked to hear her mention anything about her past. Kerry had been a closed book when it came to personal details. The only thing I knew about her past was that she had worked in Medford before being transferred to Ashland, but I'd never heard mention of her growing up in Southern California. It had taken time, but I felt happy that she was finally beginning to open up. I hoped it was a sign that our friendship could continue to grow.

"Isn't it funny how we always want what we don't have?" I kicked the fluffy snow. "I always thought it would be so fun to spend Christmas in Hawaii, but then once I took the job on the ship, I desperately missed the mountains, the cold, the snow. Christmas in the Caribbean isn't quite the same. Don't get me wrong, sun-soaked seas and mai tais for brunch aren't so shabby, but it's not like a cozy Ashland holiday."

She smiled.

"How's it going?" I asked.

"As you can see, we're being nudged out. I'm not sure what kind of involvement we'll have in the investigation moving forward. The Professor went to check in with Tim again before the team descends on the hospital."

I tucked my hands into my pockets to keep them warm as a couple glided past us on cross-country skis. "I learned a couple things that might be helpful." I gave her the rundown of my conversations with Zoe, Ernest, and Cindy.

She listened without letting a single muscle in her face shift. Her ability to remain completely passive was like watching an actor at work. I didn't know why Lance was constantly bugging me about taking the stage. If anyone deserved a starring role, it was Kerry.

"Thanks for letting me know," she said when I finished.

I thought that was the end of our conversation, but she caught my arm. "I will tell you that the Professor has been pursuing the theory that the theft was about more than money."

"So Cindy could be telling the truth?" I paused for a minute. "Actually, yeah, what about the money? Isn't it weird that there was cash in the basement if money wasn't the motive?"

Kerry wavered. "I don't know, but that line of questioning must be explored. Thomas is pulling Ernest's financial records. One of the theories the Professor is having us explore is whether the cash found in the archives was a decoy to try and throw us off the scent. We're tracing the bills, but I have to believe that the killer was smart enough to know that would be one of the first things we would do. I'm not confident that we're going to come up with any big revelations by tracing the cash, but you never know, we could get lucky."

I had at least a dozen more questions, but I didn't want to jinx anything. Why was Kerry suddenly being so open with me? Had our conversation about the wedding shifted things that much? It seemed doubtful.

As if reading my thoughts, she continued. "The Professor is highly motivated to release Javier before we potentially have to take a backseat in this investigation. He knew this would be coming, so he's wanting to get out in front of it."

"Okay. Is there something I can do to help with that?" It

felt like she was speaking in some sort of code that I wasn't able to decipher.

"Yes. We're hoping you can talk to Lance."

"Lance?" Now she was starting to make me wonder if she'd gone through some sort of body swap. "*You* want Lance involved?"

"We're going to need someone to post bail, and according to the Professor, Lance might have access to that kind of cash."

"Oh. Got it." Realization dawned on me. That was true. Lance earned a very generous salary as artistic director at the festival, but his wealth came from a large family inheritance.

"Would you feel comfortable talking to him about that?"

"Sure." I nodded, shifting my feet. My toes were starting to tingle from the cold. "I'll reach out to him right now. I'm sure he's going to come to dinner tonight anyway."

"That would be great." Kerry looked relieved. "Thanks for these. I'm sure they'll disappear." She held up the pastry box and went back inside.

I crossed the snowy street to Torte, feeling more confused than ever. Why did the Professor feel it necessary to release Javier as soon as possible? And if he, Thomas, and Kerry were sidelined in the investigation, how were we going to clear his name?

Chapter Twenty-Two

I called Lance as soon as I returned to the bakeshop. "Hey, I think we're going to have to take a rain check on happy hour." I filled him in on what had transpired. "Are you up for helping with this?"

"Darling, without a doubt. Count on me. I'll bring a check down to the station immediately, but I must know, what do you think it means?"

"I have no idea," I admitted.

"Well, then, there's only one solution. We must get to the bottom of this critical piece of the mystery," he replied. "I'm told that Torte's hosting a dinner this evening. Save two spots for me, and I'll come early so we can have a tête-à-tête, and let's reschedule our happy hour for tomorrow night. I'm sure there will be much to discuss."

With that, he hung up, and I went to tell Carlos that happy hour was off. It turned out to be better anyway. Even though the soups were simmering and bread was warming in the oven, I liked getting to be a part of setting up for events like our spontaneous Sunday Supper. I had realized lately that while I loved our growing empire of Uva, Scoops, and doing things that pushed our boundaries at the bakeshop, with growth, I didn't have as much time to spend in the kitchen. My instructor in culinary school had warned us of this natural evolution that occurred in the restaurant business. Expansion meant that my role as caption of our ship involved staff schedules, overseeing production, and vendor relationships. Thus far, I had made it a priority to be in the kitchen every day. That was one of the reasons I cherished my early morning time alone, but if things continued at this pace, we might need to hire a business manager. My passion, like Carlos's, was food and serving the community, and I never wanted to lose sight of that.

As much as I would have liked to concentrate my efforts on the case, I went upstairs to help prep for our winter wonderland dinner. Rosa and Steph were pushing tables together in the dining room. Sequoia took the last empty pastry trays downstairs. I took in the welcoming sight of the snowy windows and candles flickering along the top of the espresso bar.

"Jules, any news on Javier?" Rosa's voice was strained with anxiety.

"It sounds like he's going to be released on bail soon." I was glad to have at least one piece of good news to share.

"But how? My family has been scrambling to see how we could come up with the money." She opened a box of white linen napkins.

"Let's just say that he has a benefactor in town who is happy to help." I touched her arm. "He's going to be out soon, I promise."

Relief washed over Rosa's face. "Is it you?"

"No, but I do believe that the Professor and his team are doing everything in their power to come up with evidence that will support your uncle's innocence."

"That's good to hear. Do you know when I'll be able to see him?"

"No." I shook my head. "You could go check in with the Professor, though. I bet that he's doing the paperwork as we speak and Javier will be ready to go soon."

She folded a white napkin and placed it on a stack of others. "Okay. I'll do that once we finish."

"Why don't you let me take over?" I suggested.

"Are you sure?" She hesitated.

"Yes." To prove my point, I picked up the box and took out the remaining napkins.

She smiled. "Okay, thank you. I'll run across the street and see if they'll let me bring him here once he's released. I'm sure a Torte dinner would cheer him up."

I was hoping that she might bump into Lance. I didn't want to divulge that he was the one posting bail for Javier, but if she happened upon him, that would be a happy coincidence.

"Put me to work," I said to Steph, who had covered the long table with a white tablecloth and was setting out white plates and napkins.

"We decided to keep it simple. White for the snow." Her eyes drifted to the espresso bar. "Bethany thought we'd only do candlelight."

"That sounds great. What can I do?"

She pointed to a box of candles. "You can arrange candles on the tables. We're not doing flowers or anything like that for this one since it's last-minute."

Often our Sunday Suppers were a bit more elaborate,

with flowers from A Rose by Any Other Name next door and decorations, but I was glad that Steph had gone the simple route. The snowfall outside was the only backdrop we needed.

I placed votive candles throughout the center of the shared table and around the bakeshop. Soon the space was glowing with flickering light that enhanced the drops of white powder that continued to fall from the sky.

Bethany came upstairs with baskets of bread. "Oh wow, this looks so great. I love the white on white, and all of the candles give this such a romantic glow. It's super adorable." She put the baskets on the table and stopped to snap some pictures. "We're sold out for tonight, but I have to post these on social. I mean, come on, how gorgeous is this view right now?" Bethany pointed to the plaza. The streetlamps had come on, casting an angelic haze on the accumulating snow. A crowd of snowshoers sailed past us, waving as they glided onward toward Lithia Park. Teens carrying sleds gathered in front of the pizza shop. It looked like a vintage Norman Rockwell painting outside. "I can't believe it's still coming down. It's been snowing for hours."

She was right. There had to be nearly a half foot of snow on the ground, and it wasn't showing any signs of stopping.

I left her and Steph to stylize photos and went to check on progress in the kitchen. I was immediately greeted by a symphony of aromas that made me swoon. My stomach rumbled as I caught sight of Carlos ladling soup at the stove. Sterling arranged platters of the extra food from last night's gala, and Marty whipped butter and herbs at the island.

"You guys, it smells amazing in here."

"That's the goal." Marty grinned. "Our mission is to delight your olfactory nerves and your stomach."

"We could make that our new mantra. Put it on a T-shirt," Sterling said with a laugh. "You know Bethany would wear it."

"Or just let me sneak a taste," I said, opening a drawer to find a spoon. I walked to the stove and dipped my spoon into the aromatic vat of Carlos's Spanish stew. One bite had my taste buds dancing. The winter mountain stew had a spicy broth from the chorizo sausage and bacon, combined with white beans and onions that had simmered all afternoon with a ham hock. "This is criminally good."

Carlos nodded to Sterling. "That's because of our sous chef. He is a quick study."

Sterling wiped the edge of a bowl with a hand towel. "Team effort."

I appreciated his humility. It was a quality that would serve him well wherever he landed long-term. I had worked with my fair share of pompous chefs over the years and had learned that (like Sterling had reminded me when I was stressing out about event prep) an angry, cocky chef in the kitchen led to disaster for the staff and for diners.

As for Sterling, I wondered how long he would stay at Torte. I knew that eventually he would move on. With some more training and experience, especially under Carlos's continued guidance, he could easily land a job as head chef at one of the restaurants in town. I would be the first in line to wish him well and the first person to book a reservation when that happened, but I had to admit that I would also be heartbroken to lose him, or any of my staff, for that matter.

I shook off the thought. "Do you need anything from me? We're pretty much set up. I need to open some bottles of wine, but otherwise I think we're ready."

"Good." Carlos flashed me a sexy smile. "We will dazzle our guests with this snowy comfort food."

"And then have a post-dinner snowball fight," Marty suggested. "That should work up everyone's appetite for dessert."

I knew he was kidding, but the first snowfall always brought out in the kid in me. I was tempted to run outside and come back with a fistful of snow. Instead of giving in to my childhood urges, I brought a case of our Uva wine upstairs and opened a couple bottles of red and white. Guests began to arrive shortly after Sterling set the platters of appetizers on the table. Everyone came in wearing heavy winter gear. The sound of snow being stomped from the bottom of boots, happy laughter, and glasses clinking soon filled the room.

The windows steamed from the heat of bodies as people mingled and nibbled on our tasting bites.

Lance showed up fashionably late as always. Although this time I knew he had a good excuse because he came in with two familiar faces—Rosa and Javier.

I pulled myself away from a conversation with a fellow business owner and scooted over to greet them. "Javier, it's so good to see you." I hugged him.

Rosa kept her arm looped through his, like an overprotective mother not willing to let go of her child.

Javier looked as if he had aged overnight. His eyes sagged. His cheeks were sallow and sunken, and his posture was slightly stooped. "I owe my release to Lance." He extended his hand to Lance.

Lance made a large gesture of protest. "No, no. It's nothing, like I said. It's my civic duty to protect our art community. I won't hear otherwise."

Javier bowed his head. "I am indebted to you, my friend."

"Can I get you a drink? Something to eat?" I offered.

"A glass of wine would be nice," Javier said with a weak smile.

"I'll get it, Uncle. Red or white?" Rosa touched his arm.

"Red would be lovely." His kind eyes looked lost and empty.

"Lance, what about you?" Rosa waited for Lance to answer before heading off to get their drinks.

"Have they learned anything else?" I asked Javier.

He shook his head. "Unfortunately it doesn't sound that way. I'm convinced that someone planted that evidence in my office in an attempt to frame me. Doug is too, but his hands are tied. Evidence is evidence. Doug visited Tim in the hospital again, hoping maybe he might be able to shed some light on the horrific events of the evening, but he's still unable to recall any details about what transpired before he was attacked."

Lance made a tsking sound under his breath. "Such a shame."

"It is a shame. I certainly hope for his sake, more than mine, that he's able to recover his short-term memory. I will feel personally responsible if he suffers any long-term damage from this."

"But it's not your fault."

He sighed. "And yet I'm responsible for the museum and my staff. How can I not shoulder that?"

Lance voiced what I was thinking. "The best way you can support Tim and your staff, volunteers, and patrons is to remain strong and vigilant while the police and Juliet and I unearth the culprit."

Javier couldn't contain his surprise. "You and Juliet? You're helping with the case? Doug never mentioned anything about that."

I shot Lance a warning glance. He tipped his wineglass toward me. "No. Not officially. We have assisted the police in previous inquiries. Although it's something we prefer to keep on the down low."

Nothing Lance did was on the down low. I was shocked he even knew the definition of the phrase. At that moment, Arlo walked in, causing Lance to abandon our conversation. I was glad to have Javier to myself for a minute.

"Do you want to sit?" I asked Javier, pointing to two empty chairs at the long table.

"That would be nice." His voice was soft.

We took our wine and sat down. "Javier, I want to ask you about Cindy. Ernest told me that she had been caught stealing from the cash donations. When I confronted her about it, she admitted to taking the cash but claimed that it was because she needed it for a mailing. Do you know anything about it?"

Javier massaged his temples. "Yes. I knew about it. Ernest wanted me to ban Cindy from future volunteering and restrict her access to the museum, but she's been a loyal and steady supporter for as long as I've been there. He went so far as to recommend we post photos of her in the staff room. Like criminal wanted posters, as a warning to others. I couldn't believe he would suggest such a thing. It's an uncomfortable position. Ernest gives us his money. Cindy gives us her time."

"Do you think it's possible that she could have been involved with the theft? If she needed cash, that gives her a motive."

He was quiet for a moment. "Yes. I'm afraid that it's certainly a possibility. Not that I suspect Cindy. I don't mean to imply that. But unfortunately, everything is a possibility, and everyone on my team is a suspect. Doug made that clear in our conversations, and I can't help but blame myself. I let things go too far. I fear I've made some fatal mistakes when it's come to managing SOMA. I have been too focused on the *Shakespeare's Lost Pages* exhibit and in that have lost sight of what's truly important. Our staff, volunteers, and patrons. Now each one of them is a suspect in a murder investigation, and I must take responsibility for that."

His sentiment matched mine. The more I learned, the more I wondered if the entire staff and volunteer team at SOMA had a hand in Dylan's death.

Chapter Twenty-Three

Javier sipped his wine as more guests piled into the cheery dining room. Sterling passed around platters of appetizers, and Bethany turned on what sounded suspiciously like classical holiday music. I had a strict policy not to celebrate any holiday, be it Christmas, Solstice, Hanukkah, or Kwanzaa until the day after Thanksgiving, but I let it go for the night. It was the first snowfall, and Thanksgiving was next week.

Javier's wine went untouched as he continued. "It's hard to imagine Cindy being involved, but I discussed it with Doug, and I can't rule out the possibility. While she isn't an official member of the staff, she has autonomy. She knows every square inch of the space, and she was heavily involved in the planning and preparations for the exhibit. Perhaps I was too trusting. Doug asked about people with the contacts and knowledge base, and I have to admit that Cindy has both. She's been a volunteer at SOMA for decades. I can't overlook that. Could I have made a grave error about her? I don't think so, but this investigation is bringing everything I know into question."

"Do you know anything about her financial status?"

He shook his head. "No. I told Doug that I was under the impression she was well off. She never spoke of money, and she was available every day to volunteer. SOMA is her place of connection. I assumed that she wanted the social contact, and of course, I was very aware of her appreciation for the art world and especially the outreach we've been doing to the community to try and bring in more families and young children and students. I wouldn't have guessed that she needed money."

"Maybe she didn't." I pondered. "I guess the Professor is looking into it."

"Yes. I'm sure he will. He's doing his due diligence." For a moment I thought he was going to say more, but he stopped himself and concentrated on sipping his wine.

The dining room continued to fill in. I wanted to ask Javier one more thing before I needed to go help. "Do you think there's a chance Ernest could be involved? It seems like he's made a lot of enemies, and I know you two had a rocky relationship. Plus, there's been talk that he might have stolen the manuscript for his own private collection."

Javier flinched. "His own collection? Could you imagine? That would be a blow to everyone in the Rogue Valley and Shakespeare lovers around the world." He considered it for a minute. "His personality is such that I could see him wanting to keep such a rare piece of art to himself, except that I would suspect he would have a difficult time keeping it quiet."

"Because he would brag about it," I offered.

"Exactly." Javier smiled broadly for the first time all night.

"He takes great pleasure in making sure everyone is aware of his great fortune."

That wasn't shocking.

Javier swirled the wine in his glass, then set it down. "It's true that Ernest and I have been butting heads. I should have trusted my gut about him. I knew that he had a difficult and demanding personality, but we needed the money to bring the exhibit here, so I'm afraid I overlooked more than I should have. I'm going to have to make amends to my volunteers and the community." He sighed.

"I'm sure everyone will understand." I noticed that people were starting to take their seats. "I should go check on the kitchen," I said. "I'm glad that you're here."

"Me too." His smile didn't meet his eyes.

The next few hours were a perfect escape. I enjoyed lively conversation with Carlos, Lance, Arlo, and our other guests as we lingered around the table savoring thick butternut squash soup, the smoky melody of Carlos's Spanish stew, and hearty chicken and dumpling soup packed with onions, carrots, celery, and chunks of rotisserie chicken, just like Mom used to make. People passed around herbed garlic bread, crusty loaves of Marty's soda bread, and platters of crisp winter salad loaded with pears, toasted nuts, and crumbly cheese. The candles burned low, and the wine bottles emptied. These were the moments when I wanted to pinch myself. How lucky was I to have a thriving bakeshop and be surrounded by friends and family in the most charming place on the planet?

Our guests lingered late as we brought out plates filled with chocolate orange brownies, cranberry blondies, and snowflake sugar cookies, along with fresh pots of coffee and hot water for tea. I soaked in the sound of happy laughter and the easy flow of conversations. Carlos caught my eye from across the table. His beaming gaze and whisper of "I love you" made me infinitely glad for this moment. He and Sterling had been right. We needed this. I needed this.

It wasn't until the last of the guests made their exit that the Professor showed up. He was bundled in layers and shivering. "Apologies, Juliet. I was hoping to find your mother here."

"I think she's downstairs." I held the door open for him and shut it quickly behind him. "Can I get you anything? Dinner? A cup of coffee?" I had just made a fresh pot to get us through cleanup.

"I certainly wouldn't turn down a warm cup of Joe."

"Let's hook you up." I walked to the espresso bar and poured him a steaming cup of our Thanksgiving roast.

"How's the case coming?"

He took off his coat and warmed his hands on the coffee mug. "Ah, there's the rub. I can't quite tell you because we've been relegated to the side, as expected with the arrival of my comrades from Seattle. But that doesn't mean there aren't loopholes that my team and I will be utilizing to continue to do what we can to bring justice to Dylan and find and return the Bard's most precious work of art."

"Does that mean that the FBI has completely taken over?"

"Not completely, but it does mean that our hands are tied in terms of certain regulations and procedures. Fortunately, I've been in a similar position before and have learned some valuable lessons in negotiating my role." He held the coffee to his nose and breathed in the aroma.

"How could anyone not want your input and expertise?" I blew out the candles along the bar.

He gave me an appreciative smile. "That is kind of you, Juliet, but I'm afraid that federal law dictates my involvement." He paused to sip his coffee. "However, there has been a development this evening. That's one of the reasons why I'm late. I had told Helen there was a chance I might be able to join in the festivities, but I've been at the hospital with Tim."

"Does that mean he remembers what happened?"

"Not exactly." The Professor eyes held a hint of mystery. "Tim does not recall the moment leading up to his injuries. He maintains that the last thing he remembers is going downstairs."

That didn't sound promising.

"I see from your reaction that you're not impressed. Patience—which reminds me of Tolstoy, who says, 'The strongest of all warriors are these two—time and patience.'" He lifted his index finger. "There's been a matter that has been bothering me since the beginning of this case, which is the money that you discovered when you found Tim. Why would an art thief leave without their just *desserts*?" His eyes twinkled. "Pardon the pun, but it doesn't make sense, does it?"

"No," I agreed.

"We have a missing artifact, an injured custodian, a stash of cash, and then a security guard killed either in cold blood or inadvertently."

"You think Dylan's death could be accidental?"

"Perhaps. Tasers typically aren't lethal." He paused briefly to sip his coffee. "The coroner reports that while it is uncommon, there have been a number of instances where Tasers have caused a heart attack like the one Dylan experienced, even in young and healthy people. It's one of the reasons I stress the importance of proper training with my deputies and that use of any kind of force is and always should be the very last resort. Even if a Taser doesn't come with bullets, it should be treated like the potentially deadly weapon it is. I feel such a deep sense of gratitude to be part of a team here in Ashland where we truly approach police work as community engagement first and foremost."

"I agree. Ashland is lucky to have you, Thomas, and Kerry." I had witnessed the Professor stopping in to pick up a cup of hot coffee and a sack lunch to give to one of Ashland's unhoused. And knew that Thomas knew everyone living on the streets by name. Under the Professor's guidance and direction, the police built relationships with the community and sought to serve and connect, rather than make unnecessary arrests. "How does this relate to Tim?" I asked, trying to get back to the murder.

The Professor cleared his throat. "Yes, apologies. As I was saying, the money left at the scene has been a point of confusion for me. It potentially takes our case in two divergent directions. We must consider the possibility that our thief had no interest in the cash or, alternatively, was caught in the act and had to abandon the money. If we follow the second line of inquiry, then we must also question whether the thief successfully handed off the document. This would suggest that there's another criminal in our midst who at this moment has Shakespeare's *Double Falsehood*."

"Unless they already left town." I poured myself a cup of coffee, wanting to make sure my brain cells were firing at full capacity as I listened to the Professor's theories.

"Yes, that is an undeniable possibility as well. Then that raises the question of whether the string of events that occurred at SOMA are connected."

"Do you think they are?"

He wavered. "I believe it's too soon to be able to determine that, but Tim's revelation sheds new light on the case. While his memory is still impaired, he did make a confession this evening."

My heart sped up. What kind of confession could Tim have made? Dylan was killed after he was taken to the hospital, so he couldn't have been responsible for his death. "Wait, are you saying he was the thief?"

"Yes and no." The Professor took a long drink of coffee. "Might I beg you for a refresher?"

"Of course." I refilled his mug and waited for him to continue.

"Tim did indeed confess to stealing artifacts from SOMA. Although he insists that Shakespeare's work is not included in what he has stolen over the years."

"Over the years?" The more I learned about the museum, the more I was beginning to wonder if everyone involved was living in an alternate reality.

"According to Tim, the cash was intended as payment for him smuggling a number of items out of the basement archives. The gala provided the perfect cover. He went to the basement intending to make the trade, but was knocked out. He also reported that Dylan had caught him in the act a few weeks ago, and had been threatening to blackmail him in exchange for his silence."

"Wait, I'm confused." Obviously the coffee wasn't helping. I was struggling to keep up. "If Tim was stealing artifacts, who was he selling them to?"

"A fair question. If we are to believe him, he says that he never had face-to-face contact with the buyer. He would leave the artifacts on the second shelf in the storage room. Then he would leave the basement door unlocked and his buyer would remove the items and leave cash."

"This sounds like something out of a James Bond movie."

"I concur." The Professor gave me a nod as he drank more coffee. "Tim expressed deep remorse. Whether he's being sincere remains to be seen. As do a number of looming questions. What happened to the manuscript? Whose cash was in the box? How did the thief gain access to the manuscript, and how did they manage to swap the glass cases? Did Tim's buyer acquire the lost work? Did he have an accomplice?"

"That's a lot to consider." My mind raced to make sense of what he was saying.

"Indeed. And it's a line of reasoning that I can and will follow, regardless of my involvement in the rest of the case." He rested his coffee cup on the counter.

"I can't believe there have been so many backhanded dealings at the museum. Tim was stealing art. Cindy was using cash from the donation box. Dylan was planning to blackmail Tim. I don't know what Zoe's part is in this, but it doesn't seem plausible that she wouldn't know about some of this. And what about Javier? When I spoke with him at dinner, he seemed genuinely shocked about the developments, but he could just as easily be Tim's accomplice, don't you think?"

"I do. I don't think that any stone can be left unturned at this point in time. I wish we were narrowing in on a killer, but alas, I fear we may be intentionally being shifted off course."

"How?"

"That's what I intend to find out." He finished his coffee and handed me his empty cup. "Many thanks for the coffee. I shall go downstairs and check in with your mother. Do keep me abreast of anything you might hear."

I agreed and returned to gathering the last of the dishes, but I couldn't stop thinking about Tim. If he had admitted to stealing other artifacts, he had to be the most likely suspect.

Chapter Twenty-Four

The next morning I woke to discover Ashland blanketed entirely in white. Yesterday's snow had frozen overnight, creating a thin layer of sparkling ice on top of the fresh powder. I laced on my boots and zipped up my puffy parka to trek to Torte. Carlos was sleeping, so I left a note on my pillow reminding him that Mountain Avenue would be dicey for even the most seasoned snow driver and not to attempt it under any circumstances.

My breath puffed in bursts of steam as I slid down the hillside. I paid extra attention to my feet as I navigated the slippery sidewalk. My thoughts returned to Shakespeare's *Double Falsehood* and Dylan as I passed SOU. It felt like there was one missing piece of the puzzle, and if I could just figure out where the piece fit, everything else would fall into place.

The streets were silent as I made my way to the plaza.

The only sound was my boots crunching through the snow. I drank in the cold air and the whimsical coating of white on the rooftops. A nearly full moon illuminated my path, which was made even brighter by the reflecting snow. My first order of business when I arrived at the bakeshop, after starting a pot of coffee of course, was to text Andy to tell him to take the day off. Sequoia could easily manage the espresso bar, and I could help Rosa as a floater during the breakfast and lunch rush.

With that completed, I turned my attention to baking. Another snow day called for something special, and I knew just the thing—gingerbread waffles. I started by whisking eggs and buttermilk. Then I added brown sugar and molasses. Once those were combined, I stirred in a combination of warming spices—cloves, cinnamon, nutmeg, ginger, and a touch of rum extract. To make the waffles light and fluffy, I carefully incorporated flour, baking powder, and cream of tartar and mixed them together until they were just combined. I set the batter aside to work on a cranberry compote that would accompany the spicy waffles.

For the compote, I zested fresh orange with cranberries, added a splash of orange juice, vanilla, brown sugar, and a pat of butter. I set that on the stove to simmer on low. While the waffle iron warmed up, I whipped cream, powdered sugar, and vanilla, and poured myself a cup of coffee. I had learned in culinary school that the secret to making crisp and airy waffles is in the iron. A flip iron is essential, because it allows you to flip the waffle maker after pouring in a scoop of batter, which ensures that the batter will spread out evenly and cook perfectly on both sides.

The kitchen immediately began to smell like the holiday season. The first batch of waffles came out a dark golden brown. I topped them with the cranberry orange compote, a healthy dollop of whipped cream, and finally, a sprinkling of cinnamon.

Steph, Sterling, Marty, Bethany, and Sequoia all showed up just in time to taste my creation.

"It smells like my grandmother's kitchen," Bethany said, taking off her coat and revealing a burnt orange sweatshirt with the saying GIVE THANKS, EAT PIE. "It's actually bringing a tear to my eye." She pressed the tip of her finger to the side of her eye to prove her point.

"I hope that's a good sign," I teased.

"The best." Bethany placed her hand over her heart. "It smells like her gingerbread. It makes me miss her so much."

"Is she still alive?" Sterling asked. He had taken off his coat too. He wore his traditional uniform of skinny black jeans and a hoodie.

"Yeah." Bethany came closer to the sample plates I had assembled. "She used to live across the street from us, but she moved to Arizona a couple years ago. She decided she was done with the snow and the cold. I haven't seen her since last spring. I'm going to take a picture of these and FaceTime her later."

Everyone devoured the spicy and sweet waffles.

"Jules, these are seriously good," Sterling said as he tucked into the plate.

Even Steph broke a grin. "These might be my favorite."

"Wow, you guys. High praise for a Monday morning. I figured we needed a snow day special."

Sequoia finished her waffles. "Speaking of that, I'm going to work on a coffee drink to accompany these. I have a couple ideas in mind, especially since Andy isn't here to gloat over me."

Marty rolled up his sleeves. "I think we need actual gingerbread to go with the waffles, and I'm not talking about cookies. I'm talking about old-school gingerbread, as in a moist loaf cake that tastes like a gingersnap. What do you think, should I add that to the morning lineup?"

"Absolutely." I gave him a thumbs-up.

"I love this," Bethany said, snapping pictures with her phone. "It's only a week until Thanksgiving, and the plaza is a snowy playground. We should totally go all in on the fall flavors. I could do pumpkin chocolate brownies."

"Yeah, and cranberry orange scones," Marty added.

"Don't forget we have pie prep for next week." Steph pointed to the board hanging on the far wall, where we tracked our custom cake orders and upcoming events.

For Thanksgiving, we would be selling pumpkin, bourbon pecan, and silk chocolate whole pies along with pumpkin cheesecake, dinner rolls, sweet bread, and our signature stuffing mix, which was made from an assortment of our rye, whole wheat, and sourdough breads and then infused with herbs—dried parsley, onion, rosemary, thyme, marjoram, sage—red pepper flakes, and garlic salt. It was going to be a quick transition from Shakespearean chocolate art to family holiday favorites.

Sterling had gathered small ramekins and stacked them on the island. "Snow days remind me of hot lunch. I could do a mac and cheese with candied bacon, and roasted Brussels spouts as a side. Does that sound good?"

"You had me at mac and cheese." Marty rubbed his stomach.

Sequoia returned from the coffee bar with a tray of Torte mugs. "Be honest. Let me know what you think. A good barista always welcomes feedback," she said as she passed around samples. "This is a cinnamon fig latte topped with aromatic mace."

I wasn't at all surprised that her flavor combinations burst to life on my tongue. The earthy yet sweet fig and cinnamon mingled beautifully with the creamy latte and the final hint of mace lingered on my palate. "This is incredible."

Sequoia beamed with pleasure at my praise and that of the rest of the team. The vote was unanimous and immediate. She left to finish prepping for opening as everyone went about their individual tasks. When Rosa showed up for her shift, I pulled her aside to check in.

"How were things last night?" I asked. "Javier seemed better."

She nodded. "Yes. Thank you for finding a way to help him. I'm still worried, though. The police were very clear. They told him he must stay in town. He's basically on house arrest."

"It's better than sending him to the Medford holding facility."

"True. But I'm worried that he's going to do something drastic." She chewed on her thumbnail.

"Like what?"

"I don't know. He kept saying last night that he had to get to the bottom of this. He made it sound like he has an idea who took the manuscript." She fiddled with her turquoise ring.

"But he didn't tell you who he suspects?" I was surprised by this. Javier had made it sound like everyone connected to SOMA was still a suspect in his mind.

She shook her head. "No, but I'm worried about him, Jules. He's very upset that the lost play was stolen on his watch, and he's furious that someone hurt not one but two of his staff members. He feels personally responsible. I'm afraid that he's going to take things in his own hands."

"Javier doesn't seem like the vigilante type."

"I agree, but this is personal to him. He worked for years to bring this most beloved exhibit to Ashland, and he's absolutely gutted that the work was stolen, but even more upset that Tim was seriously injured and Dylan was killed. He feels like this wouldn't have happened if he had been more focused and not so caught up in the excitement over the exhibit and gala. I told him last night that it wasn't true. No one blames him, but he wouldn't listen."

"What do you think he would do?"

She shrugged. "I don't know, but I have a bad feeling about it. I told him that the police are on top of the investigation, and now that the FBI is here, I'm convinced that they'll clear his name, but I could tell he was only half listening to what I was saying. He's consumed with anger, revenge, fear. I don't know what else. I've never seen him like this, and I can't be sure that he won't try to do something drastic."

This was a shift. Javier had seemed subdued to me last night. But if he knew who the thief and killer were, Rosa might have a point. Or could his anger be due to something else? Was it a sign he was actually the killer? I hated to even consider it.

"What are you worried about exactly?"

"I don't know. He said that he was going to be at the museum later today. Apparently he and the Professor are having lunch today, but then he told me that he thinks he might be able to find proof at SOMA. He's not sure if the FBI will allow him inside, which is why he's talking about trying to get in later tonight."

I had a feeling that the FBI might have their team on-site at SOMA around the clock. They likely had the ability to staff twenty-four-seven watches, unlike Ashland's small police force.

"My uncle is the kindest person I know, but I do fear that this situation is going to push him to do something he would never do under normal circumstances."

"Are you worried that he's going to go after whoever he thinks stole the manuscript and killed Dylan?"

She nodded. "Yes."

There was a long pause. "I don't think he would harm whoever did this. What I'm worried about is that if he confronts a killer, he could be next."

Chapter Twenty-Five

Her warning sent a shiver down my spine. Now it made sense. She wasn't worried about Javier hurting someone, she was worried about *him* getting hurt.

"Is there anything we can do?" I asked.

"That's what kept me up last night. How do I stop him? How do we convince him that he must leave this to the authorities? It's too dangerous." She glanced around the kitchen as if looking for something that might serve as a physical restraint for her uncle.

"I'm sure the Professor will advise him. They're good friends, and the Professor won't let him take any risks."

"Yes, but that's one of my fears. I believe that's why Doug released him. Javier didn't say this outright, but he hinted that Doug suggested that he make contact with the killer."

"What?" That didn't sound like the Professor.

"Yes," she insisted, tugging the ring on and off her finger. "I think that's why he wanted to let Javier out before the FBI arrived. I think he's using my uncle as a decoy. Maybe that's part of the FBI plan too. They need his help to catch the killer, and I don't like it one bit. Javier could end up dead too."

"If that's the case, the Professor must have his reasons," I assured her. "He would never put a friend—or a stranger, for that matter—in harm's way."

"I hope you're right." Rosa folded her hands together. "I can't shake the feeling that something terrible is going to happen."

"Would you feel better if I talk to the Professor?"

"Maybe. It wouldn't hurt."

"Okay." I glanced at my watch. It was nearly seven. "I'll run over to the police station and see if I can find out any more details. Try not to worry."

Her cheeks had lost their color. She put on a brave face for me. "I'll try," she replied, with an attempt at a smile.

I made sure everything was running smoothly before boxing up cranberry scones and slices of Marty's gingerbread. The kitchen was a symphony of delectable fall flavors. "I'll be back in a few," I said to Sterling. "I'm just going to be across the street, so if there's a rush, call me and I'll be here in less than two minutes."

Sterling chopped slabs of center-cut bacon. "Since they've already canceled school for the day, I don't anticipate seeing a rush until much later. You know how many kids are doing a snow dance and hitting the snooze button on their alarms right now?"

I chuckled. "Probably a few."

"More like every kid in Ashland. They'll play outside all morning until their cheeks are red and their fingers are frozen, then they'll come in here for our mac and cheese and gingerbread." He tossed a dish towel over his shoulder.

For the cheese sauce, he made a roux with flour, evaporated milk, sharp cheddar cheese, and a touch of ground mustard. Once the creamy sauce came together, he poured the bubbly cheese over elbow noodles, topped them with herbed bread crumbs and bacon, and baked them in the wood-fired oven.

"That sounds like a perfect snow day to me." I left with a wave and went out the back stairwell to the police station. The lights were on, which I took as a good sign that at least someone was already working. Whether it was Ashland's finest or the FBI was another question.

I knocked on the door, and a man in a navy FBI jacket answered. "Can I help you?"

"Is the Professor—uh—I mean, Doug in?"

His eyes traveled to the pastry box. "Nope. He's at the college. Did you want me to leave that for him?"

"Sure. Thanks." I handed him the box. "Feel free to help yourself. I brought plenty to share."

"You haven't met my team, have you?" He peeked into the box. "These will be gone in a flash."

"No worries. I own the bakeshop right across the street." I pointed behind me. "There's plenty more if you need it."

He licked his lips. "Would it be bad if I didn't share? No one would need to know. I'm kind of a pro at figuring out the best places to stash the evidence."

I laughed. "How is the investigation coming?"

My question made his entire body go rigid. His smile evaporated. He tilted his head. "Thanks for the pastries, but I'm not at liberty to discuss any details of our investigation with the general public."

"Of course, I understand. Enjoy, and come by anytime for coffee." I backed away. The sun had risen, casting a gorgeous golden light on the snowy grounds and giving way to sharp blue skies. Every shop and storefront in the plaza dazzled, like they'd been brushed with shiny marmalade.

So much for that, I thought as I returned to Torte. I felt bad not being able to report anything to Rosa, but hopefully, if we were lucky, the Professor would stop by at some point. For all I knew, he and Javier were planning to meet at Torte for lunch. I kept an eye out for both of them as the morning wore on. But there was no sign of either Javier or the Professor by the time the lunch crowd began pouring inside for snow day sustenance.

"Do you know what the Professor is up to today?" I asked Mom when I went downstairs to grab a tray of Sterling's bacon mac and cheese and Brussels sprouts.

"He mentioned that he was going to be in meetings most of the day with the FBI. I believe he's in Medford at police headquarters. Why?"

I gave her a condensed version of my earlier conversation with Rosa.

"I'll talk to her when I have a second," Mom offered. "Doug, as you and I well know, would never do anything to put Javier—or any other civilian—in harm's way. I understand Rosa's trepidation. She's been through a lot these past few days, and I know she's protective of Javier, but worrying that Doug would endanger him is not worth her time."

"Agreed."

Mom's wise eyes drifted upstairs. "Perhaps Rosa would enjoy making her conchas this afternoon. You know what I always say, kneading dough is the best way to work through any problem."

"Great idea." Rosa's sweet rolls were always a hit amongst our customers. The sweet rolls were shaped like seashells and coated in crunchy toppings. "I'll give her a break and send her down." I felt relieved that Mom agreed with my perspective.

After delivering bubbling hot ramekins of mac and cheese and sides of fire-roasted Brussels sprouts drizzled with balsamic vinegar and olive oil, I took a turn at the pastry counter so Rosa and Mom could bake conchas together. The remainder of the afternoon passed without incident. A little before four, Lance texted to remind me of our happy hour date. I went to find Carlos and make sure that no one needed anything before we left.

Carlos laced his fingers through mine as we made the short walk a few doors down to Puck's Pub. The whimsical bar was designed to resemble a forest scene from *A Midsummer Night's Dream* with a mixture of vines and yellow twinkle lights snaking across the ceiling, keg barrels for tables, and dark wood accents throughout the cozy space.

Lance and Arlo were already seated at a table near the small stage in the front of the bar when we arrived. A guitarist was warming up on the stage. I took a seat next to Lance and Carlos slid in next to Arlo. "Good evening, dear friends." Lance gave us a half bow. "What's your poison?" He offered us a menu.

Puck's had changed their offerings to reflect the season as well. I reviewed mouthwatering descriptions of winter cocktails like their hot buttered rum served with a cinnamon stick and fresh grated nutmeg.

When the waiter approached our table, I made everyone else order first. Carlos opted for a hot toddy with lemon, orange, and ginger. Arlo ordered a winter IPA, and Lance a cranberry martini. After some minor deliberation, I decided a warm drink sounded like the antidote to the chill outside and ordered the hot buttered rum.

"Cheers to us," Lance said, holding up his jewel-toned martini after our drinks arrived. "To good friends and good libations."

"I'll drink to that." Arlo clinked his pint glass to Lance's drink.

I was glad to see that Lance was becoming more of his true self the longer he and Arlo were together. When they had first started dating, Lance had taken to ordering whatever Arlo ordered, even stooping so far as drinking beer, which I knew he hated. I understood wanting to impress a new love or trying to find points of connection. But the one thing I had learned during my time apart from Carlos was that morphing into someone other than yourself was never going to lead to long-term happiness.

"Did you see the Timbers match this afternoon?" Arlo asked Carlos.

They immediately got caught up in replaying the match goal by goal.

Lance scooted his chair closer to mine. "Well, what do you have to report?"

I plunged the cinnamon stick into my steamy cocktail. "I'm not sure. I wish I felt like I was closer to having answers, but I think I'm more confused than ever."

Lance waved his index finger back and forth. "No, no. That attitude absolutely won't do. No pity parties tonight. Let's retrace what we know."

We spent the next twenty minutes rehashing every clue and every suspect.

"You know what intrigues me most?" Lance asked, swirling his drink. "The case. Where's the case that housed *Double Falsehood*?"

"I know. That's been a holdup for me too. I mean, it's not huge, but it's not like it's a manuscript that you could tuck into a bag and sneak out."

"Exactly." Lance strummed his fingers on the edge of his glass. "What if they didn't?"

"They didn't what?"

"They didn't take the case. What if that was a lie?"

"Interesting." I thought about it. Tim had been the person who had claimed that the hinges on the case were different. He could have invented that story in order to shift suspicion away from himself. Had anyone confirmed that? I searched my memory, trying to bring every detail of the night to the forefront. Everyone had come into the main hall—Cindy, Zoe, Javier, Tim, Ernest, Dylan. They were all there when the Professor had inspected the case.

"Orrrrr . . ." Lance stretched out his words. "What if the culprit walked right out of the ballroom with the case?"

"But how? They would have been seen. It's hardly like someone could have carried a glass case out the front doors."

Lance tapped his chin. "What if they concealed it and then calmly left the ballroom with no one the wiser?"

"Tim!" I yelled. Carlos and Arlo topped talking and turned to me. "Sorry." I gave them a sheepish grin. "Tim had his custodian cart with him that night. The bottom half was draped in black fabric. I remember because I thought it was interesting that even the supply cart had been made to look formal for the occasion. He could have stashed the case there. In fact, I thought it was so weird that he took off so quickly. He claimed he needed to go get trash bags and put the cart in the basement. This was right when everyone discovered that the manuscript was missing."

Lance snapped his fingers. "Yes, brilliant."

Carlos frowned. "Are you two talking about the murder?"

"Just theorizing," Lance replied with a saccharine smile. "Ooohhh, is that the Timbers match?" He pointed to a TV above the bar, where the bartender had just turned on the game.

Carlos was too smart to fall for Lance's tricks. He caught my eye, raised his brow, before turning his chair with Arlo to watch the match.

Lance looked elated. "That's it. You've solved it. Tim stole the manuscript by concealing the case—lost play and all—in his cart, which he immediately took downstairs to the archives. We can assume that the money belonged to him. He must have been getting ready to make the transfer with his buyer when things went wrong."

"Yeah, that sounds like a good theory, but there's one gaping hole. Dylan's murder. Tim was in the hospital. He couldn't have done it."

Lance's face deflated like a balloon. "Damn."

"Right?" I took a drink of my hot buttered rum. It hit the spot, with its warming spices and the heat from the rum on the back of my throat.

"Well, he must have had an accomplice. That's the only possible explanation."

"That could be true," I agreed. The question was who?

Chapter Twenty-Six

After our happy hour, Carlos and I returned home for a low-key evening on the couch, watching a romantic comedy and eating popcorn. I tried to stay in the moment, but it was a challenge not to let my thoughts return to the investigation. My conversation with Lance did feel like a breakthrough. I couldn't believe I hadn't thought about Tim's supply cart earlier. It was the most logical explanation for getting the manuscript out of the main hall. The thief had to know that they would need to take the utmost care to protect the fragile document in order to sell it. But that still didn't account for Dylan's murder. Tim couldn't possibly have killed Dylan. So there either had to be another explanation or he had had help.

"Julieta, come, let's go to bed," Carlos said after I dozed off partway through the movie for the third time. I didn't resist, but I didn't sleep well either.

The next morning, I went through the normal routine at the bakeshop, feeling like I was going through the motions but not really processing anything. Visions of Tim racing away with his cart replayed again and again in my mind. But how had Dylan been killed? And by whom?

Twice I reached for salt instead of sugar when making our standard cookie dough for the day. When Andy asked me three times whether I wanted a coffee and finally had to wave his hand in front of my face to get my attention, I decided it might be a good idea to go for a walk and try to clear my head.

I didn't have a plan as I stepped out onto the plaza. Yesterday's blue skies and November sun had melted most of the snow. The remnants of our first storm remained in wobbly snowmen flanking Lithia Park and the red lava rock used to gravel the streets. I headed up Main Street and found myself approaching the SOU campus. The air remained cold, which served as motivation to quicken my pace. By the time I made it to campus, my cheeks felt numb from the cold. My nose dripped, and my toes tingled.

I passed bike racks with red slanted roofs constructed to protect the bikes housed beneath from the elements. I traveled along the pressed-pebble pathway toward Churchill Hall with its mission-style stucco walls and Latin inscriptions carved above pillared entryways. Leafy palm trees tucked amongst the redwoods had weathered the storm. Clumps of mistletoe hung heavy in the oaks and maples. A northern flicker fed at a tubular bird feeder swinging from the arms of an evergreen tree.

When I made it to SOMA's front doors, I was surprised to see the entrance was guarded by FBI agents. I walked past them as if I was out for a leisurely morning stroll through campus.

What are you doing here, Jules? I asked myself, as I considered heading up the hill to see if Carlos was up and wanted a ride to the bakeshop. I paused for a moment at the corner to admire student artwork on display in the windows—pottery, photography, and watercolors lined the windowsill, offering passersby a firsthand look at the results of the students' hard work.

As I rounded the side of the building, I noticed that the basement door was propped halfway open.

There was no sign of FBI agents or a police presence at this side of the building. Without hesitating, I snuck in through the open door. The basement was completely dark. Only a narrow shaft of light escaped from the crack in the door.

I inched inside, half expecting to be stopped by more FBI agents, but the corridor was empty.

My burst of fearlessness faded. Was this a bad idea?

Yes!

Every cell in my body cautioned me to turn around and leave.

But then again, the museum was crawling with federal agents, and it was daylight. I couldn't be in any danger, could I?

I inhaled, giving in to the less rational side of my brain, and continued down the hallway, passing the archive storage area where I'd found Tim. I stopped as I heard the sound of footsteps and talking overhead. That had to mean that there were more officers inside. But then why was the basement door open? It didn't make sense.

The thought forced my legs to move forward as the basement got darker and darker.

I froze for a minute, straining to hear what was being said. It sounded like someone was directing a search. I heard a commanding man's voice followed by more heavy footsteps scattering in every direction.

Was the Professor here?

And if the entire team of agents was upstairs, who had left the basement door open? Could it be that one of the agents had made a mistake and forgotten to lock it after doing a sweep of the area? Doubtful.

Again, I hesitated, but I couldn't imagine that the thief and/or killer would be dumb enough to return to the scene of the crime, sneak inside, and leave the door propped open. No, there had to be some sort of explanation.

Maybe the team was doing their final assessment, preparing to let SOMA reopen again. That made the most logical sense, right?

There's only one way to find out, Jules. I gave myself a pep talk and moved forward, stopping to check each of the side doors again on the off chance that one of them was unlocked.

None of them were.

My throat tightened as I neared the end of the corridor. What was I doing? This was a Lance move. For all I knew, Javier could be the killer. Maybe he was the one who opened the back door. He could be hiding down here waiting to sneak outside again with evidence he'd stashed away.

I was about to turn around when I felt a hand grasp my shoulder and yank me from behind.

My heart banged against my chest as my assailant clasped their other hand over my mouth to stop me from screaming and dragged me down the hallway. I dug my feet into the floor, but it was pointless. Whoever had ahold of me was much stronger.

I tried to kick and fight out of their grasp as they twisted a door handle and pulled me into one of the storage rooms.

Their fingers tightened over my lips as I twisted my body from side to side, trying to free myself.

"Quiet. They'll hear you," a deep voice whispered.

I recognized the voice.

The room was plunged in darkness. I blinked to try and get a sense of my bearings and look for anything I could use as a weapon.

But to my complete shock, my assailant released me.

What was happening?

I turned around to see Javier standing behind me holding a flashlight to his chin. The way the light cast a reddish glow on his face made him look like a villain from a comic book.

I gulped and stepped away from him, thinking frantically about what I could potentially use as a weapon.

Javier.

Javier was the killer?

Chapter Twenty-Seven

Not Javier. I couldn't believe it.

I tried to stay calm by focusing on my breathing. I needed to keep him talking and find a way out of here. Or was it better to scream? Would the agents upstairs hear me? Would it buy me enough time to make my escape? I glanced frantically around. We were in a storage room like the one where I had found Tim the night of the murder. Even in the dark, I could make out the rows of tightly packed industrial shelving units.

"Jules, you look scared, but don't be. I won't hurt you. You're not in danger." Javier's mouth moved in a strange horror-movie motion with the flashlight illuminating the inside of his mouth.

"Javier, I don't understand. Why did you just grab me?" I tried to inch toward the door. My hands were shaking so violently I wasn't sure I would even be able to open it if I could make it there before him.

He held out his free hand in a warning. "Don't move. You'll ruin everything. Please keep your voice down. We're in the middle of a sting."

"A sting?" I gulped. What had I gotten myself into?

There was a sound in the hallway.

Javier pressed his index finger to his lips and shook his head. "Shhhh."

My stomach swirled.

What was happening? Was Javier working with the police?

He waited for the footsteps to pass the doorway. Then he came closer to me so that he could whisper. "We need to get down to the archives now. Follow me and don't say a word. Be as quiet as you can. Do you understand?"

I wanted to scream no. I did not understand, but my instincts told me he could be trusted. If he had wanted to hurt me, he already could have. He must have a reason for his secrecy.

I did as he instructed, waiting for him to slowly open the door and check our surroundings. He flipped off the flashlight, plunging us back into darkness, and then tiptoed down the hallway to the first archive room where I had found Tim.

My heart pounded so fast, it felt like it was on overdrive as I crept behind him. Twice he stopped in midstride and held out his hand to signal me to stop. We waited for what felt like minutes before proceeding. The sound of voices and footsteps upstairs had stopped as well. I wasn't sure if that was a good sign or if he was leading me to my doom.

We made it to the far end of the basement. The door I had snuck in through was now closed.

Javier ushered me into the archive room first. He locked the door behind us and kept the lights off.

"What's going on?" I asked again.

He pushed us toward the very far corner of the room where tight rows of steel shelves packed with green and brown storage boxes provided us shelter. "Stay here. We have to remain quiet and out of sight. Got it?"

"What is the sting? Are you working with the FBI?"

He nodded and pressed his index finger to his lips with force.

I wished I had answers. What did this mean? Certainly it ruled out Javier as a suspect, which brought me relief and confirmed that my gut feeling about him had been right. Tim was off the table too. He was still in the hospital. That left Cindy, Ernest, and Zoe.

It had to be one of them, but who?

And the other looming question was—were we in danger?

Javier's body language and the way he was shielding me from the door made me think there was a good chance we were.

"Is the Professor involved?" I whispered.

He nodded, but didn't answer.

I could tell he was taking whatever his role in the sting was very seriously. I mirrored his silence as we waited in the darkness. The only light that cut through the musty room was from beneath the door frame at the opposite end.

It felt like hours, but it was probably minutes before I heard the sound of a key turn in the lock. Javier flipped his head toward mine with yet another warning to stay completely still. I pressed my spine into the cold concrete wall and tried not to breathe.

The door opened, and someone flipped on the lights. My

eyes revolted. I shut them tight to let them adjust to the sudden brightness. After a second, I opened them, squinting to try and make out who had come into the room.

It was Zoe.

I placed my hand over my mouth.

Zoe!

Her eyes darted around the room, peering through her glasses. Fortunately Javier had led us behind six-foot-tall boxes at the very back of the room. I felt reasonably assured that she couldn't see us, but that didn't stop my pulse from racing or my stomach from going queasy. Did she have a weapon? Was she dangerous?

I made sure to stay as still as possible as she came closer, sucking in my breath and holding it as if I were trying to submerge myself in the deep end of a pool.

Please don't let my cell phone ring, I thought. I could just imagine Carlos calling at this moment.

Zoe proceeded to walk toward the shelving unit that had collapsed on Tim. It had been returned to its upright position and restocked with a variety of boxes in all shapes and sizes.

Javier didn't move a muscle as Zoe took box after box off the shelves, not bothering to be careful in the process. For someone who was working on her PhD in art history, I was shocked by her careless abandon with the valuable artifacts. She finally found what she was looking for. She had to climb onto the bottom shelf and reach all the way up to the third level to remove the item.

I wanted to nudge Javier. What was he waiting for? Why wasn't he confronting her?

We watched as she opened a box that looked identical to the one that had housed *Double Falsehood*. She removed what appeared to be Shakespeare's lost play or some other ancient document. Had it been in the basement the entire time? I couldn't believe it. Zoe had hidden the manuscript in plain sight.

She returned the document to the box and was about to make her exit when the door burst open and a swarm of agents in blue spanned across the room with their guns aimed at her.

"Freeze right there," one of the officers shouted. "Drop the box and put both of your hands in the air where we can see them. Now!"

Zoe clutched the box like it was her last lifeline.

"Hands in the air!" the agent commanded.

She glanced from left to right before finally placing the box at her feet, standing upright, and holding both of her hands in the air.

"Stay where you are."

The agents approached her and, in a matter of seconds, had her handcuffed. One of them read her the Miranda warning while another retrieved the box she had placed on the floor.

I looked at Javier.

He motioned for me to wait.

In the shuffle I hadn't noticed that the Professor had arrived too. He stood to the side of the door frame. "Go ahead and come out now," he said.

Javier turned to me. "That's our cue." He tugged my arm and stepped out from behind our hiding spot.

Zoe spun around in our direction. "Javier! Oh no. I'm sorry. I'm so sorry." Her eyes were wide with fear, or was it remorse?

"It didn't have to come to this," Javier said, his voice laced with disappointment. "Dylan. Tim. How could you?"

"It was an accident. I swear." Her voice broke. Her eyes bulged as she glanced wildly around the room. "Tim caught me that night. I thought my plan was foolproof, but Dylan ruined it. I told him to look the other way, that if he did, I would make it worth his while. I was going pay him a couple thousand bucks and call it good. But then he got smart. He wanted more. He wanted a lot more, and threatened to go straight to the police if I didn't pay him what he wanted right then. He was such an idiot. I told him that selling the manuscript was going to take a while, but if he could just be patient, it would pay off, but he didn't get it. He wanted cash fast."

She hung her head. "I shouldn't have trusted him. I could have sent him out of the hall. Why didn't I? If it hadn't been for him, none of this would have gone wrong." She scolded herself. "It's his fault he died. If he had just listened to me."

I couldn't tell if she was actually addressing Javier any longer, as she continued to spill her secrets. "I'm drowning under student loan debt. I didn't mean to do this to you, or to the museum, but I couldn't figure any other way out. Honestly, I never thought anyone would even know. It was such a good plan. I had to order the case for the manuscript, so I ordered two. I knew I had to swap the original with the fake before we let the public in. I took Tim's cart and stashed the real manuscript beneath it earlier. He had a lengthy list of tasks from me. I thought I would have plenty of time to make the switch downstairs, but he walked in on me. I swear it was an accident. I never meant to hurt him. The shelves came tumbling down, and I freaked out. I didn't mean to kill Dylan either. I had no idea that a Taser could kill. He was young and healthy. I never anticipated that. I've been sick.

I haven't slept. I haven't eaten anything. This has been horrible."

"Why did you do it?" Javier sounded like a parent who had learned their child was in trouble. "You had such a bright future ahead of you, Zoe. I would have done anything to help further that. We could have helped you with your debt. Figured out a payment plan for your loans. You could have been running a museum at this time next year. Now you'll be behind bars."

"It was stupid. I shouldn't have done it, but I knew how tight things are with the museum. I never imagined that you could have helped with my student debt. It all feels like too much. Even with a top salary, I'd be paying it off for the next twenty years or more."

"You could have come to me."

She ran her fingers through her hair, massaging the top of her head. "I know."

The head FBI agent interrupted. "We need to take her to the station." He escorted Zoe out of the room, followed by his team.

I watched them lead her away, feeling a sense of relief and sorrow. The manuscript had been found. A killer had been apprehended, but it all seemed so senseless.

Chapter Twenty-Eight

The Professor hung back with Javier and me. "That went as well as could have been expected," he said to Javier.

Javier kindly didn't share that I nearly ruined the operation. I outed myself. "Sorry to be in the middle of this. What exactly just happened?"

"Would you like to explain?" the Professor asked Javier.

"Certainly." He placed his hand on my shoulder. "Let me begin by apologizing. As I said, I had no intention of harming you, but you happened upon us at the exact moment that we anticipated Zoe arriving. Instinct kicked in, but I hope you're not harmed." He looked me over as if expecting to see bruises.

"No. I'm fine," I replied. "I'm the one who should be apologizing. I saw that the basement doors were open, and I came in. I shouldn't have done that. I've been so obsessed with the case that I guess I didn't think it through."

"I understand, and I'm glad to hear that you're okay." He began picking up the boxes that Zoe had tossed on the floor. "I suspected that Zoe was involved almost immediately. I caught her in my office that night. She claimed she was looking for a check to pay the acting troupe, but when the Professor found the gloves, wrenches, and lock, I was immediately on high alert. I should have been more aware. You see, she had come to me about a raise a while back. I would have gladly offered her more money, but the museum simply didn't have any more to give. I explained this to her, and she seemed satisfied, but Doug learned that she went directly to Ernest, begging him to set aside a trust exclusively for staff salaries." He and the Professor made eye contact. "When the manuscript went missing, I had a horrible feeling because Dylan had actually alerted me to a phone call he had overheard a few nights before. He was working the late shift, and Zoe was in her office. She had no idea anyone was listening in. She had taken matters in her own hands and arranged to sell the lost play to a notorious underground art dealer that the FBI has been tracking in Seattle for many years."

"Is that why they got involved?" I asked.

"In part." The Professor nodded. "I had to take Javier into custody that night due to the evidence we found in his office, but I never suspected that my friend was involved, and we quickly began piecing Zoe's activities together. That's when I called in a favor with a colleague in Seattle. I would have alerted and involved the FBI in any event, but we had it on good authority that Zoe had been working with a dealer out of Seattle."

Javier continued. "I didn't want to believe it, but Dylan was very sure of what he heard. I've been beating myself up.

I should have taken the threat much more seriously. I should have confronted Zoe, but I was caught up in getting the exhibit launched, the gala, and meeting with more donors. I figured if we could at least get through the opening, then I could have a heart-to-heart with Zoe afterward. I never imagined that she would steal the manuscript at the gala. And I certainly never envisioned her hurting anyone in the process."

"Do you think she was telling the truth about that?" I felt terrible about the entire situation. It all seemed so pointless. A young man had died because of a four-hundred-year-old play.

"I do." Javier sighed, voicing my same thought. "It's such a shame. So much loss—for what?"

The Professor directed his team to recover the boxes that Zoe had been going through. "The coroner was able to confirm that Dylan was tased and that triggered a reaction in his heart. I, too, tend to believe that her intention was never to kill. However that doesn't justify her actions, nor does it absolve her from her crimes."

"Who was she selling the manuscript to? Is that connected to Tim's dealings?"

"We're in the process of trying to determine what, if any, connections there are, but at this stage of the investigation, it appears to be two different events." The Professor addressed both of us. "Tim was selling small items to local dealers who would pawn them. That's the box of cash we discovered. As I mentioned the night of the crime, there were a few thousand dollars inside, but nothing on the scale that the manuscript would fetch. Not that Tim will be let off the hook for his crimes either. But we're talking petty theft, whereas Zoe was working with an art dealer in Seattle who is well-known and, as Javier mentioned, has been on the FBI's watch list for many years now. Had she been successful in getting *Double Falsehood* out of the building, it likely would have gone underground quickly. Who knows if we would have been able to recover it." The Professor paused for a moment to hand Javier another box. "The white collar team will be following up on that lead immediately now that we have apprehended Zoe."

"How did you do it?" I couldn't believe that Zoe was responsible for everything.

"That's thanks to Javier." The Professor gave him a half bow. "He explained his perspective on the strange turn of events while in custody, and we hatched a plan. You see, Zoe had stashed the document here amongst the other items. Hiding in plain sight. But Tim caught her in the midst of trying to smuggle the manuscript out of the building. When we did our sweep of the space, Thomas found the original document, which is safe and sound in Javier's office."

"What?" I gasped.

The faintest of smiles tugged at the edge of the Professor's lips. "A sleight of hand never hurts. We swapped the original for a fake in an attempt to bait Zoe to return, which as you're aware, worked. Then we only needed to make sure that our teams were in position to catch her in the act. To be quite honest, it went better than I had anticipated."

"Did you get in contact with Zoe and tell her to meet you here?" I asked Javier.

He nodded. "Yes. That was part of the plan. Doug had me tell her that I had found the document. I made sure that she didn't suspect that I thought she was involved with the theft. I made it clear that finding Shakespeare's play in the archives must have confirmed Tim's guilt."

"Smart." I massaged my forehead. I couldn't believe that I had ended up in the middle of it. "What do you think will happen to her now?"

The Professor glanced at his watch. "She's going to be serving time for more than art theft, I'm afraid. We'll have to wait and see if Tim presses charges. Regardless, the DA will bring a case against her for the murder of Dylan. Whether or not she's able to get off with manslaughter remains to be seen."

"That's so sad. She's young. And all because of student debt?" I tried to process my feelings aloud.

"Money can cause good people to commit desperate acts," the Professor replied with a frown.

"He that dies pays all debts." They both quoted the same passage from *The Tempest* in unison.

"I wonder about her mental health too," Javier added. "She's been under enormous stress and pressure with her workload here on top of her class schedule and writing her dissertation. When you combine money on top of that, I can understand why she felt the need to do something so drastic. Like you, Doug, I don't condone her actions, but I do feel empathy for her. This is a lesson for me as well. I need to do better by my staff." He finished putting the boxes away. "Shall we head upstairs? I've got a number of calls to make and then some big decisions about what to do in terms of the exhibit."

"Are you planning to open the doors again?"

Javier shrugged. "I'm not sure."

The Professor walked toward the door. "I understand your hesitation, but let's not lose sight of what a gift the Bard's lost play is to the world. It would be a shame not to share that with our friends and colleagues here in the Rogue Valley.

Zoe's mistakes shouldn't be punishment for the community. In fact, I might argue that we need to come together more than ever now. You could use the reopening of the exhibit as a way to honor Dylan and bring healing to everyone."

"That's a valid point." Javier considered the Professor's words. Then he turned to me as we walked down the hallway, which thankfully was lit now. "What do you say, Jules? You want to put on another dessert spread?"

"Um, as long as we don't have to make new chocolate showpieces, you can count me in."

Javier and the Professor laughed. "No chocolate, I promise. Your showpieces are in good hands, and I'm thinking let's simplify for gala part two. In fact, I love Doug's idea of a community party. Let's do a Thanksgiving style buffet. Easy and delicious. How does that sound?"

"That sounds wonderful."

We talked through the details before I left. Javier's revised vision was something my team could easily pull off. Turkey and cranberry sandwiches, salads, and mini pies and cupcakes. The Professor was right. We needed to come together around the table and support SOMA and celebrate the fact that our sweet Ashland was safe again and that we were, for the next few months, the center of the universe when it came to Shakespeare.

Chapter Twenty-Nine

Javier scheduled the reopening of Shakespeare's lost play for the weekend. That gave us time to make dozens of butter rolls for the turkey and cranberry sandwiches. To go along with the feast, Sterling, Carlos, and Marty made batches of wood-fired sausage stuffing and bowls of butternut squash soup, as well as scalloped corn and shaved Brussels sprout salad. Steph, Mom, Bethany, and I made an assortment of fall-inspired mini hand pies like spiced apple with candied walnuts, pumpkin cream cheese, chocolate silk, and banana cream. Not to be outdone by pie, our dessert table would also include delectable cupcakes including chai tea, caramel apple, maple bacon, and pumpkin chip. Andy and Sequoia offered to create house-made apple cider and cinnamon hot chocolate to serve along with the communal feast.

As Thanksgiving neared, we added to the harvest display in Torte's front windows by arranging a variety of our pies adorned with leaves made from pastry crust and brushed with butterscotch, tangerine, and garnet tinted egg wash on ceramic white cake stands. We left the twinkle lights and leaves dangling from the top of each window casing and included paper cutouts in the shape of turkeys with messages about what our staff was grateful for.

Andy's turkey, not surprisingly, read: *SNOW* and *COFFEE*.

Sequoia was grateful for starlight and the season of Yule.

Mom's brown kraft paper turkey was covered with words like *family, Ashland, community, peace, hope, the future.*

But, it was Sterling's poetry that brought a mist to my eyes. He dabbled in words but had been hesitant to go so far as to sign up for a creative writing class at SOU or put his name on the list for poetry night at Puck's. That's why I was shocked when he not only allowed us to hang his poem in the window but also agreed to let it be the quote for the week on our chalkboard menu. It was titled "Gratitude":

November, she burns bright in the flickering sandstone flames of dusky twilight. When the sun sings us to sleep under Pantone skies, urging us to retreat, to welcome the early slumber. The gift of going in. Of embracing the darkness. Finding ourselves in the quiet comfort of November's gentle grace, which centers us in gratitude.

Customers commented on Sterling's soulful words as they waited at the pastry case for steaming cups of our Thanksgiving blend and pumpkin and cardamom cake doughnuts.

Rosa had taken a few days off to help Javier get things settled at the museum. Zoe's arrest had made front-page news. As the Professor had anticipated, the FBI had been able to connect the theft with the art dealer they'd been tracking in Seattle, which made national headlines. The only positive outcome of so much press was that donations had been streaming into SOMA. Before she took a much-needed respite, Rosa had told me that Javier had extended an offer of employment to Cindy, who would be taking over Zoe's role.

"Javier thinks that they've received enough in donations that he can part ways with Ernest after the *Shakespeare's Lost Pages* exhibit moves on to the next city," Rosa had said while cutting out maple and oak leaves from our hand-rolled piecrust. "This is good news for my uncle and for SOMA. He and Cindy are already planning an immersive family experience for the spring exhibit. Cindy is thrilled. She knows the community and museum better than anyone and will be helping Javier hire new staff and planning many more school field trips and free family weekends at the museum."

I felt glad for Cindy and for Javier. They both deserved to move on, and I knew that they shared a similar vision for SOMA's future.

When the day of the new gala arrived, everyone was ready to put the sad turn of events behind us and focus on the future. That was especially true for Detective Kerry, who had shown up with Thomas to serve as extra security, as a show of support to Javier.

I had finished setting up the dessert table when I took a spin through the exhibit hall to find Kerry standing guard by the manuscript. "This feels like déjà vu, except without party dresses," I said to her, noting my casual jeans and bulky, oversized cream turtleneck sweater. Kerry was dressed in a pair of black slacks and a silky gray button-down shirt. "I'm glad you and Thomas are here."

She gave me her signature curt nod. "We don't anticipate any issues. The Professor felt like having a show of force around the manuscript would help alleviate any lingering fear, but we have no doubt that Zoe was entirely responsible for the theft."

"Have you heard anything about her trial?" My eyes drifted to the manuscript under heavy glass. The old-world calligraphy was certainly beautiful, but I still couldn't wrap my head around the fact that someone had died because of this.

"Not yet, but I would guess that things will move quickly, given how much media attention there's been surrounding the case." Kerry kept her eyes glued to the manuscript, like she expected it to grow legs and walk off.

"That makes sense." I paused for a minute. "What about Tim? Has there been any update on his condition?" I'd been so caught up in Thanksgiving preparations that I'd almost forgotten about Tim.

"He's been released from the hospital," Kerry reported, sounding like she was addressing the press. "As for charges, Javier doesn't want to see him do any jail time. He feels like SOMA has been through enough. He and the Professor are trying to work out whether there might be an opportunity for Tim's sentence to call for community service here."

"Here?"

Her face was serious. "Yes. If they can come to an agreement, Tim will be responsible for the same duties, only without pay. Javier is confident that he won't repeat his mistakes. I hope he's right."

"Yeah." I appreciated Javier's trusting nature and wanting to find a solution for Tim. It gave me even more respect for him. I pointed to the hallway. "Can I bring you a plate, or do you want to come eat before they open the doors?"

"No, I'm fine, but I did want to ask you a favor."

"Sure. Anything." I was shocked that Kerry would ask me for a favor.

"It's about our wedding plans." She didn't look away from the glass case.

For a minute I held my breath. I hoped that she wasn't having second thoughts. Thomas would be devastated.

Then suddenly her body shifted. She peeled her eyes away from *Double Falsehood* and turned to me. "You know our conversation last week about Lithia Park and a picnic?"

"Yeah." I nodded. "Of course."

"Well, I like it." She swallowed twice. "I like it a lot. It feels right, and I know Thomas will be into the idea."

"You haven't talked to him about it yet?"

"No. I wanted to talk to you first."

I'm sure my face must have showed my confusion. "Okay."

"It's just that this isn't my thing, so I was hoping that before Thomas gets super excited, that maybe you would be willing to help me with the planning?"

"I would love to!" I wanted to hug her, but that might have been taking things too far.

"Would you, really?"

I made an X over my heart. "I promise, I would love to. Anything you need from me, I'm yours."

She looked relieved. "Okay, thanks. I'll talk to Thomas tonight and then maybe you and I can grab coffee after the holidays and talk through what we need in order to pull off a picnic. Remember, I'm thinking low-key."

A voice sounded behind us. "Did someone say low-key?"

I turned to see Lance strolling toward us. Even though Javier's invite to the second attempt at unveiling had been very clear about it being strictly casual, Lance wore a dark navy suit with a bright yellow tie and matching pocket square.

"Because as you two know, low-key is not my middle name." He blew an air kiss at each of us.

Kerry rolled her eyes.

"Ouch. That stings." Lance pretended to stab himself in the stomach. "Do tell, what are you plotting?"

"Nothing," I replied.

"Ha! Lies. I heard talk of weddings, and neither of you are going to get away with leaving yours truly out of the planning. What are we thinking?" He strummed his fingers on his chin with eager anticipation.

To my shock, Kerry gave him the condensed version of our idea.

"Love it. Love everything about it." Lance pressed his fingers together. "Now, picture this. We put on a bit of a performance in the bandshell for you two lovebirds."

"I don't want anything big," Kerry replied.

"No, no. Subtlety is my specialty. Imagine romance. We'll have to find the right piece, but I see a handful of actors, a love ballad, a sonnet. Roses. Wine. Yes, yes, you must have something to delight the crowd, and as an added bonus, my production would take the spotlight off of you."

He knew how to spin. Kerry came around to the idea quickly. "Oh, that's a good point. Thomas and I could do a simple exchange of vows and then blend in with the crowd."

"Exactly. So romantic. Juliet and I will put our heads together and plan the most intimate fete for you and your betrothed."

He gave her a finger wave and pulled me away before she could refuse.

"Lance, Kerry wants something small and low-key."

"As if I didn't understand the delicacy of our partnership with her. I'm with you, but, darling, really imagine how wonderful this will be. You and me planning the most romantic wedding that Ashland has ever seen. Can't wait." He kissed my cheek and danced over to say hello to the Professor.

I noticed Ernest and none other than Richard Lord in the corner of the room. Before I could duck away, Richard caught my eye. "Juliet, a word," he boomed, making a bee-line for me.

Side by side, he and Ernest bore an uncanny resemblance to one another. Maybe part of it was that they wore matching purple sweaters with the words *Parchment and Quill* embroidered on the chest.

"Did you hear the news, Capshaw?" Richard folded his arms across his body.

"Nope. What news?"

He nudged Ernest. "Me and my cousin are opening our own ode-to-Shakespeare gallery. I told you that you weren't the only one with a vision for this town."

"You two are cousins?" I wasn't surprised. They deserved each other.

"Second cousins," Ernest said, clearing his throat. "And, I told you, Richard, this endeavor is going to be high-class. None of the Shakespeare kitsch you like to display at the Merry Windsor."

"Classy. Yeah." Richard bobbed his head in agreement. "Did you hear that, Juliet? I wouldn't be so quick to claim a monopoly on the Ashland market just yet. And we're looking forward to some big partnerships for Parchment and Quill in the future. Consider yourself warned."

"Thanks for the heads-up." I plastered on a smile. "It sounds like a good match for both of you."

Carlos came up and placed his arm around my shoulder.

The sight of him in a white button-down shirt and tight jeans brought a quickness to my breath. However his appearance had the opposite effect on Richard, who stumbled on his words and made a fast exit.

I leaned into him.

"Julieta, you are so relaxed. This is good. This event is what we need. No fancy dresses. No tuxes. Good food, good friends, and good art."

"Well said."

"And then we must think about Thanksgiving. Shall we host it at our house?"

"I'd love that."

"We will invite anyone who wants to come."

Only since I'd been back in Ashland had I experienced the joy and delight of the holiday season. On the ship, there had never been time to savor the holidays. And there was the fact that it was always sunny and eighty degrees. Having Carlos in town for the holidays was going to be an entirely new experience. I was looking forward to long winter nights curled up on the couch together and lazy Sunday evenings spent cooking in the kitchen. What I didn't tell him was that I was also dreaming of what our future might hold.

Lately I couldn't stop thinking about babies. I wasn't sure what Carlos would say about the idea of expanding our family. He already had Ramiro, and we were just getting settled in our new life together. In some ways, I felt like we were honeymooners. We were finally getting to know each other at a level we hadn't been able to experience during our time together on the ship. Those years were about stealing away little moments whenever we could. Holding hands and watching the stars take over the sky late at night between shifts, and the occasional long weekend spent meandering through street markets and exploring hidden beaches. Here in Ashland, time was luxurious. Lazy Sunday evenings reading on the couch. Afternoons at Uva, sipping our burgundy and watching the sun disappear behind the mountains. Sharing a kitchen. Sharing a life. A real life. A solid life, not just part of a life.

But I wasn't getting any younger. Soon I was going to have to broach the subject with him.

For now, I enjoyed the evening. Javier beamed as he opened the doors to the museum and members of the community of all ages and diverse backgrounds funneled in. Carlos was right that I didn't feel the same sense of pressure about our food. Everyone appeared to love the casual eats and the vibe of the night.

Kids dressed up in Elizabethan costumes and drew chalk sketches of the Bard. People admired the lost play as well as the other extensive collection of everyday objects from Shakespeare's time. Our chocolate showpieces were a hit. Guests posed in front of them and snapped selfies. I couldn't wait to report to Bethany tomorrow. She would love all of the social sharing going on.

I caught up with Mom later in the evening. "How are you feeling?"

She laced her fingers through mine. "Great. Doug is much calmer now that the manuscript has been returned. He actually told me last night that he's going to take off from Christmas Eve through New Year's Day."

"That is great news. He deserves it, and so do you."

"What about you and Carlos? Have you made any plans for the holidays?"

"We were wondering about hosting Thanksgiving. How does that sound? We could do Christmas at your place?"

"That's perfect. Doug has a lot to do to wrap up the investigation in the next week, but let me know what I can do." Her eyes drifted across the room where Carlos, Lance, and Arlo were laughing together. "Carlos seems very content."

"He does, doesn't he?" I couldn't stop a smile from spreading. "I kind of want to pinch myself, Mom. I never thought I could be this happy."

"That's the beauty of life, and the gift of hardship. It makes us ready to receive the abundance of good." Her walnut-brown eyes twinkled. "What do you think is next?"

Had she read my mind?

"What do you mean?"

"I wondered what you and Carlos will be up to next. Torte, Uva, Scoops. I can't picture either of you not wanting to continue to expand." She placed more emphasis on the word "expand."

She had read my mind.

"I don't know. We'll see. For the moment, I'm going to soak up this feeling."

"As you should, honey."

The truth was I did. The time that Carlos and I had spent apart had given me new appreciation for this life we were carving out together in Ashland. I wasn't sure what was next. I didn't need answers. Not yet. I was surrounded by the best people, in the best place on the planet, and I had faith that whatever came next would unfold exactly as it was meant to when the time was right.

Recipes

Apple Cream Cheese Bars

Ingredients:
For the crust:
1 ½ cups finely ground graham crackers
¼ cup brown sugar
1 teaspoon cinnamon
6 tablespoons melted butter

For the filling:
1 8-ounce package cream cheese
1/2 cup sugar
1 teaspoon vanilla
1 teaspoon cinnamon
1 teaspoon nutmeg
½ teaspoon cloves
2 eggs

For the apple compote:
2 Honeycrisp apples (washed, peeled, and diced)
1 tablespoon lemon juice
2 tablespoons brown sugar
2 tablespoons butter
1 teaspoon nutmeg
1 small orange (juiced and zested)

For the crumb topping:
¼ cup butter (softened)
¼ cup brown sugar
½ cup oats
½ cup pecans (finely chopped)
2 teaspoons cinnamon
½ teaspoon salt

Directions:
Preheat the oven to 350 degrees. To make the crust, mix the crushed graham crackers, brown sugar, and cinnamon together, then pour in the melted butter and stir until it forms a sandy texture. Press the crust into a greased 8 x 8 square pan. Set aside. To make the filling, in a stand mixer or with a hand mixer, whip the cream cheese, sugar, vanilla, and spices (cinnamon, nutmeg, and cloves) together until smooth. Blend in the eggs one at a time. Spread the mixture evenly over the graham cracker crust and bake for 30-35 minutes, or until the center is done. Remove from the oven and allow to cool completely. While the bars are cooling, make an apple compote by combining the apples, lemon juice, brown sugar, butter, nutmeg, and the juice and zest of one orange in a saucepan. Heat over medium low heat on the stove for five minutes, then turn the heat down to low and

allow to simmer for an additional fifteen to twenty minutes. To make the crumb topping, fork the butter and brown sugar together. Add in the oats, pecans, cinnamon, and salt and combine with a fork until the mixture is like sand. Spread the apple compote over the cooled bars, sprinkle with the crumb topping, slice into squares, and serve cold.

Sweet Potato and Chili Hash

Ingredients:
2 tablespoons olive oil
1 red onion (diced)
2 cloves garlic (minced)
2 cups sweet potatoes (peeled and diced)
2 teaspoons smoked paprika
2 teaspoons chili powder
1 teaspoon white pepper
1 teaspoon salt
2 Hatch chiles (roasted, seeded, and diced)
6 eggs
Cotija cheese, for serving (optional)

Directions:
Heat the olive oil in a sauté pan and over medium heat. Add in the red onion, garlic, and sweet potatoes. Let the vegetables cook for fifteen minutes on medium low heat, or until the potatoes are tender. Stir in the smoked paprika, chili powder, white pepper, salt, and Hatch chiles. Crack the eggs over the top of the hash and cover with a lid. Allow the eggs to poach for five minutes. Serve hot. If desired, finish with a sprinkling of Cotija cheese.

Pumpkin Roll

Ingredients:
For the cake:
3 eggs
1 cup sugar
1 teaspoon vanilla
1 teaspoon rum or rum extract (more if you're feeling festive)
1 teaspoon cinnamon
1 teaspoon nutmeg
½ teaspoon cloves
2/3 cup pumpkin puree
1 teaspoon baking soda
1 teaspoon salt
3/4 cup flour
¼ cup powdered sugar (for rolling)

For the filling:
1 8 ounce package mascarpone cheese
1 cup powdered sugar
1 teaspoon rum or rum extract
1 small orange (juiced and zested)
1 teaspoon cinnamon
½ teaspoon nutmeg
½ teaspoon ginger
1 cup mini chocolate chips
1 cup chopped pecans

For the topping:
½ cup powdered sugar
1 teaspoon cardamom

Directions:

Preheat the oven to 350 degrees. In a mixing bowl, beat the eggs and add in the sugar, vanilla, rum, and warming spices (cinnamon, nutmeg, and cloves). Then fold in the pumpkin puree and combine well. Mix in the baking soda, salt, and flour until there are no lumps. Spread the batter onto a greased jelly roll pan and bake for twelve to fifteen minutes, or until a toothpick comes out clean. Allow the roll to cool for five minutes. Once the cake has cooled, invert it onto a wire rack. Dust a kitchen towel with powdered sugar and gently transfer the cake to the towel. Roll the cake up in the towel and refrigerate for one hour. While the roll is cooling, make the filling. Whip the mascarpone cheese in an electric mixer or with a hand mixer. Add in the powdered sugar, vanilla, rum, zest and juice of an orange, and warming spices (cinnamon, nutmeg, and ginger). Mix until smooth and creamy.

Remove the cake from the refrigerator and carefully unroll it. Spread evenly with mascarpone filling. Sprinkle with mini chocolate chips and chopped pecans. Roll it a final time and dust with powdered sugar and cardamom.

Gingerbread Waffles with Cranberry Compote

Ingredients:
For the waffles:
4 eggs
½ cup brown sugar
½ cup molasses
1 cup buttermilk
1 teaspoon cinnamon
1 teaspoon nutmeg

1 teaspoon ginger
2 teaspoons baking powder
1 teaspoon cream of tarter
2 1/2 cups flour
Baking spray

For the compote:
2 cups cranberries
1 orange (juiced and zested)
1 teaspoon vanilla
½ cup brown sugar
¼ cup butter

For the topping:
1 cup whipping cream
1 teaspoon vanilla
½ teaspoon ginger
¼ cup sugar

Directions:
Heat the waffle iron. In a stand mixer or a mixing bowl with a hand mixer, beat the eggs and brown sugar until fluffy. Add the molasses, buttermilk, cinnamon, nutmeg, and ginger, and combine. Then, incorporate the baking powder, cream of tartar, and flour and stir until the ingredients are combined, but don't overmix. Coat the waffle iron with baking spray and cook the waffles.

While the waffles are cooking, make the compote. Combine the cranberries, orange juice and zest, vanilla, brown sugar, and butter in a saucepan. Heat over medium high until the mixture begins to bubble. Turn to low, cover, and let simmer for ten minutes. To make the topping, whip the cream, vanilla, ginger, and sugar until it forms soft peaks. Top the waffles with cranberry compote and a healthy dollop of ginger whipping cream. Serve hot.

Café de Olla

Ingredients:
1 quart water
¾ cup ground dark roast coffee
5 ounces piloncillo (or 1 cup dark brown sugar)
2 cinnamon sticks
Orange peel
4 star anise
1 teaspoon whole cloves

Directions:
Heat the water over medium heat in a medium saucepan. Add the coffee, piloncillo, cinnamon sticks, orange peel, star anise, and whole cloves. Stir to combine, and turn up the heat. Bring to a low, rolling boil. Allow the sugar to dissolve. Remove from the heat and let steep for five minutes. Strain through a mesh cloth or strainer and serve hot in cups.

Andy's Autumn Latte

Andy's autumn latte captures the best of fall's bounty in a cup. With a touch of warming spices and strong espresso, this autumnal delight is sure to please any palate.

Ingredients:
For the latte:
2 shots of strong espresso
½ teaspoon cinnamon
¼ teaspoon cloves
1 tablespoon maple syrup
2 teaspoons simple orange syrup
1 cup milk

For dusting:
½ teaspoon orange zest
¼ teaspoon cardamom

Directions:
Add the espresso, cinnamon, and cloves to a warmed coffee mug. Whisk in the maple syrup and simple orange syrup. Froth the milk, then add to the espresso mixture, reserving the foam for the top. Stir the milk and espresso. Pour the reserved foam over the top and finish with a dusting of orange zest and cardamom.